# The
# Falcon
# Chronicles

## Lauren Elflein

PublishAmerica
Baltimore

Hardcover 978-1-4560-5657-5
Softcover 978-1-4560-5656-8
PUBLISHED BY PUBLISHAMERICA, LLLP
www.publishamerica.com
Baltimore

Printed in the United States of America

To my mom.

# Prologue

## *England, Blickling Hall, Norfolk, 1501*

A sliver of light etched itself into the wood paneling of the room, forming eerie cracks and glowing holes. Only the barest sunlight was allowed to peep in through the heavy velvet curtains shrouding the windows. A small spattering of individuals lingered tensely about, some rushing to and fro, others standing uncertain.

Elizabeth Boleyn was sweating profusely with tears pooled in her crinkled eyes as she gave one last heave. A great crying filled the room and the midwives rejoiced at the birth of a beautiful baby girl. Elizabeth fell back against her pillows breathing a sigh of relief. A serving girl rushed up with a damp cloth and patted her forehead with it gently.

Though Elizabeth knew her husband had designs and hopes for a male child, it was not yet to be. The year before she had given birth to their first child, also a daughter, named Mary. He would just have to be content with females at present.

As the baby was taken away from her she lie back on the pillows and fell into an exhausted sleep. She had no idea at this time what that crying little baby girl would accomplish in life.

# Chapter 1

## *England, 1513*

"This is Claude Bouton, seigneur de Courbaron, he will be escorting you on your journey." Thomas Boleyn was an imposing figure and he stood now cut out in sharp relief against the cool morning air. Anne looked at her father with a twinge of sadness, how long should it be before she saw him again?

Her long silky tresses of raven hair were half-loosed about her shoulders and her matching ebony eyes missed nothing. A glossy smile breezed through her countenance as she studied Monsieur Bouton and eventually set out on their long journey.

They road through the Kent countryside in a not uncomfortable coach, and Anne felt free for the first time in her life. Wisps of green flew by, leaves fluttering down to greet her. The wind kissed her nose in greeting when she was able to let the fresh air in — much to Bouton's displeasure. Blue forget-me-nots and honeysuckle were dotted and nestled amongst wildlife and rolling hills so pleasurably that she could have pictured herself running freely amidst the watercolors of nature.

Her natural ambition was leading her on this trip, as was her father's. For it was due to his negotiations and pleasurable conversations with Margaret of Austria that Anne was even allowed to make this journey. It is quite an incredible offer for one such as her, to be educated abroad and polished with that European sparkle.

They passed through old Kentish towns for a length of time before finally reaching the sea and the renowned White Cliffs of Dover.

Anne drew in a sharp breath to see the cliffs so outlined. They looked strikingly hard and intimidating, yet soft as feathering kisses or dewy snowdrops. She felt caressed by their presence as she boarded the vessel bound for the Low Countries and said good-bye to England for eight years.

## The Low Countries, 1513

"Ah, Symonnet can be quite the task-master tutor. I must say that your French is steadily improving." Margaret of Austria herself took great care in keeping up with Anne Boleyn and her education. Her father had entrusted her into her care and she was going to see to it that she came back an accomplished courtier.

Anne was one of Margaret's *filles d'honneur* and therefore served her. Margaret was currently serving as regent for her nephew Charles of Burgundy who was still too busy with Spain to worry about anything else at the time. Anne seemed to be getting on well with everyone and developing a rapport with the other Mademoiselles of honor.

"I want you to write a letter to your father and do so in French. I want him to see how you are coming along here at my court." Margaret's pale face and thick red lips inclined themselves towards Anne for her to do as bidden.

Anne curtsied and did as was told. '*Sir I understand from your letter that you desire me to be a woman of good reputation when I come to court, and you tell me that the Queen will take the trouble to converse with me, and it gives me great joy to think of talking with such a wise and virtuous person. This will make me all the keener to persevere in speaking French well, and also especially because you have told me to, and have advised me for my own part to work at it as much as I can.*'

When Anne had done as bidden she returned to Margaret's side with all of the other seventeen young ladies and listened to her as she taught them and educated them in the worldly ways of the court.

"Trust in those who offer you service, and in the end, my maidens, you will find yourselves in the ranks of those who have been deceived." She paused here and looked at each one with her sharp dark eyes. Anne was spellbound by the wisdom that Margaret always bestowed upon them and listened with rapt attention. "They, for their sweet speeches, choose words softer than the softest of virgins; trust in them? In their hearts they nurture much cunning in order to deceive, and once they have their way thus, everything is forgotten." Anne was half-nodding in understanding, hoping this was a lesson she could well put to use. "Trust in them?"

"One aught never to trust them," Anne said confidently. "It is to reproach on the God-given abilities for discernment and commitment to one's cause to be so byway laid by such obvious deception."

Margaret nodded in approval. "Then what can we learn from this? Fine words are the coin to pay back, those presumptuous minions who ape the lover. By fine looks and suck like. Not for a moment but instantly give to them their pay — fine words! Word for word - that is justice. One for one - two for two. They are gracious so to converse, respond yourself graciously — with fine words!" She looked pointedly at Anne and waited.

"Words are the common token of repayment amongst courtiers? They promise each other fine things in hopes for a reward or placement? But words may never be fully realized or paid in full when such like as these are spread about by numerous accounts. In other words, words mean nothing?" Anne's questioning dark gaze faltered for a moment.

"Quite, quite!" Margaret clapped her hands gleefully. "There is much yet to be taught but I at least can write to your father in confidence of your understanding. My other ladies are struggling to keep up with your wit and common sense my dear." She chuckled heartily and uncertain smiles went round the room.

Anne felt proud to be thus singled out and held her head a little bit higher.

## France, November, 1514

"I was in the islands of Zeelands your Majesty." Anne bowed reverently before Mary Tudor newly made Queen of France. "I humbly apologize for the incontinence of the situation. My father wrote to my mistress who did not receive your letter in time for me to accompany your entourage here to France." She again inclined her head to the proud Tudor with her sharp bone structure and auburn hair.

"It is of no concern to me now Mistress Anne. I would appreciate that you and your sister Mary are my ladies in waiting. However I do fear that my husband King Louis will insist I send most of my ladies home." Here Mary sighed and looked about her for comfort. "Mistress Diane, please be so kind as to fetch me my cream gown, we shall have to attend dinner soon."

"It was a lovely coronation your Majesty." Anne again attempted submission.

"Indeed. I am still in abhorrence however, on the selection of age in my match. It is quite a gruesome procedure, I must say."

"Yes I can imagine it would be so." Diane de Poitiers had returned with the dress and matching garments. "We must get you ready however, for I daresay the King still hopes to get a son off you."

"What is the use? He is so much older than I! He already has a daughter who is married to the heir to the French throne. What does he need another child for?"

"Why! It is to thwart the Duke of Angoulême's ambitions!" Diane was quick on the return.

"But I am a mere eighteen to his fifty-two years! That is much too much would not one say?" Mary lamented her dark lecherous fate with a man old enough to be her grandfather.

Anne pitied her. She herself decided she must have a very grand, rich, and important husband when her time came. But he must also be handsome and desirable. Not some old man such as the newly dubbed Queen Mary of France had come to wed.

# Chapter 2

## *France, January 1ˢᵗ, 1515*

"King Louis XII of France is dead." Diane quickly walked with Anne towards the privy chambers of the Queen.

"What will happen to poor Queen Mary?"

"She will be confined for a time until the Council is certain that she is not with child and carrying the heir to the throne. In the meantime Francis will ascend with his wife Claude."

"Oh I do so adore Claude," Anne gushed. A dark black velvet skirt swished around her as she walked, her tightly laced bodice showing off her flourishing figure to the best advantage. "It *is* romantic is it not?"

"I daresay it is." Diane allowed before sweeping off in a rush.

Anne curtseyed low as they entered the Queen's apartments and spoke with her in soft tones about what was to take place next. Mary was much lamenting and desirously awaiting news from her brother King Henry VIII of England.

\*\*\*

They did not have long to wait. King Henry decided to send the Duke of Suffolk, his close friend, Charles Brandon, to head up the retinue that would escort the Dowager Queen of France back home to England.

When the Duke arrived Anne was excited at the new change of pace the court had taken. From dreary and dull being under the rule of such an old and sick man, the dust began to be swept away and glitter now came through. Young courtiers seemed to crawl out of the tapestries and brilliant cloth of gold hangings strung up everywhere. Jewels and gems and pearls adorned all the latest headdresses and Francis I was handsome and alive. His Queen, Claude, was not very attractive and thus Francis took his pleasure many places elsewhere.

In fact it was not long before Anne found out her sister Mary was one of his mistresses. She sharply reprimanded her older sister for her loose conduct and morals. "Mary! Do you not want a respectable husband? Why give yourself so freely?"

"The King will see to it that I am married suitably well. And anyway the notoriety and thrill of it makes it all worthwhile."

Anne shook her dark head at her sister's golden one. "Well you are a bigger fool than I thought. I am no man's dessert; I am a wife through and through."

"Oh indeed? I hear there *is* talk of a marriage for you back home. Father has been hard at work assembling the details. He wants the earldom of Ormonde so badly he is willing to sell you off to unite the families."

Anne's face glowed pink at the news. "Truly?" She could not believe her luck. First she had served Margaret of Austria, then Queen Mary of France, now Queen Claude had taken such a liking to her that she had asked her to remain in France to be one of *her* ladies-in-waiting. But now it seems she may be recalled to England for a match. She was indeed excited.

### French Court, February 4th, 1520

Anne sauntered about the court in the wake of young Queen Claude. She knew that today, at this very moment perhaps, her elder sister Mary was marrying William Carey of King Henry's Privy Chamber. In fact, Henry VIII himself would attend the wedding! Her father had written to her to let her know the King was ennobling him as Viscount Rochford this day as well! The sweet promotions of the well placed!

Anne lamented her fate; if she were home she could attend this royal presence graced affair. She could sweep in brushing through the courtiers as though she were Moses parting the Red Sea. She could command those about her with a delicate clap of the hands or a snap of the wrist. Pearly-eyed and heady with incense would the priests be in Chapel Royal where her sister was to wed the up and coming lad. No mean feat for a girl of Mary's reputation. A wayward prostitute she determined her to be, yet there was a fixed kindness that glowed like a halo round Mary's golden head. Mary was sparkly where Anne was glossy. But alas, Mary would be the one with the husband while she continued to fester in France. She was oft surrounded by handsome obliging young men, but none would offer her the marriage she longed for.

Soon, Anne thought quietly to herself, soon.

## *Calais, Field of Cloth of Gold, June 7th, 1520*

Anne swept in with the French court in all the regality she could muster. She was feeling pert and pretty in her French hood dotted with pearls and trussed up hair in knots and pins. Her low cut French bodice was very appealing to the opposite sex and thus specifically chosen. It shimmered in the deep sea green that she chose. The green reflected a luminescence from her dark eyes that made them shine as though jet orbs reflecting the light of emeralds. She enjoyed the attention from the male courtiers and thus flashed her brilliant smile and soul-catching eyes as much as possible.

Tonight was the chance she had been long-awaiting. She could glimpse the English King and Queen and their young Princess Mary. And there was always the joy of being reunited with her family. She had not seen her sister Mary as Mary Carey. And as her father was busy with ambassadorial matters and her brother was a page for the King she hardly ever heard from any of them anymore. Her mother usually took the background on political affairs and so she never would have expected anything from her.

Anne knew however that this meeting, this organized peace treaty between the two Kings meeting here today was all in the great wake of glory for Cardinal Thomas Wolsey. She was anxious to see his scarlet pudgy bulk floating around the glorious field trimmed to overflowing with gold and silver. And this was far from an exaggeration. The triumph of Wolsey for Henry was vividly displayed. Anne looked about her, skirts swishing, at the marvelous decorations.

Her slippered feet floated across soft grass and hard stone as she went from display to display. Her haughtiness exuded from her as she admired the tapestries depicting biblical scenes and stitched with cloth of gold and silver. All around sparkled gilt, silver and gold plate and cups engraved with Henry and Catherine's symbols. Chapels that could be called anything but makeshift delivered golden cups wrought with pearls and sparkling stars in silver and navy blue tapestries shimmering endlessly on the ceilings about as though sprinkled with nighttime. It was incredible and majestic. For King Henry and King Francis could not attempt but to outdo the other. They were both young men, both athletic and muscular, both tall and considered extremely handsome by the women at court. Anne could feel the tension; regardless of the peace treaty hanging in the balance, the Kings were determined to be successful sportsmen.

Anne sauntered along, escaping from much of the chaos and bustling chambers of courtiers and ventured round the field where wine flowed from fountains in shimmering pools of burgundy and crystal. Tents fluttered in the light breeze, tents decorated and stitched with care. Burgundies and creams in soft hues with Tudor roses adorned hilltop after hilltop. The sun shone brilliantly, illuminating the hard work of Wolsey's men.

As Anne looked on the court that Henry had brought with him she was impressed to find that no one had been left out. The strapping and somewhat terrifying Duke of Buckingham strode around as though he were the King and not Henry. He was a descendant of Thomas of Woodstock, King Edward III's son, and had a better claim than Henry to the throne; he was not to appear so arrogant. In fact Henry had kept him quite nicely and treated him as a trusted friend and advisor. But Anne quickly saw the cockiness dripping through his layered doublet and decided he would be someone to watch.

The Duke of Suffolk, now lately the husband of the Dowager Queen of France was there as well. Tall and broad with dark graying hair he stood out as a man to be contended with. He was indeed one of Henry's closest friends. Anne knew that William Carey was about somewhere, as was the rest of her family. She noticed Thomas More the great humanist scholar as she passed through another throng of people. She knew she would be reprimanded if she were gone too long, she was after all a lady-in-waiting to the Queen of France and had duties to attend to. But Queen Claude had understandings in regards to Anne's family being present.

Once Anne found her brother and sister in the teeming crowds surrounding the banquet hall they ended up scampering about as if children again.

"I hear Father has indeed made a match for you with James Butler, the heir to the earldom of Ormonde. Wolsey is arranging everything." Mary twinkled at her sister before slipping away once more to flirt with the Kings as best she could.

"You know, I've heard some names that they call her Anne," George, as handsome as ever, whispered in Anne's ear. His height and dark coloring made him all the more attractive, and as far as she'd seen he was indeed getting the ladies' attentions. "I do believe she is called the infamous whore," George continued. "It is not a good reputation to have."

"You already have the reputation of a poet and slayer of all female hearts." Anne teased.

"I am friends with Thomas Wyatt you know."

"Yes, aren't we all?" Anne laughed. "He was our dear neighbor George."

"Yes well now the King of England has taken a liking to his works and he is at court all the time."

"I daresay you two get along charmingly." Her fierce black eyes flashed like coal being lit in a fire.

"Mmm...oh Anne. Do let's dance and enjoy ourselves! These rooms with their enormously rich trappings deserve to be used and admired."

"Oh my dear brother!"

Mary's golden head flashed like fire in the sun as she bounced about from male courtier to male courtier. "Does her husband not mind?"

"Not in the least. It would seem that our good King has taken a liking to her if you understand my direct meaning."

"Indeed?" Anne was amused. Her skirt rustled as she shifted her weight from foot to foot. "That does not make me feel like dancing George. I am quite tired from merely walking around this enormous place. It is grand!"

"Oh Anne. You are not jealous are you? You know he discards all his mistresses rather quickly. His latest, Bessie Blount, bless her soul, gave birth to a son last year, Henry they called him."

"So I have heard," Anne remarked dryly. "And now she is nothing to him."

"That did not stop the fireworks and blaze of glory her bastard son received. You know he is called Fitzroy and is being established in a double dukedom!"

"He intends to make him his legitimate heir?"

"Catherine as yet has but a living daughter, the Princess Mary, and the rest have all died. The Queen was most displeased at the display put on for the bastard."

"Her anger is to be commended. I do not want a husband who is not loyal to me. I want a husband who loves me for me and is loyal to me through all the years. I have seen enough whoring around for my taste. I am chaste and saving my maidenhead for my true love."

"Oh Anne...." George sighed and tapped her gently. "You are a very good woman."

She smiled brightly and could have chilled winter itself with her steely look. "I intend to live my entire life as one, and die as one too."

# Chapter 3

## *England, December 1521*

Anne walked quietly as her soft slippered feet swept the floor and her dress brushed in a hiss and whisper like running water over the stone threshold. She was home.

A glorious hush fell across the court as she walked elegantly along, her head held high, her chin protruding. Her pale face appearing pearlescent, and her long neck accentuated by the deep cut of her gown. Her French hood poised regally on her head, she looked as though she herself were royalty.

She was being escorted to the Queen's apartments where she was to become a lady-in-waiting to Queen Catherine herself. Mary was already situated in the household and was waiting to welcome her home to the English court.

A murmur arose as Anne passed through the crowded hall and out of sight. She was indeed markedly grown up and quite beautiful, though not in the usual sense of the word. She was not buxom in looks, she was not voluptuous. Nor was she golden and honey colored like the sun, but more pallid and lifeless like the cold moon. She was night and day compared to her sister. But there was some sparkling quality that brought her to life, which made her glitter. What was it?

Anne arrived within the Queen's Privy Chamber, the most private and hallowed halls of the Queen and curtsied low as the rotund, aged Queen waved her hand in acceptance.

"Mistress Anne Boleyn, sometime lady-in-waiting to Queen Claude in France I hear. You are to be commended on your education and upbringing. Your father did you a great service in this." Her heavily Spanish accented voice grated on Anne's nerves. It was inconceivable that after being here in England for most of her life that she could not speak English in an English voice.

Anne therefore decided to affect the opposition and speak in a lilted French accent when regarding her Queen. She curtsied again and made reverence. "Your Majesty is too kind. I humbly accept your comments and seek to do you the greatest service in return." Just as expected Catherine did not look pleased at the decidedly French dress and language and appeared affronted. She waved Anne away and explained to her what was expected of her as a lady and what she should wear.

Once out of earshot Mary caught up to Anne, catching her embroidered sleeve. "Dearest sister! How have you been tucked away in France?"

Anne hugged her tightly and pulled away slowly. "Things were absolutely marvelous in France! Father brought me home to marry Piers Butler and to serve the Queen here; he determined my education was finished."

"I hear the French King was none too pleased at your departure."

"Oh merely because he suspected Henry of foul play. He thought if I was being recalled that the King was going to declare war on France."

"Ah, I see," Mary shrugged. "The vanities and affairs of men are no place for such lowly creatures and chattel as women. Would you not say?" She lifted an eyebrow and affected an unintelligent composure. "I do declare that all women are here merely for reproduction and no greater pastime."

Anne laughed at her sister's folly and grasped her hand. "It is good to be back. Do I hear tell that you are the King's new mistress?"

"I have been his mistress for some time Anne. "

"Yes and I suppose it has only helped the Boleyn's to prosper, and your good and faithful husband no doubt?"

Mary's golden waves bobbed as she nodded. "It has been rather a grand festival for the Boleyn and Howard family. The Carey family as well. I suppose I really am mere chattel to be sold to the highest bidder; in this case, the King of England himself."

Anne looked worried. She knew indeed that all mistresses were discarded eventually and not with much ceremony or pomp. Soon Mary would be cast aside for something new, and then where would their family be? The rewards would cease and Mary may be disgraced. Anne thought about this and decided that she herself needed to make a suitable match to increase her family's power, wealth, and standing in the English court. But she wanted to be in love.

"I heard of the Duke of Buckingham's demise," Anne said softly.

Mary's eyes clouded over, a troubled look dwelling within. "It is said he crossed Cardinal Wolsey and plotted the King's death. His head was struck from his body. It was terrible."

Anne pictured the proud duke, lowering his bulky well muscled frame onto the straw-strewn scaffold. Witnesses scuffling about before him to watch his death; to watch the last iota of life alight from his eyes, the last breath inhaled by his lungs, the last twitch of his lips, the last muscle holding him upright before it was all sucked out of him before their very blood-thirsty eyes. They would drink it all in as he lowered his head to the block, proffering his arms, signaling his admittance to the end. She can see the headsman wielding his ax high overhead, letting it sing in the air for a moment, sun filtering off of its metal surface, sharpened to a fine point by rough stones and knives. She can almost hear the gush of wind as it rushes to meet the flesh below it, hear the thud of the head and the dull noise as the blade meets the wood. She can see the blood gushing and pooling in his now defiled body. She can see maidens, most likely Buckingham's relatives, scooping his head up in a cloth that quickly soaks through to burgundy with his dark sticky blood. She can see young men lifting and heaving his body into a wooden crate to be deposited into the cold hard ground. Then the workers will come and sweep up the straw and use filthy muddy rags to sop up the blood, making ready for whatever victim shall next be here for execution. She can see the crowd, their faces drooping in anticlimactic sorrow — the show is over.

With that the vision is gone and the room spins slightly before her. She steadies herself and looks at her sister with sadness. "Executions are never a pretty sight. They are gruesome and for the glory of none. Traitors must suffer, regardless of their standing. The duke grew too heady with his own scent of importance. We must learn a valuable lesson from his arrogance."

## England, York Place, Shrovetide March 4<sup>th</sup>, 1522

The Great Chamber was lit with torches as everyone finished their supper. Rich tapestries and arras sumptuously decorated the room. Near the end of the chamber was erected a castle with towers that was decorated with banners with torn hearts, a woman's hand gripping a man's heart, and a woman's hand turning a man's heart upside down. The tower on one end had a cresset burning and tucked away beyond sight within the towers were musicians playing haunting melodies.

Anne was also hidden from sight inside the towers and was feeling prickly with excitement. She was wearing a dress of white satin with the word and role Perseverance picked out in embroidered gold on her dress. On her head was perched a caul and gold Milan bonnet stitched with priceless jewels that had cost the King a small fortune. Anne felt sumptuous indeed. She glanced around at the other ladies with her: Beauty, Honor, Kindness, Constance, Bounty, Mercy, and Pity. The Duchess of Suffolk was of course Beauty; her own sister was Kindness, and another face Anne was coming to recognize: Jane Parker played Constance.

Below them on a smaller level of the towers' construction were young boys from Wolsey's Chapel dressed as Indian women and representing evil virtues, Danger, Disdain, Jealousy, Unkindness, Scorn, Malebouche, and Strangeness. These young men were guarding the women against the chivalric enterprise that was soon to take place.

Anne giggled lightly as the show began and all eyes in the court turned to the castle. Eight great strapping men appeared in cloth of gold caps and long blue satin cloaks from a chamber. These men portrayed Amorousness, Nobleness, Youth, Attendance, Loyalty, Pleasure, Gentleness, and Liberty. But the man leading the group was dressed in a fiery crimson red satin burning with flames of gold, leaping out to lick those standing too close, singeing those around named Ardent Desire.

As these young knights strode forward attempting to rescue the hidden virtues trapped inside, now revealing themselves in all their angelic displays the evil virtues below began shouting at the knights. The boyish voices squeaked as they spoke out against the knights: "Back! Back we say! These virtuous ladies are ours now! Back!"

Anne with the rest of her virtues began throwing comfits and sweetmeats down to the knights below. The flames of the leader's garb flashed in Anne's eyes, a glowing desire was discerned there. The knights began gallantly throwing oranges and dates at the towers to take down the evil virtues who finally surrendered much to the delight of the crowd. Anne was soon sequestered and taken down out of the towers onto the dance floor below. She watched as the crimson clad savior danced with the Duchess of Suffolk and spun her round and round. She watched the white satin flutter in the air as she twirled. Fat diamond drops tasted of sugar, dew nestled into icicles, endless sprinkles of hyacinth clustered into a hidden place safe inside Anne's heart. She felt love hit her throat. She stopped looking at the crimson hero and instead turned her attention to a new man. A man she had not noticed before. For of course the crimson hero was the King, but this other man, who was he?

Henry Percy, heir to the earldom of Northumberland.

***

"She is your sister!" Thomas Wyatt stood with Anne and George and exclaimed remarkably about Anne's presentation at court and her beauty. "Why, Mistress Anne, your hair is like star-spangled gossamer. It shimmers and breathes when it moves. It flutters like the wings of butterflies and hisses like the wind kissing roses!" Wyatt breathed deeply.

"I daresay you have quite forgotten you are already married!" George playfully swatted the poet.

Anne's cheeks blushed a faint seeping pink tone which pleased Wyatt to no end. His eyes twinkled as he took her in. "You truly are a spectacle Anne."

Anne stared him down now, embers flaring in her lustrous eyes. "I do believe you are too informal with me Master Wyatt." Anne inclined her head, traced impatient fingers through a trestle of ebony hair and sauntered away.

"Ah, the brunette. Always elusive." Wyatt chuckled to George as Anne moved pointedly out of earshot.

Anne's breath caught in her throat as she espied her special suitor once more. He seemed to be a larger than life figure looming on the outskirts of her thoughts. He was imposing and dominating, a specter of intellect and wit. She could feel his sparkling charm emanate through his cloth of gold and blue satin, creamy and whipped, soft and smooth. A sigh caught in her throat and her chest heaved against her boned bodice of the purest white.

The word 'Perseverance' glimmered in gold thread picked out across her chest, illuminating her greatest virtue. If she must persevere to make Percy her husband, persevere she would.

## England, 1522

Anne was teasing her sister mercilessly, tendrils of her hair springing loose as she laughed. "Is it true that at the jousts Henry's motto really was '*elle mon coeur a navera*'? I don't have to tell you what that means do I?"

"She has wounded my heart," Mary said shamelessly. "What can I say? The man is hopelessly in love with me. He is a true romantic."

Anne sighed wistfully. She herself was in love and could not speak of it. Would he then resort his pastime unto the Queen's chamber where Anne's eyes went forth as messengers, bearing the secret witness of her heart?

Indeed yes. Henry Percy was now often in the Queen's Chambers, but on whom should his eyes fall but Anne. No other for him, only

Anne. His deep brown eyes and matching chestnut hair fell in waves about his head that was simply tantalizing to Anne. She longed to run her slender fingers through it and smell him. "How I long…." Anne realized she was speaking aloud and admonished herself internally. "I long for a good man to take care of me," she finished lamely.

Mary nodded her head and continued with her stitching. "Ow! Take care!" Mary pricked her thumb with her needle. Anne laughed and continued with her own needlework. "The Queen is very demanding with her sewing."

"I believe that is a good virtue. Sewing for the poor and your husband is a good pastime," Anne said stoutly, but her eyes were on the roaming figure of Percy. Anne knew he was to inherit a wealthy estate when his father passed away. But that was not the prime figure that accounted in her eyes, it was his solemnly handsome face and the way his eyes glossed over when he looked at her; as though his heart was aching just as pityingly as hers. She sighed and felt her heart rate subside. She must be very careful.

"Oh you know that Gilbert Tailboys is the lucky wedded husband of our own Mistress Elizabeth Blount?" Mary looked at Anne sharply; was that a questioning look?

"The King finally married her off respectably? I bet it was Wolsey's doing more than the King's."

"Yes, well, either way it is all arranged. I do believe Tailboys is prospering from the match. A discarded mistress brings her own sorts of rewards." Here she paused and seemed to revert to internal debate. Anne pitied her sister, for the affair with the King would end for her just as it had for Bessie Blount. If Mary became pregnant that would signal the absolute end to her reign as mistress.

# Chapter 4

## *England, St. Giles Church, November, 1524*

In the pretty little chapel situated in Jane Parker's home seat of Great Hallingbury, Anne gathered to watch her brother marry the young woman. Jane's father, Lord Morley, had tired endlessly on getting the marriage contract between the couple just right in case anything should happen to George then Jane would be provided for directly by Thomas Boleyn himself.

Anne was proud of her father; he had been made Viscount Rochford when Mary married William Carey, who knew what more was in store for their family if the connected marriages continued.

The church was filled with a handful of courtiers, but most was Jane's own family and a few of her maids. Soon Jane's bridesmaids were flitting down the aisle with lovely sprigs of rosemary stuck in bunches on their dresses, and within their hair. They were there to ward off the devil with confusion as he lay in wait for the vulnerable bride about to enter the scene. With bright colored garlands of flowers clutched in hands and held aloft in came Jane wearing deep crimson velvet. Her golden hair flowed about her dotted with tiny white buds and pearls entwined. The crowning glory was the woven floral garland circlet draped round her head. A golden jeweled girdle was fastened round her waist glinting now and then as the sun trickled through the stained glass windows. It cast rainbow prisms dancing about and filled the air with lighted gems. To weigh her down even more a fur-lined satin mantle was draped round her shoulders and made her appear regal and elegant; its length tugging on the floor as she moved.

Bride-men stood guard around Jane as she met George to await the ceremonial process. Music and song guided the way in melody through the process. The priest then waited to commence the ceremony.

"We are all here," his deep voice intoned dryly, "To join together two bodies into one body. I must now enquire about the dower of the woman."

The necessary documents were presented and thus the priest continued. Anne fidgeted and looked sideways at her sister and her husband. They looked contented and excited to see another happily married couple. Though it was for land, money, title, and convenience, George and Jane seemed to like each other well enough. Anne decided she was pleased for him, Jane was a nice girl, and they should get along fine.

"George, will you take Jane as your wedded wife — to love her, and honor her, keep her and guard her, in health and in sickness, forsaking all others, for as long as ye both shall live?"

George stood regally in cloth of silver and shone vibrantly. A smile spread across his mouth revealing pearly rows of teeth as he said, "I will."

"Jane, will you take George as your wedded husband — to love him, keep him, and obey and serve him, in health and in sickness, forsaking all others, for as long as ye both shall live?"

"I, Jane, take thee, George, to my wedded husband to have and to hold from this day forward, for better, for worse, for richer, for poorer, in sickness and in health, to be bonny and buxom in bed and at board, till death us do part."

Jane's meek smile peeped out from under the tresses of blonde caramel hair and long eyelashes. George placed the ring on a Bible for the priest to bless.

"God, I beg you to ensure that the wearer of this ring will abide in thy peace and continue in thy will, and live, and increase, and grow old in thy love." He then sprinkled it with holy water and George placed it onto Jane's fourth finger of her left hand.

"With this ring, I thee wed, with my body I thee worship and with all my worldly property I thee honor," George said while slipping the ring on.

The priest finished praying and everyone exited into the main section of the church. George and Jane went to the altar steps where her pert little bridesmaids shifted her dress about so she could kneel with more ease. Anne stood and prayed for George and his new wife with the rest of the congregation. She felt her eyes grow moist and realized once more how much she loved her dear brother and his quirky ways.

His sandy hair flopped over his ears and his eyes were warm. The couple then left into the presbytery while clerks held a canopy over their heads and prayed for their union and nuptials. Anne waited until it was all over and finally found a chance to speak to her brother. She decided to be teasing.

"She is quite wispy and willowy is she not?" Anne commented dryly to George as they stood to the side while everyone round them commenced to dancing and feasting.

"Oh and you are quite waspish I should say!" George declared testily.

"I meant no harm George! She is actually rather lovely and has a sweet temperament and demeanor. I am sure you shall get along very well and be very prosperous." Anne sweetened and George relented.

"Anne, Anne, Anne."

"Are you happy dear brother? You seem truly happy."

"I am Anne. I am very happy. Jane is a dear girl and I believe she will make a most excellent wife." He paused and looked sheepishly at her, amber eyes appearing wet. "I *am* sorry that father gave up the Butler marriage. It seems it just ran out of luster. I believe father is working on the King to receive the Ormonde titles regardless of marriage between the joint-heirs."

"Never mind that brother! Enjoy your *own* wedding day instead of fretting about mine!" Anne waved a hand merrily, feigning joy and happiness. Inside she had shriveled a little when the Butler marriage came to a standstill between Wolsey and her father. The negotiating ended and other, more important marriages were taking place, including her brother's this very day. It was of little consequence, she consoled herself, and she would soon catch a much bigger fish with a bigger pond to swim in.

## England, Greenwich, December 29<sup>th</sup>, 1524

Anne patiently waited yet again for the chivalry to commence. She was waiting hidden in a mock castle all to Henry's specific construction. The Duchess of Suffolk and Jane Boleyn were crouched with her, along with her freshly pregnant sister Mary. The court was very happy that the production could go forth today as it did not snow and it was not so very cold out. The sun sparkled and brought a glow of warmth to those taking part in the revelry.

Anne could just make out the voice of the heralds proclaiming outside in the tiltyard in a screeching voice:

"Although youth had left them and age was come, and would let them to do feats of arms; yet courage, desire and good will abode with them, and bade them to take upon them to break spears, which gladly they would do, if it pleased her to give them license."

Anne could picture Catherine's smug wrinkled Spanish face demurring to the heralds her consent for the jousting and play-acting to begin. She would be sitting in the audience on her throne looking every inch the matriarch of the performance. Anne stifled a giggle as she pictured her puckered face in displeasure of her comments.

She could hear the crowd gasp in amazement as the heralds revealed themselves to be Henry and the good old Duke of Suffolk, Charles Brandon. A soft smile played about her lips as she relished the thought of her act; she had always enjoyed such performances in Margaret's court, now she was a part of it in England. She had been trained for these activities half of her life.

Within the tiltyard below was the castle that Anne and her fellow courtiers were hiding in. It was a magnificent structure that had been coined as the Castle of Loyalty or *Chateau Blanc* for the being of such purity and virtue as white as snow. Fifteen young knights of the court paced about in front of the castle guarding it from the would-be attackers. Anne was happy that two of her greatest admirers were in fact defending her honor now; Percy and Wyatt.

But with Henry and Suffolk on the scene the crowd was raging and the tables would shift. Older than the young knights they may be, but in bad shape they most certainly were not. Henry's reddish gold hair and golden eyes shone brilliantly in the rays of sunlight setting the yard ablaze. His over six foot tall frame was muscled and toned and Henry had always been known as a keen sportsman in the tilt. Suffolk himself with the gray hair seeping round the edges of his brown was still strong and strapping; and the fight in him would never be put out.

Thus one by one they challenged the Youth and defeated them mercilessly. Lances poised and split in shattering sprays of wood to the hollering and cheering of the crowds. Horses' hooves thundered down the line sending dirt up in swirls of wind choking the masses and blinding their view.

Anne and the other ladies revealed themselves, wearing sparkling cloth-of-silver with pearls stitched on the bodice and sleeves. Sheer silk stockings of white with white satin ribbon stitched with cloth of silver clung to Anne's legs.

The ladies cheered and yelled for the King and Suffolk until the battle was finished and the injured attended to by Henry's physicians. Francis Bryan lost an eye that day, but was none the angrier for it. He declared he lost it with good intentions and would 'see to it' that the women of the realm were always well defended. Henry was quick to point out that they still lost and the maidens were still unprotected.

However as the winners stood on the tiltyard below, in shining silver armor, Henry's chestnut horse trapped in cloth of gold, he looked every inch the King and waited patiently for the ladies to descend from the castle.

Henry raised his helmet and watched as each lovely angel of purity alighted on the dusty ground. He dismounted with Suffolk and together they walked over to escort the women out of the yard. Suffolk immediately went to his wife and leading her by the arm and the cheers of the crowd exited the arena. Everyone now assumed the

King would take his mistress' arm; however his eyes seemed quite taken with another altogether.

Anne's raven hair was free and flowing about her in long tendrils. Her silver dress billowing up around her like stardust, revealing the matching bows of her stockings underneath. Anne modestly adjusted her dress and glided forward like a cloud. Henry's eyes never left her as she came ever closer. He grasped her hand tightly when she came within reach and found himself lost in the depths of her endless fire pit eyes. "Who are you?" Henry asked dumbfounded.

"I am Anne Boleyn your Majesty."

"Boleyn?"

"Indeed, I am Mary's sister." She inclined her head to him gravely, but not without a hint of irony. The blue sapphire ring on Anne's right hand suddenly flashed in a brilliance of sun and color. The light catching the King's eye and making him smile.

The sparkle in Anne's eyes and the intensity portrayed through them was not lost on the King. He returned the stare and still they stood their hands interlocked and unmoving. The crowd began to murmur and Catherine rose from her seat, she was ready to congratulate her King who wore her favors and could not understand what was happening. Was something wrong?

Henry snapped to attention with sudden alacrity and walked with Anne while Mary and Jane were left to be escorted by their husbands who were among the defeated Youth. William Carey and George Boleyn were left to ponder the actions of the King. George knew his sister well enough and William his wife well enough to judge that she was hurt if not a bit jealous at the sudden attention bestowed upon Anne.

The tiltyard towers twinkled in the light, an architectural accomplishment whenever a spire catches sun droplets just so. Running across the towers in a connecting link was the tiltyard gallery where all the jousting equipment was stored and where the men were now heading. Henry had recently had new stables built and the horses would be led there to rest amidst their snug hay.

Anne pictured the horses choking on the dust floating up in motes as they lay amidst their straw beds. Strong hands would brush their muscled bodies, letting their chestnut and black coats, silver and spangled coats, shimmer in rippling beauty. Their glossy orbs would twitch as they tried in vain to assess what was happening to them. Their trappings, saddles, and bridles would be beat and polished to its royal sheen for whenever the noble constituents would deem to ride again.

*\*\*\**

Once inside the court Anne was led to her dining table with the other ladies as Henry assumed his place with Catherine. Though all around did not miss the pointed glances cast Anne's way throughout the meal. Bets were placed that Anne would be positioned as the next royal mistress within a fortnight. But Anne had no such illusions or intentions. She would not settle for anything less than a prosperous marriage, and one was within reach. For Henry Percy and Anne had become quite entangled with one another.

A promise of marriage had been made and Anne saw them as good as married now. She would call him her love and expected the real wedding and consummation to take place forthwith. However, she knew a contract would have to be worked up between their families at some point. Should they marry in secret?

Her mind twirled passionately as she gazed longingly to where he was seated with the other young knights of the court. It seemed that tonight all eyes were on Anne. Percy studied her face and Wyatt did not miss the exchange. But most disheartening to him of all was the King's attention, albeit silent attention.

Thus when the dancing portion of the festivities commenced, Wyatt approached Anne and immediately set to work. "I have a riddle for you Mistress Anne."

"Alright Wyatt, let's have it then shall we?" Anne asked somewhat intrigued and somewhat impatient to be by Percy's side.

"What word is that that changeth not, though it be turned and made in twain? It is mine answer, God it wot, and eke the causer of my pain.

It love rewardeth with disdain; yet it is loved. What would ye more? It is my health eke and my sore."

"Oh dear Master Wyatt! I would hope the answer would indeed be your wife!"

"The answer to the riddle is Anna...." Wyatt trailed off in uncertainty and could not suffice to meet her eye.

Cardinal Wolsey was strutting about in his crimson robes, assuming a haughty air as was expected from him. He did not go anywhere without a long train of servants carrying silver crosses blazing forth his trail while he was escorted on a donkey. It was all a performance with Wolsey. Anne watched as he approached Thomas More who bowed his head reverently at the most trusted minister in the kingdom.

More's dark hair was coarse and beginning to be peppered with grays, but he stood tall and erect and there was something in his presence that affected respect. Anne could admire his strength of will and determination to live a Godly life, she just did not agree with his principles and did not assume they would ever be warm acquaintances.

While the two of them had their heads bowed in consternation and conspiracy Anne left Wyatt scrabbling for words as she went to dance with her beloved Percy, the King's sharp eyes never leaving her person.

## England, 1525

Anne felt triumphant as she sauntered to Mary's chambers. Henry it now seemed was forever turning his back on her sister. Anne had known this would happen all along and was grateful to know her intuition and court smarts had been wiser than that of her elder sister. For now Mary was in labor, giving birth to a new baby. The mystery surrounding the child was whether or not it was Henry's or her husband William's. Anne tended to give credence to it being William's as Henry had blown hot and cold with Mary long enough to suspect this.

Anne helped the midwives and dipped cloths in warm water and then cold water to dampen Mary's sweating face. She dabbed her pale skin splotched with red marks from straining and shied away when

Mary moaned out like a wolf. It was a frightening scene to watch someone give birth. It seemed time hung suspended and everyone held their collective breath while the world waited to see if she would deliver successfully. But all the time there was a flurry of activity going on around them. Anne knelt beside Mary's bed and carefully stroked a strand of hair away from her face.

"There, there dear sister, all will be well." Anne's gentle soothing voice soon calmed Mary's near hysterics and as she gave a last heave a cry rent through the room.

"It is a boy!" The midwife stood triumphant with a bloodied apron tied round her waist and her hair knotted up in a white towel. "It is a boy!"

"Henry…." Mary said sweetly, purring at the soft downy head of the fresh newborn. Henry was gently handed to Mary in swaddling cloth and Mary pressed him to her bosom humming gently. Anne felt a twinge of jealousy at the choice of name and then remembered her own male suitor and silenced her heart.

"He is beautiful Mary," Anne said softly and brushed her fingers through his smooth blonde hair. "It feels like a duckling." She giggled. Mary smiled at her and nodded, kissing the soft head and cooing.

***

"The King is done with Mary it is said." Thomas Boleyn loomed large as ever in Anne's life, as domineering and as powerful. But she loved him nonetheless.

"I certainly pictured that this day would come," Anne said calmly as they walked together through the teeming mobs of courtiers all vying for the King's attention. They passed through a hallway and out into the open courtyard. The sun was shining but the air was brisk. Anne shivered and slunk closer to her father.

"Yes, we all knew it had to end eventually. It is a wonder the King does not create the child into a duke as he did with Blount's bastard."

"Hmmm…" Anne murmured. "I doubt not. It was scandal enough the first time, why do it twice? Nay, he has his heir waiting if all else should fail. Maybe he is convinced the child is not his."

"True." Boleyn stroked his chin deep in thought. "I am sorry that the Butler marriage did not culminate as planned. I had wanted to marry you suitably and have you situated by now. Your elder sister is married and you are of age." He paused and looked at her sparkling black orbs. "I believe you would be happy with a man to spar with." He chuckled and then resumed his pace.

"Indeed, I should like to be married. I feel I am getting old. Now that the treasures will stop piling on from the King we must look to the future." Anne stepped over a broken stone on the ground and paused to gaze at the clear blue sky. "I want someone to be happy with."

"Happy? Happiness is not a part of rewards and power. Happiness is a byproduct of a successful match. Most couples do not find love, but may find a sort of peace and prosperity together. Most simply take mistresses and lovers."

"I do not wish to live that way. I am passionate father."

"That I know. You take after your ancestors, and you have a bit of myself in there if I might say." He winked and watched birds flutter across their landscape. "We must take care and find you a husband. Shall we?"

Anne's heart beat very fast. If he only knew that she already found one!

\*\*\*

Anne rushed back and forth across the room. "Wolsey found out? How!?" she demanded hoarsely. Tears streaked her cheeks, staining her pale beauty. "He is sending me away?"

"I am sorry Anne. I truly love you. I must leave court as well. My father is very angry with me and threatens to disinherit me from the earldom." Henry Percy bowed his dark head, illustrious curls framing his face. He had a boyish look and an innocent air about him. But he was backing away, inching towards the exit, backing away from her.

"So you are leaving me?"

"Wolsey says I must! My father says I must! I am to be married to Mary Talbot."

"No!" Anne's face was contorted in pain. "You mustn't!"

33

"Wolsey and that Cromwell fellow of his demanded it. I have to obey the King's wishes; he is very displeased with me. As a prominent courtier I am supposed to seek the King's permission when taking a wife. I have made an offer of marriage to you, but I must withdraw."

"No! No!" Anne's face was dark, her small tongue lashed out like a cat's, and she raised her small fists as if to scratch him.

"Anne...." Henry's eyes were searching, deep flecks of gold and amber washed across their surface. His eyes spoke of love, his voice spoke of separation, distance.

"Will I ever see you again?" she whimpered pathetically.

"You will."

"But with your wife."

"Yes."

"I swear I will make Wolsey suffer for this! He will not come out of my unhappiness unscathed! He is the cause of this! One day he will wish he had never crossed me!" Fire hissed from Anne's nostrils, Percy could almost imagine smoke issued forth as well, a dragoness breathing fire.

"Oh Anne..." Henry Percy, Anne's first true love, left her alone at last.

The embers in the fireplace shifted and sank into a deep red and orange glow as they became mere ashes. A soft sigh escaped her lips like wind bending the boughs of tired old trees in the forest. She pursed her lips and flicked dust off of her jeweled sleeve. She sucked in a deep breath and held back crystalline tears that threatened to spill over in redoubled force.

Her love left her. He left her.

# Chapter 5

## *England, June 1525*

"But father I do not want to go!" Anne raged and stormed about her chambers throwing stockings and ribbons. "I will not go!"

"Anne! Calm yourself! Remember who you are!" Thomas Boleyn's sharp words cut short Anne's next protest. "Wolsey wants you rusticated and therefore you must go home, do your penance, and come crawling back to court on your knees when summoned once more. If you should be so lucky after the scandal you've caused!" Thomas's gray eyes flashed at Anne. "It is a shame I have such a harlot for a daughter!"

"Father!" Tears threatened her eyes as his words sank in. "Father, I did not go so far with Percy."

"Oh Anne...." Thomas's eyes crumpled and tears welled up. "I know that. I did not mean it. Mary is the harlot daughter, not you Anne." He cupped her face gently in one palm and wiped a tear from her cheek. "All will be well. But you must tarry in Hever for a time. It is for the best. You must regain royal favor."

*England, Autumn 1525*

"That dog Wolsey summoned me back," Anne snorted.

"It would sound as though *you* are the dog to be summoned." George laughed heartily.

Anne swatted him. "That is not funny George!'

"We must all obey Cardinal Wolsey or we shall be damned for an eternity in purgatory. Didn't you know that? Only Wolsey can save your soul," he winked. "And you have been quite the naughty courtier! A lady-in-waiting to the Queen! For shame Anne!"

"Oh George....How is the Queen faring these days?"

"Haven't you heard the latest gossip?"

Anne shook her head.

"They say she no longer bleeds. The King is furious as he still has no male issue, and it would appear he may never get his heart's true desire."

Anne's face flashed sadness before she replaced it with a hardened look. "She was much older than him when they married."

"Well, she was sent here to marry his elder brother. She was Arthur's wife, it is too bad he died, things might have been so much different."

"You do not love your King?"

"I do, I do, do not mistake me. There was simply gentleness from what I've understood that Arthur possessed. There is the clear Tudor streak of passion and derision in Henry."

"What a philosopher you are! Indeed you are spending too much time with Master Wyatt!" Anne scolded teasingly.

***

Anne sat sewing in a circle with the Queen and the other ladies in waiting. Anne's sister-in-law and her sister were still serving and it was a great comfort for Anne to be around familiar faces. Everyone stitched quietly until the Queen left to take Mass for the fifth time of the day. The Queen's ladies were not required to be as pious as she herself was, but were still expected to imbibe religiosity.

Once the Queen and a train of maidens with Lady Worcester and the Marchioness of Exeter also attending her had left, a few gentlemen thought it prudent to seek audience with the Queen's ladies. George Boleyn came flitting in with Thomas Wyatt, William Brereton, and Nicholas Carew. In the past Henry Percy might have joined them, but as it were, he was now absent from court. Sent home to his father's lands of Northumberland to also be taught a reminder of how disobeying the King's will was fatal.

"Where is Francis Bryan today?" The ladies were giggling and talking amongst themselves. William Brereton stepped forward, eyes flashing. "Why! Every lady knows that I am the most sought gentleman of the court!"

Amid raucous laughing and George teasing Jane, Wyatt took his opportunity to approach her. Anne placed her stitching in her lap and neatly folded her hands together adopting a serious and pious pose. "Yes Master Wyatt?"

He bowed low and then kneeled before her. "I must seek the favor of one of your rings your ladyship."

Anne chuckled heartily. "Lady I am indeed Master Wyatt? But nay, you may not take a ring from me. I do not bestow my favors on you."

He leaned forward and whispered urgently in her ear, "But I would seek to have you, to make you my own." His lips lingered tantalizingly close to her, sending a chill up her spine.

She recoiled and snapped at him, "I am no man's mistress! I trust in God to send me a husband and I trust you will not make such overtures to me again!"

Wyatt reached out a hand and snatched a bright sapphire ring from Anne's finger. She gasped in shock and fright as he did this and bowed to her once more. "Thank you Mistress Anne." And with a flourish he was gone.

*** 

Anne finally had a moment to herself. It seemed she hardly ever had a time like that anymore. She breathed deeply in the fresh air. She was walking through the royal gardens at Greenwich and she felt more alive than she had for some time.

A gentle breeze was blowing through the air, but the weather was starting to turn crisp and chilly. The trees were no longer green and vibrant; a haze lingered in the sky. A lazy pair of birds flew overhead and were quickly gone; their gentle chirping fading with a flap of wings. Water trickled from a nearby fountain, and perfectly trimmed grass was starting to crackle underfoot. Anne trod lightly, her soft black slippers barely making a breath over the soft dirt. The sun caught her jewelry's reflection and sent glitter dancing through the air, framing her in a halo of light. Her velvet dress dragged the ground; she lifted her skirts revealing matching stockings underneath.

She suppressed a desire to be a young girl again picking her skirts up to her thighs and running about freely laughing wildly. The urge died suddenly in her when she saw the King standing like a sentinel on the path ahead of her.

She immediately dropped her skirts to their modest length and heaved a deep breath, her breasts pressing tightly against her bodice. Her favorite necklace, pearls looped round her neck ending in a brilliant gold 'B' for Boleyn with pearl-drops hanging from it felt heavy against her clavicle.

She curtseyed low as the King approached her, long legs striding quickly across the ground. "Mistress Anne," he spoke her name in a whisper, as if afraid that if he said it too loud the person would disappear before him, like mist on a moor.

"Your Grace." Anne again inclined her head to him. Twinkling sparkles of glitter danced about from Anne's dusting of jewelry. A glint of gold from a single ring on her finger, to a tiny shimmer of the pearls glowing iridescent round her neck.

"I have much desired to speak with you Anne, much desired. You have haunted my waking dreams and come to me at night to whisper in my ear. But I much desire to hear you speak these words of passion to me now."

Anne was reeling, her head spinning. The King was intending her to be his mistress? Anne fervently shook her head, dark locks flying. "Your Majesty I must humbly decline." She bowed deeply, hands flicking skirts, and then began backing away from him. His reddish gold hair flashed in a streak of sun, a snarl lit his face.

"Anne! I must speak with you! Desist this haste you are making from my side! Are you thus insulted and repulsed by my advances for your most humble suit?"

"Why, your Grace, I am both flattered and pleased that you would take such an interest in such a lowly courtier as myself. However, your Grace must understand that I desire nonesuch but my husband to take my most precious gift from me." The sleeping embers in her eyes, ignited into flames.

"Why Anne....how very noble of you. I apologize and submit myself most humbly into your forgiveness and mercy, beautiful mistress. I forgot my chivalry in my advances but will now embrace you wholly as a virtuous maiden who I shall be patient to wait for."

"You will wait a long time your Majesty, as I will submit to none but my husband."

The lion inside Henry nearly exploded into a roar, but he quieted himself and straightened his royal personage, puffing out his chest. He reached for Anne's hand, grasped it lightly in his own large one, caressing her delicate fingers. He brushed the gold ring nestled firmly on her finger and plucked it right away. Anne was transported to the scene with Wyatt but banished these thoughts as the King slipped it on his own finger, kissing it as he did so. "Mistress Anne." He inclined his head and moved swiftly away from her.

Anne was now left to serious contemplation.

## England, Shrove Tuesday, 1526

Anne watched from her seat near the Queen and the rest of her ladies, as Henry trotted out on his gallant steed. Anne wore feathers in her hair and a pale choker round her neck. Her hair was as smooth and wavy as black velvet. She smiled as Henry drew close and only then did she notice his device. Henry was wearing a brilliant jousting costume of cloth of gold and silver making him reflect the sunlight harshly. But this was not what attracted Anne's attention most deeply; it was the words embroidered on this costume that moved her so. *Declare, je nos.* Declare, I dare not. Stitched with mastery above these words was a man's heart engulfed in flames. Anne's face turned pink as she heard the murmurings of the other courtiers around her noticing the same emblem. Would any know Henry was speaking to her? From one heart to another? Emboldened by the flame of love? Enraptured in the honey, the milk, and the seed of a planted admiration? Would any watch as the flame engulfing the man's heart licked up and took his soul? Would any note that inside those burning flames lay the wings of a ruffled Falcon? Would they know it was Anne?

Henry's eyes glowed with a fervent desire; a hungry lust. He held his lance high, facing the ladies of his court. Catherine's eyes were alit with adoration for her husband; her love was so bright as to never be extinguished. Such pride shone forth through her very stance. What dedication did this plump Spanish woman show her husband! For even the peasants of the field would beat their husbands bloody upon hearing sharp words slither past their teeth. But never so with Catherine. Not for risking rebuke or retribution, but for a deep-seated sense of duty and love would she forever stand by her husband.

In this quality Anne could almost concur with Catherine. A woman's place was by her husband, both adoring each other with unveiled desire. Each one dancing a set or singing a song that mirrored the others'. Each one living their life to complement their lover. If right for Anne, then left for Henry - perfect opposites in synchronicity and harmony to reciprocity of good will and nature.

The wind whispered through branches of trees, making them moan softly in protest. A butterfly flitted about on golden wings but Anne was not to be distracted. Clouds drifting lazily overhead went unnoticed by the spectators below. All eyes were on Henry and his flaming badge.

Anne knew it would not be long before all eyes were on her.

## *England, Spring 1526*

The crowd erupted into hearty cheers as the King knocks over the wood against Wyatt's last bowl. "I believe it is mine then Master Wyatt." The King points to the felled pieces and indicates the win with a tilt of his head.

Thomas Wyatt was fretfully gazing at the golden ring sitting pertly on the King's finger. He attempted to control himself but it was as though something snapped inside of him. "It is debatable your Majesty, as I say it is mine."

The crowd began murmuring, uncertain as to who had won the game.

"Wyatt, I tell thee it is mine."

"If it may like your Majesty to give me leave to measure it, I hope it will be mine." Wyatt, his brown locks rippling over his forehead swiftly removed the ring he had stolen from Anne. The sapphire blue nestled within glowing brilliantly in the warm sun. The sapphire seemed to mesmerize Henry for a moment. Wyatt proceeded to use the ring, tied to a ribbon, to measure out the distance to determine who the winner was.

Henry now in a furious rage suddenly threw up his hands admitting defeat and stormed away from the scene. The crowd's cheers now died in their throats at the look of disdain and fury etched on the muscular King. He strode away, each step thundering in the ears of those left behind, but most deafeningly did it roar in Wyatt's.

✳✳✳

"Why does Master Wyatt possess a jewel from you Mistress Anne?" The King burst into the ladies' chamber without warning and all fell to their knees humbly before their sovereign.

"Your Majesty!" Anne instantly groveled.

"Be gone!" He dismissed everyone but Anne from the room. Catherine was saying her prayers and was gone for the moment, or Henry would not have dared this audience so publicly.

"I repeat to you now Mistress Anne, why does Wyatt have your jewel?"

"Your Majesty he stole it from me!" Anne cried piteously. Henry's face instantly softened a notch from unmasked fury to a gentle understanding. "He meant to have it from me as an act of chivalry, but I declined him. So he instead took it from me and I was powerless to stop him. It was but a meaningless bauble and I decided it was not worth the effort of obtaining it from him. I ask your Majesty's forgiveness."

"There is nothing to forgive my dear. I was most heartily mistaken." Henry now merely looked baffled and slightly embarrassed. This caused Anne to smile and eventually laugh.

"Oh your Majesty, do not think I would even consider any other but you. I would never give a lowly court poet the attentions that I would deny your most royal highness."

Henry now smiled broadly and cupped Anne's soft chin in his hand. "Oh Anne…" He looked into her deep soulful eyes and felt he could drown in them. And happily.

"Your Majesty…." Anne lowered her eyes in obeisance and folded her hands in front of her delicately.

"The Queen! The Queen!" a herald yelled loudly, the ladies were reassembling outside of the privy chamber to attend the Queen on her way back from prayers. Anne could picture her now clutching her rosary beads as though a lifeline. She bowed to the King and moved back a few paces just as the Queen entered the room with her retinue of ladies.

"Your Majesty!" Catherine fell instantly to her knees in the most humble of submissions. "My Husband, it is so good to see you here in my rooms. I only lament that I was not here to entertain you, I was at prayers submitting to Almighty God to send us our longed for Son and Heir." Catherine's light hair and eyes fell flat in comparison to Anne's. They were lacking a certain sheen and shimmer. Henry's vivid gaze for Anne died on Catherine. An instant wall was erected between the two, forming tension in the room. Catherine still had not noticed that Anne had been alone with Henry.

"What can I do for your Majesty?" Catherine asked sweetly, her pudgy cheeks puffing into a bright, but obviously forced smile.

"Nothing, I came to see how you were, that is all. It would appear you are well and so I must be leaving." Henry turned on his heel without waiting for a response and without a backward glance. He was gone in an instant, just as quickly as he had come. Anne felt new life growing inside her, a new goal, a new conquest, a new reason to fight.

No challenge had ever been put to a Boleyn but that the Boleyn had conquered all. Anne must now conquer.

\*\*\*

"Well Mary, how feels it to be a mother?" Anne laughed heartily as her sister sighed heavily.

"Oh Anne, why can you not be more pleasant?" Mary sighed, her eyes shining with tiredness. "It is so very exhausting to have gone through such an ordeal."

"But you do not even have to take care of your child! That is what the servants are for! How can you be so tired?"

"I suppose it takes some strength from a woman when she gives birth. Take our good Queen for example, she—"

"Yes, she has had many miscarriages and stillbirths and yet after all these years of marriage to our mighty King Henry she has only produced one living child — a daughter! What good is that to the succession and safekeeping of this realm?"

"God's teeth Anne! Watch your tongue! The words you speak could be construed as—"

"Treason? I think that is not so likely." Anne's sly smile confused Mary but she remained silent. Anne slapped her hand and looked back to her book of hours. "I am working patiently on my knowledge of our Lord."

"I can see that you have been very fervent lately. In fact, I looked in your trunk Anne and you have many forbidden books. Books that are burned, books that *people* are burned for possessing! Would you so lightly flaunt yourself a heretic?" Mary's face flushed slightly as she spoke, and her stitches got further and further apart on her sewing until she angrily pricked her finger and squealed. As she began to suck gently on her finger Anne answered slowly.

"It is not heretical to follow God's will in all things; it is heretical to follow the clerical will in all things. The Pope has assumed a power that is beyond his to wield. He believes he is God here on earth, but the truth is that he is not. Henry should be free to rule his people, not

43

bow to the Pope every time he has an idea or question. The authority of Rome has gone too far. Too much is at stake."

"Anne, what are you talking about? You could be in the Tower for this if not much worse! I do not want to hear another word!"

"George agrees with me." Anne's words struck like a knife. Mary's face held horror, seeing that her siblings were turning from the true religion set forth by God moved her deeply. Anne felt differently. She felt that the true religion set forth by God was the freedom to worship Him the correct way. Anne was most certainly anticlerical and wanted the Catholic Church reformed. Mary could not fathom this notion of thinking, but Anne was convinced that eventually she would see the light.

"Father writes to Erasmus, who also has revolutionary thinking, humanism."

"Oh why don't you talk to Thomas More then?"

"Tsk." Anne shook her head violently. "I feel he will never be an ally."

"An ally?" Mary's blonde brow arched. "Indeed Anne, are you starting a war?"

"I just might be Mary. I just might be."

\*\*\*

Graceful as the night, as quiet as the stars above, as black as the ebony sky, Anne moved about her chambers with care. Her father had insisted on sending her home to Hever when Henry had made clear his intentions to court her. Now her brocade skirts swished about her in agony, in torment, in loss of love. Like gossamer waves of the ocean her hair rippled about her unbound and free. Her skin as pale as the glowing surface of the moon shone bright as the twinkling pinpricks of light peeping through her window. Anne moved catlike towards the slit in the heavy velvet and pulled it shut, desiring darkness. Her lithe body swiftly crossed the floor and returned her to her silk canopied bed. The Boleyn's may not be the wealthiest family, but her father made certain they lacked for nothing.

Now in the still coolness of the night, inky blackness crept up on Anne and she languished in it. She could feel the sweet cooing melodic voice rocking her to sleep. She supported herself on her elbows, knowing she should have allowed her maid to change her into her night gown, but she had felt so desirous of being alone that she had sent her scampering with a flick of the hand.

Her creamy skin like milk or butter glowed in the black of the room as she laid her head back to rest on her goose feather pillow. Her head sunk in deeply, surrounded by cushion and silk. She lay there, piercing eyes wide open to the canopy above her, interwoven flowers and vines entwining in constant growth across the material. She imagined herself stuck in embroidery, forever stitched in fabric, forever weaving in and out, forever on display. She shuddered when she realized this was quite similar to being a mistress to the King. There was no private life for a courtesan, Anne was no fool. She pinched her rosebud lips in her fingers in consternation, making blood rush to them. This was an old trick some of the French courtiers had taught her. Pinch your lips and pinch your cheeks and color will flood into them making you more desirable.

A circlet of stars danced before Anne's eyes, mesmerizing in gold and amber hues, now turning silver and a luminous white. As her conscious thought drifted into waking dreams she felt the crown alight on her head and she herself rose up as a star in heaven.

Some time later her maid entered the room and woke her up to be undressed.

# Chapter 6

## *England, Hever Castle, Spring-Summer 1526*

Anne sat in her dressing gown, resplendent in forest emerald green, a striking contrast to her inky locks, sending glass bottles of fragrance and cosmetics clattering across her dressing table. An enormous looking glass was erected in front of her, sending back vivid images of Anne's wild eyes. Sharp as ever, as fierce as any eagle soaring the heights above, her chin jutting out, Anne slapped hair pins and ribbons down on the table in exasperation. "I do not want to be cooped up here like some animal in the menagerie!" This comparison of Anne to a caged lion or panther made her chuckle with delight. Her feline prowess could not be suppressed. She stared deep into her own eyes, sunlight glinting off of the glass at weird angles, sending shafts of light shining through the transparent bottles now scattered about her. Anne was speaking to no one in particular, having risen early when the maids came in to clear out the chamber pot and ask if she was in need of anything. Anne scoffed at the maid who once again was sent, tail between legs, scurrying out of the room like a whipped dog.

Anne heaved a sigh, her breasts swelling against her tight fitted bodice laced over her silk chemise. A jeweled comb lay nestled in a velvet box, sapphires and rubies glinting off of its golden surface. What a gift it was, and from such a humble suitor. No less than the King himself! It did not arrive unaccompanied, but came bandying a thick sheet of vanilla papyrus on which was scrawled in masculine script a love letter.

A mirthless laugh bubbled up inside her. What an impression she had made! Her! A simple Boleyn. What did she have to offer the world? She had wit and charm, a feisty repartee, and best of all, a sensual appeal. Anne recognized lust in men's eyes and spun it to her advantage. They would not have her, but if they thought they could why not reap the benefits? Anne felt cynicism biting at the edges of her sarcasm and irony. The problem was not that Anne was not virtuous, by far she was a most Christian and humble lady of society, but she must not shed a certain *seduction* and *appeal*. In this world it is essential that she appear to be what men most desire, as women are seen as nothing but chattel. Anne knows she is more, but will have to prove it her own way.

She fingers the comb, shaped like a butterfly, wings flayed in delight, antennae twitched to the side ever so slightly. It was such a delicate and intricate thing; no, not the comb, her life.

Now she takes the letter in her hand, small fingers caressing the material like the kiss of the sun on a snow covered field. The mere touch could melt it away. Anne's shallow breathing makes the paper flutter, as though coming to life under her care.

*In debating with myself the contents of your letters I have been put to a great agony; not knowing how to understand them, whether to my disadvantage as shown in some places, or to my advantage as in others. I beseech you now with all my heart definitely to let me know your whole mind as to the love between us; for necessity compels me to plague you for a reply, having been for more than a year now struck by the dart of love, and being uncertain either of failure or of finding a place in your heart and affection, which point has certainly kept me for some time from naming you my mistress, since if you only love me with an ordinary love the name is not appropriate to you, seeing that it stands for an uncommon position very remote from the ordinary; but if it pleases you to do the duty of a true, loyal mistress and friend, and to give yourself body and heart to me, who have been, and will be, your very loyal servant (if your rigor does not forbid me), I promise you that not only the name will be due to you, but also to take you as my sole mistress, casting off all others than yourself out of mind and affection, and to serve you only; begging you to make me a complete reply to this my rude letter as to how far and in what I can trust; and if it does not please you to reply in writing, to let me know of some place where I can have it by word of mouth, the which place I will seek out with all my heart. No more for fear of wearying you. Written by the hand of him who would willingly remain yours,*

*HR*

True, this was not the first letter his royal Majesty had sent her. Nor was he mistaken in thinking she had been rather vague and ambiguous in her own replies to him. Downstairs in her father's study sat a freshly sharpened cream quill and an inkpot ready to be dipped into. The black liquid congealing together until the point of the feather meets it in a marriage of writing capabilities.

Anne tapped a finger against the paper and then a finger against her sharp teeth, jutting out angularly as she bit her lower lip. Thoughts trickled in and out of her mind like a running stream as she attempted to gather her thoughts on this, the latest of the love letters. He had in fact, taken to signing his initials with a heart entwining her initials with his. It was all a bit astounding to her. She watched him roar about his palaces, pacing like a caged lion amongst his counselors, or as he saw them, his jailors. All feared his wrath, all bowed before him in great obeisance. None dared cross bows with the King. His reputation for war and ruthlessness was growing, a great abscess that would continue to convulse and stink in putrefaction until Anne, his loving Angel rescued him. And thus she was quite dumbfounded that she could see one person in two such completely different ways. It was as though there was the King, and then there was Henry. There was a public figure, and then one just for Anne. But, what was he to Catherine? Here Anne chewed more firmly on her lip, realizing in so doing she was forming quite the bad habit.

Running an invisible line across the words on the paper that said: *"I beseech you now with all my heart definitely to let me know your whole mind as to the love between us..."* What 'love' did he imagine there truly was between them. Her finger hovered over that word, love, that inescapable word that so conflicted with her emotions. She tucked a strand of hair behind her pale naked ear, unadorned now with the queenly jewels she so loved to adopt. A huff of air emitted from her now half parted lips in frustration. Love. She had felt love once, and that love had been taken from her, bitterly. She imagined his red rotund figure moving about like crimson silk. Fluttering and flowing in all holy importance. Sitting pompously on his hairy mule, the beast straining under the great bulk of its burden, heaving in great consternation as each hoof hit the earth in dusty clomps. It was unbearable! His chain of office gold and gleaming thick and fat about his meaty neck and shoulders; glinting in the lights of flickering candles sitting in fat stumps of dripping wax. Dimly lit rooms with arras hung draping round him, tapestries of Queen Guenevere bestowing her queenly essence upon Sir Lancelot, or the Queen of Bathsheba, or King Solomon. Gilt cups, gold cups with jeweled rims splashing bits of fine red wine as thick swollen lips close their wetness around the rim. Gulps of wine staining the rotting teeth to a blood-red; the look of which is comparable to a wolf having finished with its sheep dinner. The telltale fur in tufts at the corners of his mouth. This is the vision she has of Cardinal Thomas Wolsey — the destroyer of hopes and dreams.

Thus as she sits there, staring from the word 'love' to her pallid reflection in the mirror does she know that she will have her vengeance. She will wreak her havoc on Wolsey, the thief of love, the specter of doom and humiliation. For where was Percy now but married to the homely and thick figured, doe-faced Mary Talbot! How dare Wolsey interfere with Anne's heart! Now the King longed to have it she would win.

As Anne considered her reply to Henry, forming witty quotations in her mind, peppering it with charm and vivacious anecdotes, she begins to see how her future might be. She must be more than simply a mistress. Once had, soon discarded. No one taught her that better than her own notorious golden-haired sister. Though Mary was much like a Greek goddess straight from mythological tales, or a sculpted beauty forever poised in glorious seduction, she was now fobbed off on a husband who was only promoted due to royal favor of the sexual kind. Mary bowed to the King's wishes without thinking of her future life. William Carey was a kind man, to be sure, but Anne had more desire than for a simple kind man. She wanted a man with passion and desire. A man to whisk her away and grab desirously at her voluminous skirts. To cup her china face in his hand and whisper words of affection in her ear. To dance merrily with her in a room warm from a blazing fire, the hearth casting eerie glows of red then orange flames dancing along the stone walls. Brilliant candelabras lit in anticipation of the night lasting forever. To eat off of plate inscribed with all of her initials and badges. How many gowns she would own! Of velvets and silks and brocades! The French hoods she would have made! The embroidered sleeves and the stockings! The girdles and the jewelry! The gloves and muffs and glorious slippers for her delicate small feet! Layers and layers for her dresses, shifts and dressing gowns. Jewel encrusted fabrics and saddles! Tapestries and coverlets and all things imaginable! No expenses spared for any woman of her standing! Or so it shall be.

Her thoughts again return to Catherine. The Spanish Rose no longer. A Spanish Thorn indeed. For how prickly she is! How disagreeable! How pious! She is in constant muttering of prayer, Latin seems to be her first language anymore, and the image of the cross is ever present in her mind. At times she will kneel where she is, falling to her knees in abject humility. She will cry and weep as though she were losing fat droplets of blood from sore red eyes. It is a painful thing to watch. But the Queen is desperate for an heir, and is unable to deliver one. Anne pities her in a deep dark corner of her soul that she never visits and rarely remembers exists. But the pity does exist, it is there, and we must not forget it in the coming years.

## *England, Hever Castle, January 1ˢᵗ, 1527*

Anne studied the great ship with care. It was lavish in the extreme. Her father had paid to have it crafted, smiling genuinely while twirling a piece of dark hair around his aging fingers. He chuckled when he handed over the fee to the craftsman, even patting the old man on the back. The ship had four decks and was made covered in silver and gold plating, detailing every nook and cranny of the ship. It was tall and it took Anne both hands to hold it to her chest, the weight of it surprising. On the front of this maiden ship was a large diamond dangling precariously and catching the light at odd intervals of frantic spinning. This was a gift for Henry, his New Years' present which had to be extravagant. For everyone knew that New Years' gifts *must* be splendid and sumptuous for the King. It must go above and beyond what one would normally give to another courtier.

And herein lays the majesty and altogether cleverness of her gift. Anne was the ship, and no matter what storms she was tossed through in life, if Henry, her diamond, was guiding her she would be safe. He was sure not to fail to see the hidden message. Henry could be far too clever by half at times, thwarting her subtle gestures.

Nevertheless, Anne now sat with the ship boasting its pride in front of her on the small intricately wrought table at which she sat. The table's surface gleaming bright as she flicked the diamond about with a sharp nail. It was by no means a small diamond, but a fat one which seemed as fresh as having just been cut from a large stump of diamond rock. It felt weighty in her hand and she would sometimes sit there just letting it rest in her palm, feeling the heaviness of its symbolism rather than its actual weight.

Soon men began arriving with a velvet lined box to lay the ship to rest in. It nestled in amongst its velvety cushions without protest, and the men closed a jeweled lid over it before leaving with it to be delivered to His Royal Majesty.

## *England, Greenwich, May 5ᵗʰ, 1527*

Anne's new crimson dress sways gaily about her frame; she is blooming like a flower. Her small dainty hands clasp her partner with a gentle ferocity as he spins her about and then catches her to him. Her partner you ask? Oh, King Henry VIII. His young daughter Princess Mary floats about in unfeigned illness and weak legs with the French ambassador De Tuerenne. Anne is certain to flash bright rows of pearly teeth at him whenever he merely glances in her direction. But Anne realizes no one is really paying her all that much attention. She adjusts her gold girdle inlaid with deep rubies and fidgets with her matching earrings, hanging heavy on her ears.

Henry's hands slip from Anne's waist to just a fraction lower with every movement he makes. Anne is starting to feel a violation coming on and quickly exits his grasp with dignity. She bows out of the dance while the lute's eerie sound continues to repeat in her ears. It is still echoing there in fact when she exits the room into a hallway lit with flickering torches. Guards stand like statues at the far end where the entrance is, but she pays them no heed, taking them to truly be made of stone. Though she knows their ears are all flesh and their gossiping lips just the same.

She sucks in a huge gulp of air, her nostrils flaring at the smoky scent that rushes up them. The audible lashes of the torches' tongues snake out at her in fury. She backs away from them and leans against the wall in a fire-free zone. The coolness of the stone she can feel through her thick layers of dress and it feels like sweet nectar after the dry desert air. Anne can feel perspiration forming on her forehead underneath layers of curls and waves, and inside her bodice where her arms meet her ribcage. She shivers despite herself, the stones cooling the hot sweat to an icy sheen.

She brushes absent-mindedly at her gown, smoothing her skirts and flicking off dust. She knows her face is flushed and that there's no reason to pinch her cheeks like a French whore and slowly her breathing returns to normal. Just when Anne thinks she is finally recovered and may return to Henry's overtures and advances, he comes bustling out into the corridor to find her.

"Anne! My precious Anne!" His golden-red locks fall into his eyes most becomingly. Sometimes he is as innocent as a young boy. But then the innocence washes away and is replaced with a lusty grip. "Anne…" He leans forward and pins her body to the wall with his own. She can smell wine on his breath and tries to turn her sensitive nose away from the revolting smell. His unshaven face rubs raw against her cheek and neck as he nuzzles her roughly. "I loved your gift you know…." he purrs into her long neck and against her small earlobe, her earring bouncing against his nose in protest.

"Yes…yes…I knew you would." Anne tries to affect a breathy voice to show eagerness to please. But in reality she feels a bit revolted. She swallows her repugnance, knowing she is just not herself tonight and shoves him back a step so she can see his eyes. They look back at her with confusion but a swelled happiness.

"Oh Anne…I love you so." He tries to kiss her but she extends a long spidery arm to stop him.

"I have explained everything to you Henry. I will commit myself to you, but I will not sleep with any man but my husband."

"That is why I am making you my wife!"

She looks down, no longer able to meet his eyes, staring instead at his cloth-of-gold doublet with his fur lined cloak shrouding his broad shoulders. He really is handsome. He shifts on his feet and lifts her face to meet his eyes. "I will make you my wife Anne Boleyn."

Anne knows he means it. He has already sent Thomas Wyatt on an embassy to Rome. To what? Canvass opinion? Or to get him out of his way to seduce her? She is uncertain, maybe it is both! Why not kill two birds with one stone after all? Henry is a man of means and he means to have her no matter what.

In fact the thought is rather frightening and Anne shudders against him. He holds her tightly though, not seeming to notice her physical cringe. "I do so love you sweetheart." His gravelly voice is not to be drowned out.

## England, May 17<sup>th</sup>, 1527

The Night Crow glides about her chambers laughing hysterically. "I am the *most happy* woman ever to have lived! I want to soar like the falcons above and crest the winds with glitter dust sprinkling from my hair. I want to be vivid in the memories of all those who come after me and for them to say 'Long live Queen Anne — the true Queen of Hearts.' I want to spread the Word of God and indulge in the happiness that life has to offer. I will be a great patron of the arts and my name shall forever more resound through these hallowed halls."

Jane Boleyn laughed with Anne. It was indeed a true laugh, a burbling joy that her family should be raised thus. Nothing but success could come from these assignations between Anne and the King. And now, on this very day, Wolsey had opened the Secret Trial of the King's Marriage. It was all a very big to-do, but very hush-hush lest the Spanish Pig should discover.

Anne had worked painstakingly, finger-prickingly, unerringly, on stitching the words 'The Most Happy' onto an emerald piece of satiny ribbon. She had whole-heartedly adopted this motto and wore the ribbon on her body at all times. It was ever-present like her now very recognizable 'B' necklace. She flaunted herself, gathering up yards of fabric in her hand, and twirling about the room. She did not flinch when anyone snickered behind their hands at her, turning their noses up at her approach, or becoming quite quiet as soon she enters a room. Anne laps up the attention and does not let the harsh opinions of others taint her success. If the King loves her what else should matter?

Indeed, behind locked doors and guarded chambers, within hallowed halls few are allowed to traipse, Cardinal Thomas Wolsey sits with fingers interlocked much perplexed as to what the King's wishes are. His bright employee Thomas Cromwell has been running errands for him up and down the city and farther still. He brings him constant news of the King's attitude, as Wolsey has shuttered himself away in a veil of hard-work. Indeed, he does not stir for hours at a time, pouring over biblical text and the Papal dispensations for the Aragon marriage. He is tired; his fingers rub his skull back and forth, while the wrinkled jowls hanging limp on his neck warble to and fro with this motion. He has been preparing for this day ever since the King confided in him about his troubled conscience and his new love, Anne Boleyn. Now today is the day they will open the King's Trial.

Anne is utterly unaware of the Cardinal's true feelings on the matter, and does not care one whit for them anyway. He must bring her a satisfactory answer or *she* will not be very satisfactory with *him*.

Oh Anne longs to make Wolsey pay for all his mistreatment of her. She vowed it, do you remember? But she knows her own issue, the King dubs it 'The Great Matter', to her 'Our Great Matter', must be resolved first and Wolsey is the one to get the job done. Who knows, maybe if Wolsey completes this task with much groveling at her feet, she will forgive him in the end. Perhaps not.

Anne meanwhile, attempts to manifest and embody everything she believes a queen ought to be. She does not think so very ill of Catherine for being religious, it is the *religion* itself with which she is unsatisfied. Catholicism is her religion too; Anne admits somewhat stubbornly, it is the religion of England and its kings! However, the clerics that run the religion are very flawed, as humans always are. The Pope is worshipped as some kind of God and Anne is quite fed up with it. She will embody the true Christianity for all to see and practice after her. She tucks a stray lock of black hair behind her ear, nervously fidgeting with her Boleyn necklace. The 'B' dangles dangerously, skewed as though it is a horizontal line with two humps in it, like a camel. Anne slaps it back upright and watches as the pearls hanging on for their dear lives vibrate and purr against her soft breastbone. Anne's sharp hook eyes miss nothing. They soak up every detail of a room. They take in every item a person before her is wearing. They assess the words coming out of servants' mouths to be truths or lies, and watches as their bodies flit in uneasiness as she sharpens her claws for condemnation.

The truth is, Anne is highly suspicious of all who now support her. Jane Boleyn and Mary Carey she trusts implicitly as they are family and will only succeed should Anne succeed. But other young maidens or aged matrons with crinkled faces with sweet honeyed words but false eyes ring dangerous in Anne's ears. These tolling bells of warning must not be overlooked; not just anyone can be counted on in these delicate times of uncertainty.

Anne shifts her weight back and forth between her feet, still prancing about the room dancing and laughing. She has been given very large chambers now that bring her very close to the fire-headed King. Jane and Mary are with her and stifling giggles as Anne jumps about giddy as a child.

Jane's pasty face is for once quite aglow, and Mary's plumper waistline wiggles as she joins in the mirth. Thanks to Anne they both sit indulgent with French hoods pinned expertly to their heads. Oh, anything French is *very* much in style, Anne has brought that Frenchified air to the English court and now everyone is shedding their English gable hoods in favor of donning the King's *maîtresse-en-titre's.*

\*\*\*

"Oh indeed! My badge looks quite beautiful crested upon these fabrics! Oh and he is gifting me plate! Gold plate Mary! Gold! With *my* Falcon forever displayed, engraved onto its glittery surface. None shall soon forget that *I* am the Queen-in-Waiting! Hah!" Anne clapped her hands merrily with her sister as they sat contentedly in front of a deck of cards. Anne much enjoyed gambling, but was content at the time to merely play with Mary. She had been exhausted lately what with thoughts of marrying the King and having new dresses made to match all the gifts of jewelry Henry kept dispatching to her. Gems lovingly nestled in precious metals, inspiring thoughts of wickedness! But Anne nevertheless found virtue in all things. She prominently and quite contentedly wore these jewels, boasting the gift-giver, but never flaunting herself. After all, though the court believed there was a rendezvous of sorts inspiring between her and the King, they did *not* know that she was going to assume Catherine's rightful place as Queen of England. All thought certainly Henry would tire of his raven and dispose of her just as quickly as he had discovered her. Only Wolsey and Cromwell were doing the King's secret bidding; were in on the King's true contrivances. For yes, the world was coming to understand, albeit slowly, that Henry was unsatisfied with his marriage and was looking into the validity of it, they assumed still that he would come to his senses, read the magical dispensation and all would return to normal. However, Catherine could clutch, and would clutch, her dispensation like a life-line, like the blood of the Savior Himself; it would do her no good. In the eyes of the Catholic Church Henry and Catherine were lawfully wedded. But Henry had other thoughts and Anne helped prove them to him.

In fact, even now she sat mumbling through thin lips the verse which would be her rescuer in this trial. "Leviticus 20:21 - And if a man shall take his brother's wife, it is an unclean thing: he hath uncovered his brother's nakedness; they shall be childless." Anne licked her lips in relish as she finished and Mary giggled across the table from her, flaying wildly her hand of glossy cards.

Rushes covered the hard floor to soften Anne's every step. She snuggled her feet in deep to the carpeted surface and sighed happily. "I daresay the Pope cannot argue with God's word."

"But argue he will," Mary said rather fixedly. "If a Pope dispensed it in the first place it would mean to say that God agreed the marriage between Henry and Catherine was alright. So if anyone were to say now that it was not alright would be to argue God's word."

"But the Bible says—"

"It matters not. The Lord speaks to the Pope directly, hence the reason why we take the ruling of the Pope so seriously. Really Anne, you'd think you didn't understand Catholicism." She shook her head sadly in remonstration of her wayward sister. "How indiscreet you are."

"Indiscreet! Sister the King of England means to make me his wife!" Anne looked both ways, eyes darting fervently, covering her mouth with a delicate jeweled hand. She lowered her voice substantially. "I mean to say that I shall be indiscreet in the near future."

Mary smiled slowly, a happy glow that encompassed her whole body. Radiance could shimmer out of Mary in a way it never could from Anne. Mary had a certain *kindness* that Anne rather lacked in the general sense. Anne could be specifically kind, but not wholly kind. It was therein that Mary rather lacked the sense of grappling power and lust for riches. She was far from dense or stupid, but she had a higher sense of purpose that the other Boleyn's sometimes shed in lieu of advancement.

"Our dear Uncle Norfolk is suddenly quite interested in our fortunes," Anne comments wryly, the dry nasty tone croaking out of her throat as though just waking up from a deep slumber. "He never cared so much before what became of me," she scoffs now, ironic and menacing. "I daresay he expects to share in my rise. Whilst I am on the ascendant he will cower before me, but if ever there was a chance….he would pluck it from me like a lightning bolt." Here Anne's harsh eyes softened, and the angular lines of her face melted away. "But he is my mother's brother, and I believe he does love me. I will not leave him out of my success." Anne lightly flicks her skirts to spread them out more modestly about her legs and cover her peeping feet, snuggling them deeper into the carpeting.

She looked from Mary her sister, to the eyes of Mary Magdalen peering intently at her from a tapestry nearby. A gift from Wolsey. Dear Wolsey. How he was struggling to please her. The first trials regarding Henry's marriage to Catherine had failed rather miserably for them, but he was placating her nonetheless. The deep swirling colors of the tapestry seemed to illuminate in the room, drawing Anne's face towards it. She stared hard, watching as a mirage of images swept across it in the stillness. She could quite see her Falcon badge circling round the image back and forth, back and forth, lust in its eyes. A hunger, a thirst, a desire to be the best. And ever present below it was Mary, her sad eyes pleading with Anne to look away from the Falcon, to look to God, turn your eyes away she seemed to plead. But Anne paid no heed to this imagination of thought; she was ready, not greedy, but ready. The vision before her faded, the tapestry hanging heavily on the scrollwork holding it up, and Mary her sister waving a small hand in front of Anne's face. "Anne? Anne?"

"Sorry," Anne said suddenly, coming back to reality. "Oh are you not so excited about my plate! It has my badge imprinted on it!"

Mary laughed a barking laugh, a note of jealousy ringing sharply in Anne's ear. But no, not kind effervescent Mary; no jealousy lurking there. "We already discussed that Anne!"

Mary fingers the fabric Anne proffers with the embroidered Tudor roses and Anne's Ormonde Falcon. She feels the seams with her finger, rubbing the stitching up and down, fully appreciating the craftsmanship. Mary pictures in her mind a stooped wrinkled woman bent over a flickering candle lovingly and painstakingly pushing the needle in and out to form this regal bird. "It *is* lovely Anne." Mary's voice is soft and hushed as though she was speaking reverently in church. Anne smirks in obvious satisfaction with the approval and flutters her eyelashes beguilingly. Mary understands why everyone is held spellbound by Anne; she is luminous and yet opaque. She is vibrant and yet simmering. She is open but secretive. She is the epitome of female lusciousness, yet lacks a certain fashionable image. She is unique. Everyone who sees her realizes this and none of it is lost on her elder sister.

Anne pushes hair out of her face, tangles coming loose from pins. "I daresay Mary I am going to be indebted to you very shortly." Her face is contorted as she studies her cards and then laughs. "You shall not make the Queen pay you surely?"

"But you are not the Queen."

"Not yet Mary….not yet."

\*\*\*

Thomas Cromwell shuffled into the room with reverent bows, hands flapped over his only slightly pudgy stomach. He was dressed well and rather expensively, Anne noted as she admitted him into her presence. His face had a sharp intellect vividly and most clearly written across his countenance and demeanor. It was a certain manner, a certain adopted air, a certain feeling of *nonchalance* that gave Anne this impression. It reminded her in fact, of herself. His dark hair fell rather flat on his head but his eyes were far from dull. They engaged her intensely the minute they connected. Anne inclined her head in obsequiousness, in acceptance of his presence.

"Master Cromwell," she said imperiously.

"Lady Anne," he said; hooded eyes now downcast in reverence. "I come to bid you good tidings and inform you on the status of my journeys for the Cardinal."

A flash of red silk through Anne's mind before she waved a hand to clear the vision before her. "Of course, of course."

"As you know, all did not go entirely as planned, the Council rests it has not the ability to judge this matter. Wolsey himself has submitted the case to Rome." A flutter of Papist propaganda at the edge of Anne's consciousness, a shudder she cannot suppress.

"Ah," she sighs, a puff of air exhaling with rigor. She stifles a yawn and sinks into a nearby chair. "Do sit if you wish Master Cromwell."

His birdlike neck darts up and down as he shifts into a seat still deferring to Anne. "I cannot say I do not understand the King's mind in the matter. I know he means to take a new wife." He stares fixedly and pointedly at Anne. "I am uncertain that the Cardinal believes this to be wholly attributed to...." he trails off not wanting to insult her.

"To me? Is that what you are afraid to utter? You fool, Wolsey may not assume to know the King's mind in any matter. He has overindulged his bulbous chins enough." Anne thought she could detect the faint widening of Cromwell's eyes before he adjusted his expression into unread-ability. This frustrated Anne as she lacked the impassivity of emotion that so many of these sharpened courtiers possessed. However, Anne considered herself of the noblesse now, not a common servant to the King.

"Nevertheless, the case being remitted to Rome will not bode well with Henry's will. He wants this done and over, but with Catherine falling on her face, knees scraping cement, in front of the Pope, all will go awry."

"Catherine will not publicly object to her Husband's will. She will submit to him and plead with him until her face is pink with effort. But never can she go against him in this."

"Surely Rome will accede to Catherine! She holds the dispensations for her marriage to Henry and will grip them with a mighty fist even in the throes of death!"

Cromwell's face paled, Anne noted, even in the subtle glow of candles and it was a bit unnerving. Indeed, Anne was crossing boundaries it was impolitic to discuss, especially with one's inferior. She heaved her chest high, forcing out what was not there, sharp collarbones protruding more than any breasts. She smoothed her creamy skirts and slushed them around like froth. "I am at my wit's end you see. This is only the beginning of what I foresee to be a long and possibly fruitless journey. I must be able to count on you as an ally to do what you can for Our Cause. I know that you care for our good Cardinal, just rest assured in one thing — if he should fall, all who cling to his crimson tide will be sucked asunder as well."

Anne pictured Cromwell desperately grasping Wolsey's red robes and then in the Cardinal's great deceit watching as the robes turned into blood red waves. Sucking and spinning, pulling Cromwell into their depths; listening as he splutters and flails before finally being sucked down into their depths for an eternity. A shiver passed through the room.

"My Lady." Cromwell, somewhat removed, more formal, stiff, not unfriendly, stood and bowed slightly once more. Anne returned this by standing and dipping a half-curtsey before Cromwell shuffled back out of the room, whipped soundly.

Anne's mood soured substantially when Cromwell left. She cupped a hand to her face and felt herself wilting like a flower. She could feel her petals dropping, melting like crystal icicles hung precariously overhead. She was fading away. But she must bloom! One must not let the failures of others keep one from rising above!

With a shake of her head and a pinch of her pale cheeks, Anne felt life rushing back slowly. The blood coursed through her body, swimming quickly to reach her cheeks and fill them with that red rosy glow. She licked her lips and realized they were dry and cracked. She passed her tongue quickly across them, moistening up the peeling skin.

Anne studied her delicate hands, placed piously in her lap, folded like a church steeple. She examined her nails and her cuticles and made sure not a fleck of skin was out of place. Her hands were elegant and regal, and she took great pains to keep them that way. She would tuck them in fabric or wear soft gloves for protection. She would slip them inside voluminous sleeves to keep the elements at bay. Jewels often sparkled furiously from their position upon her long fingers. But little did Anne know however, that many took it as an odd facility. Anne shutting her hands out of sight so often was a rather curious occupation. It led to speculation about a deformity, but Anne was not privy to such musings and would continue her odd protection of female delicacy.

Anne paced about her chambers, all servants banished to the outer rooms to deliver her some privacy. There were rumors about her and Henry of course, the court understood she was a sort of "plaything"; therefore Catherine was not in dire need of her services as lady-in-waiting any longer. Henry had installed her with her own comfortable lodgings and said to shirk the rest of her duties for pleasurable pastimes. Anne made progress of this suggestion by pulling out a well-thumbed, ear-marked book from her trunk. Wrapped in elegant fabrics and hidden in the depths of the trunk were her banned books. The ones Thomas More would love to wrap his thick fingers around and strike a flame to. He would love to watch their writhing torment as flames engulfed their words and message. He would lap it up like a dog, panting in excitement as the last ember faded away.

Thus Anne would read and study and excel in the knowledge that she would share with her King. The knowledge that would decide the fate of many; the knowledge that one woman possessed could change a nation. Anne intended to wield that power like the glory of those before her. Like Margaret of Austria, her beloved tutor in all things sophisticated, she played the Queen of the Amazons with naked sword held aloft in her hand. Anne could even cite Catherine's own success over the Scottish when Henry was at war in France. Catherine's regency bought the life of the Scottish King and it showed a remarkable streak of determination in the Queen of England. Anne must compete with that. The fervor, love, and vigor of a Queen so dedicated to her husband that she slaughtered a King. Anne sighed;

she would join the ranks of the remarkable women. She would own a title in the hallowed halls of those "who came before".

Thus, in the snug warmth of her dark room, with a few candles burning, wax ebbing slowly away, did Anne sit down to read her destiny.

# Chapter 7

## *England, June, 1527*

Henry storms into Anne's rooms with nary an announcement and she drops into a stiff curtsey, caught unawares. "Your Majesty," she says humbly. When he dismisses the servants surrounding his regal wake he bids her stand up.

"Anne. I have just spoken with Catherine."

A *frisson* bristles in the air. A palpable pulse beats wildly in the room. Anne's eyes grow slightly wider, her orbs opening to drink in all her Lord might say. His face seems frozen in time, his expression twitched somewhere between confusion and frustration. Anne's cheeks grew pink as excitement at the situation dawned on her like snowdrops tickling her hair, nestling in and melting against her black head.

"Oh Anne. She did not take it well. She wept most loudly, most un-queenly, and begged me not to leave her. She claims to be my rightful wife. She says she never consummated the marriage with my brother Arthur before he died. I do not believe it, I cannot believe it, and I will not believe it!" His legs shook in their hose, and his hands were clenched in tight fists. A fury lit his eyes as he recounted this and they seemed to glow the same gold-red as his hair. Soft prickles of hair were sprouting up on his chin and spreading across his face; the beginnings of a beard. His nose twitched ever so slightly as he turns from red to a whitish pallor.

"Henry; my perfect sweet Henry. I cannot imagine what Catherine has to say will hold very much weight up against your wishes and powerful words," she paused, taking a tentative step forward, feet slipping on the stone floor. "You are the King of England, none can contest you." She snaked a hand up along those prickly hairs and rubbed it up and down, fingers entwining in the golden sprouts. "You will have your way."

These calming words had the effect of a sudden bright sun awakening through clouds on a storm-wrought, wave —tossed sea. The frothy foams settled up and down the shoreline, caressing the sandy beach. This was Anne's hand trailing up and down Henry's face. He beamed at her appreciatively. "Oh you are right sweetheart; I should fear the will of no man." The rough demeanor in which he said this served not to encourage Anne so much as to frighten her.

## *England, Summer, 1527*

"So. It is agreed then. Henry has formally asked you to be his Queen?" Thomas Boleyn shrugged his broad shoulders and then settled into a slouch, more comfortable out of the ever-opened eyes of spies around him. His hardened face was beginning to show its age. Crow's feet spread inexorably out from his eyes in mock salute to Anne's nickname, however insulting it was intended. Tiny crinkles formed around his tight, thin lips and seemed to be widening like fissures in a rock formation.

"Yes father," Anne said quietly, her French hood seeded with pearls making her look every bit the regal figure. "We have officially agreed to be married. He is going to ask the Pope for a dispensation covering all areas regarding wedding me." An invisible glow wafted off of Anne as she stood there proud and serene. The King loved her and wanted to be with her for an eternity. That should say something about Anne's iridescent charm and outgoing, spicy personality. Her father had always appreciated her general wit and knack for understanding. Religion and literature, philosophy and art were major foundations of the Boleyn household. Anne had upheld her end of the bargain that is between parents and children and become quite learned and sophisticated. She had been polished to an elegant sheen by her time overseas and now her father knew it was well worth the effort.

"What a blessing you shall be to the English people. They deserve a lady as noble as you to guide them in all things Godly and humble." He smiled, genuinely pleased at his daughter's success. "I daresay I never dreamed that we could achieve *this*."

Anne disregarded his use of the word 'we', knowing full well it was through her own intellect and prowess that she captured a King in her web. Anne shook her head furiously; she was not some spider, some black widow, devouring the flesh of her lover. No indeed, she loved Henry! Passionately! And wasn't that what she always wanted? However much her family had helped afford her a generous allowance for gifts and clothing and jewels, it was through her own efforts alone that the King worshipped her every step trodden on a filthy ground. It was no matter that he groveled to no one, he groveled to Anne. She believed chivalric tradition established that this was proper; Henry should seek to do his mistress every possible good. To be charming and heroic; great imaginings of silver swords unleashed, glinting in the light with great fat rubies and pearls glittering in Anne's hair, sending luxurious waves floating through the air. It was a painter's dream. A love unbound and undisturbed. A perfect river to flow in harmony, eroding the foundations of the earth around them, but never ceasing to be swift and constant.

Anne paced to the window set in the far wall of the room and pressed her face to the thick glass. A puff of air, her breath, spread out like ripples in the water as she exhaled on the window. Her eyes roamed freely about her, she thought she could detect smoke billowing in the air in the distance, like a dragon's quiet huffings whilst slumbering. Black swirls faded to a dim grey seemed to hover uncertain in the air. Like a thought billowing into life Anne surmised it was most likely the work of Thomas More, burning heretical books again no doubt. Their leafy pages shriveling into nothing as the flame did its work. Leather-bound volumes were not the standard, rather flimsy things could be found distributed amongst the poor Lutheran-followers. Anne did not tolerate *all* of Luther's teachings, no she upheld the Catholic standard, but she *understood* many of his principles. She did not condemn him nor condone him in the widest sense of the words.

As her nose started to lose sensation pressed up against the window most uncomfortably and unladylike, Anne adjusted her bodice and stepped back from the glass. She turned towards her father who lounged catlike, supine, stretched out in a lavish manner. "Ah Anne, we are finally quite free." The little wrinkles dabbling his chin stretched out into nothingness as he grinned broadly. "My girl to be Queen! Indeed!" He chuckled heartily at that and Anne smiled placating, not really desiring to have this conversation. She was much more desirous in fact, of snuggling deep into Henry's strong arms. Feeling the sinewy muscles contracted tight against her body protectively; smothered in his embraces. This was where Anne's mind was taking her, on a circuitous route back to her love, her prince, her Henry.

Ironic in her mind only perhaps, that her first true love was also named Henry. But what a fickle love that turned out to be. How quickly he could be bought and turned. How quickly he glanced shamefacedly away; berated like a little boy by his father, threatened by Wolsey. An imposing figure he did not cut, a true man he did not form.

Anne relished the fact that Wolsey was currently far away, two hundred and fifty miles away, in France. Wolsey was seeking to attain 'Eternal Peace' at a summit meeting between the European countries. His success previously of a 'Universal Peace' had led him to believe he could trump even that. But in so doing he had politically removed himself from the power plays made by the English Court back home, and his duties concerning the Great Matter of Henry's divorce now fell into other more capable hands.

## England, Beaulieu, Summer 1527

The royal progress this year had been somewhat stunted. The court had moved around year after year almost continuously. Visiting castle after castle; being sheltered by Henry's forced friends and confidantes, and being housed in Henry's own structures and battlements. Indeed, this year was quite different! The royal party was moving solemnly and commenced upon the old Ormonde estate to stay for some time. Anne was slightly nostalgic of her first dreams when returning from France of marrying the Ormonde heir; however she checked herself upon realizing she had instead ensnared a King for a husband, making her his consort-in-waiting. Anne was now openly queening her power over others and taking what she could get. She did not consider herself greedy; rather she considered these things her due.

The party commenced upon the hall and consisted of Anne's own aging Uncle Norfolk, and the sometimes-in-favor Duke of Suffolk, along with the Earls of Oxford, Essex, and Rutland, the Marquess of Exeter, Viscount Fitzwalter, and her own father Viscount Rochford. Anne lamented the gathering of nobles, knowing full well it would decrease her own wielding power over Henry. When he is oft surrounded by his counselors she is pushed aside to hear these great men's opinions. Though she knew that the Duke of Norfolk and Viscount Rochford, her flesh and blood, would indeed opine in concurrence with herself, she did tighten her grip round Henry's leash. She felt he was bound to her as a lapdog might be. She was forever trailing after him, or he after her. It would seem he could not stand to be apart from her for even a moment too long. A lovesick puppy indeed!

Anne thought of the puppyish eyes and flopped over hair that he sometimes affected. It was endearing if not grating on the nerves at times. When Anne longed for a serious conversation, Henry would sometimes cuddle up in her lap as though an infant in need of tender care. Or when Anne felt particularly inclined to romance Henry would be rampaging about his wife's uselessness. It was all very frustrating to Anne who sought nothing more than her own happiness.

The conclave of privy counselors gathered about the King like seagulls flocking to food on the beach. Anne had indeed seen this rather frightening sight on her many journeys. Sandy beaches, grains tumbling over grains to forever grapple for the surface, loosely fall about soft slippers as she would pad through towards the water. Tossing gently the waves to shore, to forever have them tossed back is quite frustrating for the ocean. It cannot seem to rid itself of this excess of water no matter how forcefully it throws the froth up to the sand. And in its reluctance to leave again it drags, nails biting in and scratching, the sandy floor sending wet grains scattering in bubbles all round. It reveals monstrous crabs and ocean life buried underneath the deceitful sand. And amidst the spray of salt on the air, stinging her nostrils, and the gentle mist of water tickling her lips tantalizingly, seagulls would flutter overhead menacingly. It would remind Anne of crows seeking death below, circling and circling until such a time as would be convenient for the feasting of flesh, the sucking of blood and juicy moist meat. The seagulls affected her in the same way. She would be quick to throw away a comfit or sweetmeat so the seagull would ravenously attack the sand encrusted treat, spewing the grainy mixture back out as the beak clomps decidedly appeased on the morsel. It made her shudder to recall their evil beady eyes that seemed to bore into her skull. And thus did she picture Henry's trusted 'advisors'. They eyed her with that same knowing, and insightful stare. As though they could see through her thin layer of skin, translucent before these men. It unnerved her in such a way that she could never express nor admit. But she flaunted herself before them as though not a care in the world could touch her delicate frame.

Anne left the men to their own tidings and meetings, knowing full well Henry would apprise her of any progress made in regards to decisions on their Great Matter. Meanwhile Anne longed to be alone with her thoughts, her Lord, and her Book of Hours.

When Anne had dismissed all but a serving girl from her presence and was situated most luxuriously in the chambers provided for her, close to Henry of course, she sat with book in hand and dipped quill at the ready. Anne opened her Book of Hours and studied the blank inside cover. It seemed the thing to do was make an inscription. She had had this in mind for some time; it is simply what one does. She held her quill hovering over the blank creamy surface and thought. It must be something meaningful, this book must proclaim to all who would ever behold it that indeed it belonged to the most noble and formidable Anne Boleyn. The proverb suddenly came to Anne's mind 'a day will come that shall pay for all' and thereby struck her white feather to paper inscribing in permanent blackish purple ink '*le temps viendra*' The Time Will Come. In a sudden burst of artistic feeling and energy she drew an astrolabe and her signature next to this phrase of virtue.

When she had finished she drew back and blew gently on the ink. A couple of bubbles dotted out in bleeding tears of black until coming to a permanent standstill. Forever stamped upon this Book of Hours are Anne's religiosity, knowledge, wisdom, time, and cultural excellence. A new artist at court who had been painting everything in sight and who had become a great painter under Anne and Henry's joint patronage had been extremely struck by such tools as the astrolabe, the celestial globe, cylindrical sundial, the quadrant, the polyhedral sundial, and the torquetum to name a few. His name is Holbein, Hans Holbein. Anne and Henry strove to cultivate a true Renaissance court, from great painters and literary works, to humanist scholars and Cambridge men to embody everything a sophisticated England should be.

Her dear brother George and her great admirer Thomas Wyatt were themselves artists in poetry and satire. It drew the collectively held breath of the court into a puff of air released in mirth and thankfulness. It is hard to be thus laced up every day not knowing where the blow will come from. About the throne, thunder rolls.

\*\*\*

"Secretary Knight has been sent on an embassy to Rome, to meet with Pope Clement VII to achieve a dispensation freeing me to marry immediately, all impediments aside. " Henry's grin bespoke the great depths of his heart and the meaning that lay therein.

"Oh I am so happy dear heart! I am glad that the Cardinal is too busy to attend to this matter personally, he did not seem to care very much for it in the initial secret trial." Anne still smarted from the failure of Wolsey to arrange anything but a satisfactory answer into Henry's inquiries. Nevertheless, even if Henry was willing to sidestep Wolsey now, he was not entirely out of favor, and would forever be in the shadows, clinging to the end of Henry's cloak. If only something could be done about this. Wolsey must either join up or prepare to be slaughtered. The idea of Wolsey as a suckling pig to be slaughtered, then plumped and stuffed, apple shining brightly from his mouth made Anne smile.

Henry inclined his head to Anne, sending shafts of delight shuddering down Anne's spine. This King, this great man, this Godly prince was hers! He loved her! For everything that she is, and everything that she is not, he loves her.

***

Anne is walking amidst greenery, taking heart in all the abundance of life around her. There are blooms budding on the intricately clipped hedges. The grass is so fine and shorn so short that Anne can barely feel its green carpeting beneath her. It crunches gently as she walks, skirts sweeping it free of loose petals and dirt. At length she tarries near a fountain, burbling crystalline droplets of water. She is tempted to rest along its stony ledge but contents herself merely gazing into the murky depths. Though the liquid spurting out is clear as a winter sky, the water pooled up all round the arcing fountain is green and the sides of the pond are slick with black slime. In the darker recesses Anne can detect flashes of gold and silver as small fish dart about in fear. Pinpricks of light must glimmer through every once in awhile when the filmier stuff shifts aside. The pooling light most assuredly frightens the fish as much as a pale hand darting in and searching in vain for its prey.

A beam of sunlight warms Anne's back through her thick brocade fabric. She feels stiff and unaccustomed to so much maneuvering and dancing and talking and thinking. It sounds so feeble reverberating round her brain; but the honest truth is Anne is being whisked one direction then another. All the courtiers are paying court to her, all the ladies maids, well, nearly all, are flocking to her side in regroup formation for battle. Anne waves her banner high 'The Most Happy' and shouts with a gallant stride and a boisterous laugh 'Let them grumble!' it seems to strike fear into the heart of the enemy's camp. Even so there are those stubborn enough to cling to Catherine, to grope her and defile her, to believe in her virtuosity. A great burbling laughter forms in the pit of her stomach, Anne grips her muscles tight in an attempt to repress this mirth but finds it issuing forth, rushing through her throat and out her tight lips. It starts as a small eruption of giggles but transforms into an unladylike bellow. It is the swirling emotions of the hurt, confused, and excited. The pressure bearing down on Anne from all sides is sometimes more than she can bear to handle all at once. Thus the laughter.

Just as Anne is catching her breath she finds she must steel herself for another round. Henry and his usual retinue of followers and guards are heading towards her with all due haste. Anne quickly flips her skirts about and falls into a low curtsey. "Your Majesty," she says quietly as he reaches her person. The guards fan out and the followers fall back.

"It is a disgrace! It is an outrage!"

Anne is instantly aware of all her shortcomings and grapples to think what she might have done; what trouble she might have caused his weary Majesty.

"The Pope has been captured by Charles! That prude! That strumpet! That peacock filled with vile detestable pride!"

Anne must stifle more giggles as she pictures the Emperor strutting about with emerald and sapphire feathers, gluttonously preening them before all to see. Beak nodding in earnest as he spreads his fan as wide as it will reach. But then Anne actually hears the words, the devastation registers in her ears.

"Catherine's *nephew* has captured the *Pope*?" What hope would they have of a dispensation with Clement under Charles' thumb?

"*Yes*," he says the word deliciously slow, as though chewing it, sucking the life from it, savoring every morsel, before realizing it is sour and rotten and spitting it out with vehemence. "Agh! Charles invaded Rome and sacked the Vatican! The Pope scrambled to take refuge at Orvieto! What are we to do now!?" He lifts his large frame and settles on the stonework of the fountain that Anne had resisted the temptation to do.

His faithful servants pressed closer to his royal personage but Henry waved them off with a calloused hand. Anne smooshed her

72

skirts in her hands and settled down beside Henry. She took his hand in hers and patted it gently, as though soothing a child who has just broken its favorite toy. "There, there…" she says softly, brushing her lips close to his ear. "All will be well. Mightn't Secretary Knight still seek an audience with his Grace?"

"Yes….it is *possible*," he conceded. "But what *point* would it make? The Pope is sure to discard all my scruples as mere trifles and declare my marriage valid. He could not risk his captor's fierce anger."

The full weight of their predicament settled firmly on Anne's shoulders. In her mind this was enough to snap a decision from her.

"Fine," she said, suddenly smarting from wounds too deep and too many to count. "You are wasting my youth! I could have been respectably married by now! What is the purpose in this interminable waiting and indecisive power? I am certain this is not the correct path." Anne stood and bowed to the King, much more shallowly than previously. She then whipped her dress round and started to march away.

"Anne! Wait there." He stood and met her on the dirt path. "Please. Forgive me and my callous behavior. You blame Wolsey no doubt."

"Indeed I blame Wolsey! It is his fault we are at this stage in the very discussion! He should have ruled on it here in England; remitting the case to Rome has done what for us?"

Anne spread her arms wide as though emphasizing a point, regarding an unseen villain. Her hair tucked up high on her head and her firm and fashionable hood squeezing it all together made her face appear tight and withdrawn. Her already pallid complexion was shot with anxiety and thus doubled its original pallor to a deathly white. Her black eyes shone fiercely, appearing as two pieces of black glass rolled round and round betwixt two fingers until at last forming perfect orbs. Her nostrils flared in her small nose and her lips pressed so tightly together as to disappear entirely inside her mouth. Pinched cheeks and frequent shallow breaths puffing out her chest and she formed the perfect picture of despair. It softened Henry's heart instantly.

"Oh my sweetheart." He reached out and instinctively pulled her to him. She breathed in the scent of him, fresh pine and sweat, and sighed in utter relief. Her passionate flare and temper seemed to entice Henry to love all the more. Tears pricked her eyes and threatened to spill over but she sucked them back in by sheer force of will. She must be strong, now more than ever.

"We will not be foiled in this Anne. We *will* be married, and Wolsey *will* do his part as much as anyone else." He turned away not daring to look down at her quaking form; Wolsey had come to him and begged him not to go through with this. Begged him on his knees to turn away from this foolishness. It had cost Wolsey a quick banishment, but Henry knew it his heart he would relent again, he would let Wolsey come crawling back on all fours, fat trickling over in bulbous waves under his crimson robes. What to do with a man like Wolsey?

"All will be alright sweetheart, all will be alright," he murmured to her as he felt her hysterical breathing and near-sobbing subsiding. Now gentle breaths were pressed against him as he stood there awkwardly holding his love, his mistress, and his consort-in-waiting while his servants looked on in wonderment. "All will be well."

## England, December 1527

Anne was tentatively happy to be reassured by messengers that in fact, the Pope had finally escaped Charles' clutches. On December 6th, Clement disguised himself as a gardener, and walked right past his jailors in Castel Sant'Angelo and took refuge as was originally intended, at Orvieto. It was through this miraculous delivery that Secretary Knight had managed an audience with the Pope at long last. After months of waiting and frustrated deliberations Knight finally saw the decrepit old man, hunched over with a stiff back, but still fingering his heavy cross reverently.

Anne sat holding her missive from Knight and was greatly unnerved by the contents. Though happy she could be that plans were finally being put into motion, the Pope was sending a papal legate to England to act with Cardinal Wolsey in holding a trial determining the legitimacy of Henry's marriage. Back and forth, back and forth. Anne pictured a swing floating absent-mindedly in the wind and decided *that* was the process outlined.

*I cannot see, but in case the dispensation and the commission be put into execution at this time, the Pope is utterly undone, and so he saith himself. The Imperial troops doth daily spoil castles and towns about Rome; monsieur de Lautrec, the French commander, is yet at Bologna, and small hope is of any great act he intendeth. The Pope thinketh that he might by good color say that he was required by your Ambassador here and by M. de Lautrec to issue the commission, to whom, being here with great power...he could not say nay.*

In totality, the Pope had issued this special commission to be brought to England, but of course there were no guarantees. The Pope seemed to be dangling a carrot that if Henry would help Francis' troops defeat Charles' then he would be more inclined to help his cause. Anne tapped her forehead in frustration, teeth clicking in her skull. This was not agreeable. Anne doubted if this commission and this papal bull were anything more than mere fiction to buy the Pope some time. A trial in England? Pah! The Pope did not mean to carry through with this; he is stalling. Anne could see through it all instantly, why did Secretary Knight not?

* * *

Anne sulked quietly in the Queen's lodgings at Greenwich. Due to propriety's sake Anne was not to participate in Christmas festivities, it would still be the role of Queen Catherine. For Anne to say she understood this was to admit a falsehood, she was not in the least understanding. To hide away a mistress was only to acknowledge her as thus! She could picture it all now, today was December 25th, the first day of Christmas, and the festivities would last until January 6th, Epiphany, or Twelfth Night.

Henry would wait impatiently for all presents to be delivered unto him and graciously accept each in turn. Then everyone would gather excitedly in the great hall and the Lord of Misrule would ride in on a hobby horse. Plays would have been organized and mummers would come in acting out the various scenes. Henry's fool would laugh and dance about, causing others to merrily chime in. Songs and carols would go round the room, boasting a jolly and festive scene. Wyatt would no doubt be in attendance reciting some new satirical piece he had written about the trivialities of Tudor Christmases.

Mark Smeaton, Wolsey's reappropriated musician would be strutting about playing the lute with elegance and fervency. He would be accompanied by drums and whistles and pipes played in the gallery. The tables would be laden and heavily burdened with boars' head and peacock pie. Ale and wine would flow freely into every mouth that is opened. Holly would be hung on every rafter, from ceiling to floor, strung up for all to see. Mistletoe would glisten at random intervals, and candles would shudder as rushes of air would send them into chills. Ribbons of crimson and velvet would be snuggled and entwined about women's hair, with garlands and shimmering stones.

Anne sat stewing, jealous and angry. Catherine would preside over Christmas, but what of Anne? Was she to be thus pushed aside for an unwanted wife? It was all she could do not to march in on the party anyway, and break up the merrymaking with a tantrum of her own. Let them grumble! For she is going nowhere. She is here to stay.

All should be paying court to her. Be wondering what to buy *Anne* for Christmas, not Catherine! A smug look crossed Anne's face as she thought about future Christmases. She would place silver candlesticks and silver crosses on the tables, fresh meats and pies sizzling in their cookware as they are placed on the slick table. Runners of emerald green would dash across the table, holding up the plate of gold and the jewel encrusted cups. Smeaton would play for *her* and Wyatt would recite for *her* and Holbein would paint for *her*. Her choice of holly and garland would be displayed, and her idea of Christmas tapestries, plays, and revels would be performed and shown. Anne would be the elegant and regal Queen residing over the land.

But not yet.

She can see Wolsey in her mind's eye chatting with Cromwell and Thomas More, discussing her, debating her, plotting her ruin. "Why *she* isn't invited!" Cromwell would remark, and More would wink knowingly.

"Well, she is only the King's *mistress* after all." And venom would spew forth as his holy lips spoke the word 'mistress.' For it is not a word the likes of Thomas More often has the opportunity to taste, to sample, to flavor. It is not common for a man who flogs himself daily and is known to wear a hairshirt underneath his clothes to utter the word 'whore', 'prostitute', 'concubine', 'mistress', and yet since Anne came into the picture More has expanded his vocabulary concerning 'fallen women'. It is very distasteful to him, but he has come to appreciate the finer nature of the underbelly of society. And he dubs that Anne is the Queen of *this* world.

For all More's infamous purity, his own family is rather a mish mash. Anne knows he has one daughter who he favors above all others and she clings to his bosom for spiritual nourishment. But she also knows there are those within his household who are wont to resent him. She thinks Cromwell respects him but disagrees with his principles.

Cromwell is a man who is more alike to a cipher. He is someone she does not really understand. She has attempted to dissect his personality but comes up dry every time. He is an enigma she will not soon discover the key to. He can be discreet, he can be secretive, and he can be trustworthy, but there is something in his manner that rather revolts Anne. A sense of something *lurking,* something *unseen*, that bothers her. It is like a demon, a possession, something hidden and seething underneath the surface. Breathing, longing for escape, but trapping itself within until the timing is right. And then…then it will be loosed to eat upon her flesh. Anne shivers, taking it as a whim of fancy, rather than premonition.

She slinks to the door and speaks with her maid. She wants a tub brought up and filled to the brim with steaming hot water. She will bathe now and rub her skin raw and pink with the thought of cleansing and purifying her worldly body.

It is not long before the tub is hauled in and sat rather clumsily on the floor by the young maid Anne employs. Nan is her name and Anne rebukes her for her clattering before she scurries out to carry in smaller tubs and pitchers filled with boiling water. Nan takes these and slowly, slowly, empties their contents into the tub. The sound of rushing water fills Anne with the need to relieve herself, but she waits until Nan has left to use the chamber pot. Once Anne has disrobed of her own accord, she slips neatly into the water which emits continual bouts of rising steam and heat. The mist permeates Anne's hair and immediately it is damp and a sheen of perspiration outlines Anne's face as it begins to glow pink from the heat. The chill air stings and burns like shards of ice smacking her face, thus balancing out the fiery water. Let the snow fall outside! Let it cling like a child to its mother as it covers the countryside in a white blanket. Deceitful in its name, for this blanket keeps no one warm, least of all the ground which shrivels up frozen underneath it.

Anne sinks deeper into the water, letting her body rest and relaxes in the depths of the tub. She lays her head back and feels the edge of the tub pressing sharply into her neck and the base of her skull, she ignores this as her mind turns once more to the Christmas she is not having.

Certainly she ate a nice meal of Christmas treats and drank enough wine to make her more than slightly tipsy, and she took in stride the lovely gift of pearl earrings Henry gave her, but this does not replace the presence of Anne at Court!

Henry knows this; that is why he is placating her to the best of his abilities. He promises he will make up for it very soon, when she is his wife. She begins to doubt the words he says, but what can she do? She may wield power over him, but if he is not her protector, if she crosses him, she will be fed to the wolves that seek to devour her flesh every second of the day.

As the mist rises from her bath and begins to coat the walls with a damp smell Anne splashes her hands under the water and giggles like a child. "Merry Christmas Anne Boleyn; merry Christmas," she says it to herself, for no one else has. The weight of this thought strikes her with the fact that she is very much alone no matter how many others are surrounding her. Alone, in the midst of a crowd, so alone. No one can help her with the burden she must carry; it is up to her and God.

# Chapter 8

## England, New Years', 1528

"Oh, he does not want to appear to be 'living in sin' with me at Greenwich. He wants our reputation to glimmer with the light of the angels. However are we to prosper if I am not there to see it through?" Anne lamented to her mother who sat with tight lips and pale face.

"Daughter, sometimes the will of men must be allowed, we cannot *always* have our way." She clucked her tongue and looked to the sky rustling clouds in thin drifts of wispy white across the blue expanse. It looked bitterly cold outside.

"I just want this to be over."

"You must have patience child, patience is a virtue. Ecclesiastes 7:8 'The end of a matter is better than its beginning, and patience is better than pride.' Proverbs 25:15 'Through patience a ruler can be persuaded, and a gentle tongue can break a bone.' Ah…but I'm not done yet Daughter, Proverbs 19:11 'A person's wisdom yields patience; it is to one's glory to overlook an offense.'"

"Does that last one by any chance refer to Cardinal Wolsey?" Anne's pointed look shot through Elizabeth Boleyn.

"Well dear, 'Vengeance is Mine saith the Lord.'"

"Mother!" Anne was exasperated. "Do you think I am doing wrong?"

"You have kept your virtue Anne; I can commend you on that alone. It is a commodity not often seen these days — morality."

Anne smiled sheepishly. "Oh dear."

"God in Heaven, show us the way."

## *England, February, 1528*

Anne shuddered despite the warmth of her room. A fire blazed with ferocity in the hearth and spits of orange flame lashed out at random intervals. Ash dusted the grate and spilled out in a mock-salute to uncleanliness. Anne cuddled her knees to her chest in her shift. She was alone save for the maid coming in to occasionally stir the fire with a metal poker and ask Anne if she desires anything to drink or eat. Absent-mindedly dismissive, Anne waves her out again and again. Her stomach growls in resistance to its emptiness, but she cannot inspire herself to eat. Thus she grows waspishly thin.

It was mere days ago that Henry declared joint war on Spain with France. Soon after this debacle and the half-hearted gesture of Wolsey's great speech in the Star Chamber to convince all the nobles of the land what a wise move it was, Henry seemed to withdraw and back out of the thing altogether. Anne was unsure where it was all going or what Francis' role in it seemed to be. But Henry had gone so far as to have Mendoza, the Imperial ambassador arrested and thrown in the Tower. It was a lot for Anne to process, knowing all of this was because of her. All of the pain, the political unrest, the church's destruction, the undermining of the Pope, it was all due to her. She understood Henry's fickle nature and had cultivated it to her own reaping, but that did not change that he could decide an entirely different fate for her in an instant of doubt or indecision. It was scary to know how easily Henry could change his mind, or be made to see something in a different light.

A log shifted in the fire, sending a display of sparks and ash alit with burning embers in a spray of light resembling fireflies drifting through the air. They slowly descended and settled atop the logs once more, sleeping in warm content. Anne adjusted her knees so she could rest her chin upon them where she sat. To her right lay her open Book of Hours, notes on a paper beside that; but the most astonishing piece of work sitting here was *The Obedience of the Christian Man and How Christian Rulers Ought to Govern* by William Tyndale. She shuddered to think what Thomas More would say to this book, or even Henry himself. She had not revealed *all* her secrets to him after all. But Anne knew this book spoke the truth, she had discussed aspects of it with Henry before, based off of her own opinions and pieces she had learned through Tyndale's work. She had hinted around about it with her siblings and in the end whole-heartedly embraced Tyndale's work. In this moment, Anne decided she must present the book; in its entirety to Henry has a gift. There was no other way but to simply confront him. Pussy-footing about the subject could shed a ghastly light on the subject, whereas shoving the whole meal down his throat was sure to make him swallow.

The King is answerable to God alone, not the Pope. There is no need for an intermediary; cannot God speak directly to the King? This as a basic principle outlines the thoughts of the book. Anne has voiced this often enough to be content Henry will likewise mew graciously at her to disclose more. He will be so thirsty for her well of knowledge she will let him suck her dry.

## *England, Greenwich, March, 1528*

"I shall not let Knight come home!" Henry declared loudly. Knight had been stranded in France for some time now as Wolsey had regained his ascendancy.

Wolsey had vigorously attacked the papers sent home by Knight as soon as Henry had waved them triumphantly in the Cardinal's face. He had annotated and devoured every inch, every sentence, word, and period that the papers had to offer. In the end he found them so seriously flawed and so prejudicial as to be utterly worthless to Henry's cause. Thus the in-between status Knight had adopted in Calais.

Just a few days ago Wolsey's henchmen who he had dispatched to Rome posthaste upon determining the original documentation null and void, Foxe and Gardiner, had finally met with the Pope and gained some ground. Clement had conceded to an out and out trial of the King's marriage to be decided in England by Cardinals Wolsey and Campeggio. It was merely *getting* Campeggio to England that would prove the most difficult task. Wolsey was very familiar with his fellow legate and knew that Campeggio had been seriously afflicted with gout for some time. Thus traveling would be slow and arduous and Rome was quite a long way to travel.

Gardiner and Foxe were also requested to do some canvassing of university's opinions on the matter of the divorce to be able to understand what the *theologians* thought of the case rather than the *legal* minds who so opposed Henry and Anne's views. Thomas Cromwell had said someone suggested this option to him and might they secure these opinions?

Anne's impatience might be her undoing as she paces restlessly about the King's privy chamber. Henry sits, leaning back dangerously in an intricately carved chair, while Wolsey sits across from him, hands resting delicately on the glossy table surface, his back straight and head high. He seems to be enjoying his return to power, Anne thinks snidely.

"We shall have our case tried here, though I can easily tell you Catherine will want the case tried in Rome." Wolsey clasped his hands together, steeple shaped. "Let Knight stew and think about what he has done," he adds as an aside to Henry's outburst.

Anne looked on with repugnance but it was Henry who answered. "She cannot openly defy me, and surely the Pope will bend to *my* will and not a *woman*'s." Anne looked affronted afresh but squelched the feeling and sugar-coated her features.

"Cardinal Wolsey," caramelized words fell from her lips like water dripping from a melting icicle. "What you are doing is greatly appreciated and will be thanked more fully when the success has been realized." She paused. "We will be forever grateful to you for your services."

Wolsey inclined his head in recognition of this acceptance.

"Gardiner tells me that the Pope refused to agree to an outright dispensation for you to marry, but remitting the case here for trial has been whole-heartedly embraced. We have only to await Cardinal Campeggio's arrival. I feel, you are right, Catherine's voice will be drowned out in the uproarious unification of all under your banner, your Majesty." Wolsey's words now dripped with honey. Anne wiped the disgust off her face quickly and fell to a chair with a harrumph. Her skirts billowed out and settled around her like dust off an overlooked shelf. She smashed her arms into the table and adopted a pouting expression. It was going to take so *long* to get anything done.

Just as Anne had assumed before, Henry had bowed out of the war with Spain most gracefully after uprisings in the counties had changed his mind for him. When public opinion was thus overwhelmingly heard, Henry could not turn deaf ears to them. Now Henry had to fear the possibility of France uniting with Spain against him in a counter-plot to seize power and strength. Anne knew how much deterioration in the faith of himself cost Henry the upper hand. When he lost his courage and his masculinity soon he lost the strength to command. He needed cosseting and encouraging. His temper raged to that of a trapped kitten to a devouring panther, it was all more than Anne was used to handling, but she executed her role very well.

The truth of it was that Anne loved Henry so much she was willing to sacrifice a little dignity and play the game. Henry understood her as so few did, and appreciated the qualities about her which she had always strived to make shine in a brazen light. But so many women of the day did not understand the depth and importance of a well cultivated mind; a higher standard of thinking; an exploration in the arts. Anne had a mind for things more developed for men, and could thus share a wealth of knowledge with Henry that forever sparred debates and councils betwixt the two of them, which ended in a heated affair of Anne wrapped in Henry's strong arms. The passion inflamed could consume them both.

George Cavendish appeared by Wolsey's side after a few more moments of discussion between the King and his Cardinal. He had a head of auburn hair which was slightly shorter than was fashionable, but he had kind eyes. He did not often fix these kind eyes on Anne. But she knew he complimented her grace and behavior to those who would listen. She supposed he probably called her a minx as well, but no matter he is merely a servant of that dog Wolsey. A smile played at her lips as Cavendish spoke quietly to Wolsey, out of earshot of Anne.

Mumbling mouths and weary eyes betrayed the man as he murmured back and forth; he appeared ill-at-ease. Every now and again a word drifted across the room to tickle Anne's pink ear: "Cromwell....it's a matter for the council to decide....surely Catherine will concede.... not a virgin...witnesses to be rounded up....for heaven's sake!" Anne turned raptly to face Henry while Wolsey trundled about with a worried expression lighting up his jovial face.

"I am informed Catherine is writing to the Pope to have the case tried in Rome and repressed in England."

"But you just confessed to me that Catherine would never openly defy me!" Henry's tongue lashed out like a snake, hissing and licking the air. Tasting the scent of fear wafting off of Wolsey's fat frame. But Wolsey was robust and resilient.

"Your Majesty, this was unforeseeable, who would imagine your 'loyal Queen' would take it open herself to so betray you?" Wolsey melted the King's anger but then quickly refroze it in Catherine's direction. Yes, he seemed to be thinking, spray your venom into *her* blood. She is Spanish anyway.

Anne twisted her face up in consternation while fingering her embroidered sleeves. "Ah....I must declare that I agree with the Cardinal." Anne's face cleared and imbued intellect and vivid thought. "After all, we have long suspected Catherine of treachery, but none would have imagined she would subvert the wishes of her husband! She gropes the floor and begs for God to grant her mercy, yet she openly would defy her Lord? Her liege! Her husband! It is condemnable. It is a tragedy and we must not let her win."

Wolsey's face was grateful and Cavendish saw this moment to step from the shadows and nod his head in concurrence. "Your Grace," he said, not directing this to either Henry or Wolsey and dropped a paper onto the table before exiting with a humble bow.

Wolsey lifted the paper off of the table rather gingerly, noting that Anne and Henry now possessed wild hungry looks like foxes that haven't eaten for days. He unfolded the creamy surface one fold at a time, and delicately opened it to its fullest extent.

"Ah…it is a missive from Stephen Gardiner. He says they are on their way home with the papers and a promise of Campeggio soon to come."

"Good. Good," Henry said, all curiosity evaporated. Anne herself seemed to wilt where she sat. Her 'B' necklace lacking luminosity and instead merely sitting dully against her chest.

### England, June, 1528

Anne sat absent-mindedly brushing her dark luscious locks, watching her hand's slow elegant motions in the looking glass before her. Nan, her maid, came into the room and began straightening bits and making her bed. "I'll have your bed pans warmer for you tonight Mistress." Nan said in her funny accent, nodding her head as she spoke.

Anne smiled at her in the mirror and continued brushing, humming a tune to herself. "Which dress do you think I should wear to—"Anne stopped midsentence as she watched Nan clutch her stomach, drop the bed linen, and fall gasping to the floor. Anne rushed to her side, grabbing the silver ewer off her table as she did so, pouring cooling water onto the maid's face as she lay convulsing on the floor. Great gobs of sweat broke out instantly all over the poor girl's body, beading and pooling on her face making her appear incandescent. It is a horrific sight.

Gently, gently Anne dabs the water on Nan while she screams for help. Anne knows what this is; Nan's pained eyes speak it all too plainly. The Sweating Sickness.

*** 

Anne, in great delirium has been sent from court. She sits in her bedchamber at Hever, listlessly counting the cracks in her ceiling. She cannot seem to keep still, she fidgets almost constantly. Nan died of the sweat shortly after first collapsing with it. Henry rode posthaste from Greenwich and sent Anne and her father back to Hever to convalesce. Is she sick? No. Not entirely. Anne feels her body grow warm, her breathing is shallower, but she doesn't feel the worse for it. Her father moans a little every now and again, she can hear it through the walls. Is he sick? She doesn't know.

Anne is stuck in her night gown, her housemaids are afraid to change her often; no one wants to come near her for fear of catching the sweat. After all, she was heavily exposed to it by Nan. She decides to lay now. The room is dark, her bed is warm, and the air is eerie. The windows are shuttered and the fire is blazing despite the heat of summer. The bed pans are hot under Anne's blankets and send up wafts of steam in Anne's imagination. She shivers despite snuggling tightly under her bulky coverlets. Her hair is loose and sweaty, tangled in knots around the nape of her neck. Her face is flushed from the heat of the room, and she can hardly see for the light not being allowed entrance.

Anne falls into a fitful sleep where she dreams she is Queen, the heavy gold crown of St. Edward the Confessor placed upon her brow. And she can still feel the weight of the crown while she is carried to a scaffold piled with faggots. She is tied to a stake in the middle of the faggots and the wood is lit on fire. She burns and burns while screaming heart-wrenching cries, the crown slipping over her face and hanging round her neck like a heavy necklace. She can see her own face reflected in its gold surface and a sob is cut short by someone shaking her into wakefulness. She finds she is sweating so profusely that she can hardly breathe; her maid is standing over her, hovering worriedly with a man she does not recognize.

Delirium has started to set in. A great throbbing pain courses through Anne's stomach and she clutches at it in agony. Perspiration staining her face, running off in streaks like rain on a window. Shuddering and quaking Anne calls out to the man before her. "Madam, my name is Dr. Butts; the King has sent me to attend to you. He also bid me bring this letter to you, but I see you are in no state to read its contents at this time. He was informed you were ill and now that I find you are indeed, I will help you as best I can." Anne could hardly see his face for her blurred vision. He seemed to be a looming white figure, ghostlike, wavering about the room. He had soft eyes that looked like snowflakes, glistening tenderly at her through a film of glass. A red bulbous nose contradicted these eyes and cried out for attention. Wisps of grey hair clung to his head as he removed his hat and laid it aside. By now Anne knew, it was growing dark outside, she must've slept for hours.

Dr. Butts excused the maid to fetch him water and towels and set about to help Anne. "We must get you to sweat my Lady. The more sweat that issues forth the more the poison will leak out of your body. If you can make it through this night you may yet live."

Anne moaned and writhed about on the bed sheets. They were soaked through with sweat. When the maid returned he commanded her to take the sheets away and burn them and to return with fresh linen. She bobbed a curtsy and dropped a nod of the head, and exited stiffly. The doctor then returned to his task of plumping up the bed covers and tucking Anne in tightly. He stoked the fire and added two new logs to freshen the heat. He lit lamps and candles and illuminated the room with an eerie red glow. Anne passed in and out of consciousness, unaware that the doctor was losing hope for her life.

Once dreaming again Anne felt she was swimming through a river, clear and crystal as ice, feeling refreshed and having the ability to breathe in the bubbles. Swiftly, swiftly she cascaded through this water before she felt her body being lifted up, up, up to the heavens. Soft, white, dainty wings sprouted from her back and she took off flying across the countryside. She passed York Place and Greenwich, Beaulieu, and came to rest overtop of Hever Castle. Anne knew her body lay inside, sweating and breathing hard this very instant, she felt a hard pull on her dream-body and cried out, groping helplessly at the thin air surrounding her. Stars twinkled out of sight as Anne's will began to grow stronger to live. Soon she woke up; her black eyes wide, her tangled hair drenched and sticking to her face and neck. "Good...good....possibility to live...strong-willed...." Anne heard mumblings and murmurings but was still uncertain of their sources. The deep monotone of a priest's voice could be heard filling the room at odd intervals. She felt all wet and sticky and soon fell asleep once more.

\*\*\*

"You have made it through the worst, you will live." Dr. Butts stood before Anne with a happy face and a light heart. Anne lay propped up on fluffy pillows in her bed. Her face was pale and looked near death; her normally sparkling eyes and countenance were hovering near ugly and dull. She seemed heavy for all her small stature. She heaved a great sigh and managed a weak half-smile.

"I cannot thank you enough Dr. Butts." Anne felt tears stinging her eyes. A couple of splashes fell in a spattering on her brushed out tresses of hair and her smooth chest and neck. "I really mean that. I know it was not in your power to decide my fate, but you sacrificed your own safety to do all you could for me. I…" Anne felt too weak to talk anymore. Her voice was coming out barely above a whisper and at first she was uncertain if the good doctor had even heard her.

Then she saw him give a curt nod and say "You're welcome."

Then with a tip of his re-donned hat, he turned on an immaculate heel and hobbled out the door. Her maid came in then and curtsied before running to Anne's bedside in triumph. "Oh Mistress! I was so worried about you! You said the most frightful things! You looked like death warmed over! I felt shivers to see you groan, I thought someone was walking over your grave! Oh! Oh!" Tears streaked down the poor girl's face, her chubby cheeks blotched with splotches of red.

Anne smiled feebly. "There, there, I am all right. You were very brave and strong too."

The maid seemed ready to fall over with this praise. "Oh thank you Mistress, thank you!"

"Tell me, how is my family?"

The girl's face fell instantly. She took a half-step back and seemed to stumble.

"Girl?! Tell me!"

"S-sorry Mistress, it was only that the Viscount caught the sweat as well, and was sick something mighty terrible. He has recovered though, but he is not doing very well right now."

Anne's countenance faded and she felt herself falling asleep again. The letter from Henry as yet unopened on her side table.

*There came to me suddenly in the night the most afflicting news that could have arrived. The first, to hear of the sickness of my mistress, whom I esteem more than all the world, and whose health I desire as I do my own, so that I would gladly bear half your illness to make you well. The second, from the fear that I have of being still longer harassed by my enemy. Absence, much longer, who has hitherto given me all possible uneasiness, and as far as I can judge is determined to spite me more because I pray God to rid me of this troublesome tormentor. The third, because the physician in whom I have most confidence, is absent at the very time when he might do me the greatest pleasure; for I should hope, by him and his means, to obtain one of my chief joys on earth — that is the care of my mistress — yet for want of him I send you my second, and hope that he will soon make you well. I shall then love*

*him more than ever. I beseech you to be guided by his advice in your illness. In so doing I hope soon to see you again, which will be to me a greater comfort than all the precious jewels in the world.*

*Written by that secretary, who is, and for ever will be, your loyal and most assured Servant,*

*H. (A B) R.*

# Chapter 9

## *England, Greenwich, June, 1528*

"My husband is dead." Mary's face trembled, tears threatening to spill over her already stained face. "Dead Anne! Dead!" Sobs now wracked her body but still she held the tears in. "I loved him so very much!"

Anne thought sharply that it was a pity Wolsey did not die. He survived the sweat as well as she. But poor Mary's husband William Carey did not survive his bout. It pained Anne to see her sister thus afflicted. "Oh Mary! If it were but in my power to take your pain away!" Her voice was laced with distress and she compressed a fist to her forehead. Were there not enough problems for Anne to contend with but to add her sister's grievance to the list?

Anne noted the fact that her sister appeared rather whey-faced and dowdy, her hair not quite fixed, her dress not quite laced up, her garters not quite pulled up. Anne sighed and breathed deeply. "You will always be well provided for."

Mary wiped a trace of snot off of her nose and lips, the gooey substance sticking to her sleeve in a streak of mucus. "Oh Anne, I know you will look after me, I just wish I had not loved him so."

"Look to God, for He will guide you through all misfortunes."

Mary sniveled but looked relieved. "Yes," she said quietly and hobbled along with Anne. "What duties await us today Sister?"

And like that a widow is ridded of her deepest sorrows. Though Mary had donned mourning black and stood starkly against every backdrop, she could not grieve forever. Anne studied her sister's face and detected a hint, a trace, of feminine excitement. Was Mary indeed looking for a new husband already? Mary had given birth to a daughter not long after the son of questionable parentage, and had their futures to think of. Mightn't it be appropriate to seek a new father to dower and provide for the children?

"Oh, we shall laugh and be merry. I cannot stand one more problem arising. I have written a sort of love letter to Cardinal Wolsey."

Mary's guffaw echoed in the hallway. Anne could almost picture it bouncing agonizingly swift across the stones.

"Hush Mary! It was a letter of pleased sobriety. I am happy he is recovered, pah, and indebted to him for his services, pah, pah, tsk, tsk."

"Whatever is to become of your sinful nature Anne?" Mary's small eyes grew wide with fear. "You lie as though it were the honest truth. You do so jauntily! Saucily! It is quite wrong!"

"Mary…." Anne trailed off and looked about. "What would you have me do? I have to embrace him for as long as he proves useful to Our Matter. There is nothing else to it. He has interfered unsuccessfully in my life for far too long. I shan't keep allowing such contrivances to pass as suitable." A fury etched itself deep into Anne's soft features, hardening her shell of determination. "It is not for Wolsey to decide what the King needs and wants."

"I suppose it is for *you* to decide then?" Mary raised a delicate pale eyebrow, a look of pain still visible within her eyes. So she really does love William then, Anne thinks solemnly. Such a shame.

"Well, in fact it is. I am to be Queen and I will not be led around by this fool like a hound chasing a stag. I am the one running, running, and I shall never be caught."

Mary nodded slowly, a small tear trickling down her cheek, unseen by Anne. The hallway was fairly dark and dust swirled in the air near windows where peeps of light streamed through.

"What shall I do now then Anne?" Mary asked suddenly, feeling very uncertain of her future.

"No small wonder you are confused Mary. But I will find you a new husband if you wish it, when the timing is quite correct." Anne sauntered on. "You will serve me when I am Queen Anne. You will be my most trusted lady-in-waiting."

"Along with little Jane no doubt?"

Anne laughed merrily. "Little Jane, Little Jane, pretty Little Jane! How our brother adores her!" her sing-song voice melodic as she speaks. "I daresay he chose well. She is a confidante that I trust implicitly, as should you Mary. Sisters are hard to come by." She nudged Mary's arm and felt instead of playful resistance, weak compliance. She crumpled like a ragdoll beneath her weight.

"Mary? Are you quite well?"

"Yes, just deflated. I feel like all the air and life has been sucked clean out of me. I feel empty and light. I could float away if I only let myself." Gold tendrils promised to tug loose of their haphazard pins stuck in her head at painful looking juts. Her rosebud mouth was pinched and pink. The black of her dress drowned her small body.

"Oh Mary, Mary, Mary," Anne murmured holding Mary up by her own weight. "You must rest and mourn your husband privately. You are too weak to be walking about. Let us take you back to my chambers and have food brought up to you. They will be clamoring about in the kitchen, banging brass pots and filling silver goblets. All just for you. Fresh mince pie steaming, piping hot. If you like we can have Mark Smeaton come to the rooms and play the lute for you. We can make it a merry time."

Mary's face brightened infinitesimally. "Yes Anne. That sounds very nice."

## England, July-August, 1528

Anne fidgeted in her seat, reading more love letters from Henry. She had been sent home to stay with her mother for awhile. Anne was quite tired of being sent back and forth just to keep things appropriate. Cardinal Campeggio would be arriving in a few months, and Henry did not want Anne in the way muddying up the affair. Thus Anne languished about her rooms, pacing the floors endlessly until her mother, belowstairs, was forced to chide Anne for making the floor boards squeak.

With a puff of pent up air released Anne set to work on studying her book. She wanted to be ready to present her arguments to Henry and felt the need to be diligent.

Thomas More was bent on his heretical burnings. Evermore it seemed smoke choked the air and blackened even the prism of light seeping through the most expensive stained glass. It filled the city of London with dread, and the surrounding countryside was awash with trepidation for fear of more lessons taught to the 'simple folk'. It had never occurred to Anne before just how close these heretics touched to home. She could be painted as one herself.

She shuddered involuntarily, her glossy hair shivering of its own accord. She let a single breath escape and pushed her silken locks back behind her shoulders. The poor men who had died in the fish cellar of More's college. How dare he be so foolish as to have these supposed heretics clapped up in a salty cellar without due process! There were no charges, only the smell of rotten papal views and this landed them in a dank musty prison. Some of the students shut away had died, and the others had been released only to be re-imprisoned at More's bidding in the Tower of London. She had heard tell however, that one clever man, named John Frith had fled to the Continent to find William Tyndale and escape persecution of More's lusty gaze. It seemed More only saw hellfires when he looked out at the world. His eyes could only discern faggots and flame.

Very soon she would spit in More's face by presenting Henry with the very works he is seeking to roast in his almighty witchhunt. Soon it would be More's face that felt the heat of the flames and the smell of singed fabric as he looked upon his own death.

Mightier giants had been felled, and none could stand in the way of Mistress Boleyn and Almighty God.

\*\*\*

Lautrec has died. Anne sits pouting in her room, picturing a blood-wrought battlefield. Ah, if the French are to be thus defeated, none will stand and oppose Charles!

## England, September-November, 1528

Unbeknownst to Anne who occupies herself with idle pastimes, Cardinal Campeggio has finally arrived in England, unscathed, though much stricken with pain from his gout. He hobbles along with a rough hewn walking stick, his hand wearing down a pattern on the end. Those around him swear they can hear his bones creaking and ready to snap under the weight of his frame. He is withdrawn and wrinkled, dark circles forming half-moons under his rheumy eyes.

Henry stood up before his counselors and announced that: "Divers great clerks have informed me it is directly against God's law and precept and if it be adjudged by the law of God that Catherine is my lawful wife, there was never a thing more pleasant nor more acceptable to me in my life. Both for the discharge and the clearing of my conscience and also for the good qualities and conditions that which I know to be in her. So that if I were to marry again, if the marriage might be good, I would surely choose her above all other women."

If Anne had heard these words echoed through his Star Chamber resoundingly, piercing the heart of no man, ringing true in no word, she would have indeed been viciously sharpening her claws. She would have plunged them deep into Henry's chest; renting a scar and watching the blood seep out in satisfaction. But Anne was kept in the dark of these fabrications and thus had time to mope about wondering when the tide would turn.

Anne was sitting at a table filled with correspondence, but her favorite was a particular missive intercepted and copied word for word by her agents. It was from Ambassador Mendoza to his master Charles V.

> *The lady who is the cause of this King's misconduct, perceiving that her marriage, which she considered as certain, is being put off, begins to suspect that the*

*Cardinal of England is preventing it as much as he can, from fear of losing his power the moment she becomes Queen of England. This suspicion has been the cause of her forming an alliance with her father, and with the two Dukes of Norfolk and Suffolk, to try and see whether they can conjointly ruin the Cardinal. Hitherto they seem to have made no impression on the King, save that the Cardinal is no longer received at Court as graciously as before, and that now and then King Henry has uttered certain angry words respecting him.*

Anne smiled to herself, twirling the letter in one pale hand, fingers gently teasing the paper. It was true; she had been secretly meeting with her father and the two dukes in hopes of forming an alliance. Indeed, the alliance had been formed rather quickly, like plaster taking to mold they had clung to her and her opinions in regards to Wolsey. If there were one thing the oddly grouped courtiers could agree on, it was their bilious distaste for Cardinal Wolsey.

The pompous man had grown too big for his robes, and set about collecting every jewel and treasure in England. He closed monasteries and diverted the money into his own personal coffers rather than the King's Exchequer. It was abominable to be sure! Now her father and the dukes were persistent in trying to bring Wolsey down. His star had risen high enough, it had burned bright enough, and now the light must fade. A black hole must form where Wolsey once shone.

Anne sat the intercepted missive down and began toying with yet another letter, the black wax seal broken and sitting in two pieces on the table. The thick wax looked like a chunk of coal, softened and melted down. It was an unmistakable seal, one that sent shivers of anticipation down Anne's back. It was from the Vicar of Hell. Or Francis Bryan to be more exact.

He had always had a reputation for being ruthless and hell-bound; he captivated women and stole their virtue. Debts meant nothing to him, pride was his only currency. He would slice a man's throat just to see what color his blood would run. He was dark, his hair falling in short night sky waves across his head. The shadow of a beard was always present on his chin. His features were well chiseled. His good eye was haunting, it struck a musical note inside their beholder, but one that was off-key, out of tune. It seemed to ask where its partner was, where the matching eye had gone. In the chivalries of Anne first returning to court, Bryan had lost this eye in a joust. He now wore about an eye-patch, lending ever more credence to the mystery and thrill surrounding his character. Thus Bryan had been chosen to usher in new advice and progress by being sent to Rome to continue spying on the Pope and to hopefully make some headway.

Anne always liked Bryan, he was a willful man, but not without his useful qualities. His gravelly voice sent chills down her spine, made the hairs on the nape of her neck stand on end, made her feel as though the kiss of death was upon her, but he had a trustworthy air. He had a demeanor that one may tell him their worst fears and come away relieved and safe. Yet, what did he do with these secrets once he had them? Did he bury them into the recesses of his brain? Did he tuck them into his heart for safekeeping? Or did he use them to buy and sell loyalty and favors at court?

## *England, Greenwich, December, 1528*

Du Bellay, the French Ambassador: "*Mademoiselle de Boulan is at last come thither, and the King has lodged her in a very fine lodging, which he has prepared for her close by his own. Greater court is now paid to her every day than has been to the Queen for a long time. I see they mean to accustom the people by degrees to endure her, so that when the great blow comes it may not be thought strange.*"

Henry stationed Anne at Durham House for the beginning of December, but by Christmastime Anne was stationed in her own establishment at Greenwich. Though Henry still presided over the festival with Catherine as his Queen, Anne was beginning to realize recognition for this role. Henry's placidity and mealy-mouthed composure was due to the fact that Cardinal Campeggio was present this year. Before the trial began they could not risk tongues wagging and prejudicial accounts driven like nails in a coffin into Campeggio's tired old head.

Henry was in fact, nearly tripping over himself to bandy about with Campeggio. Every pleasantry, every nicety, every kindness imaginable was bestowed on Campeggio like holy oil on a king, or christening water on a newborn babe. It was enough to make Anne's stomach turn. She cringed every time she saw a flash of crimson, the bitter taste of Wolsey ever present in her mouth. Then the uncertain gait would alert her to the true identity of the bloody cloak and she would dip a nearly invisible curtsey and vanish before she had a chance to register in his filmy brown eyes.

Thus it was for Anne, disappearing round corners like a ghost, melting into a tapestry, finding herself tucked behind courtiers like a human wall. Falling into a curtsey, a reverent bow, and all the while the beholder is expecting her to rise when in fact, she is already gone! Gone? Where did she go? Who *was* that raven-haired, sallow-faced girl? Was that a lady-in-waiting to Her Majesty? Ach, no, I believe it was the King's *mistress*. A hissed breath a tight-lipped voice would utter with disgust. Surely not his mistress! Would she dare show her face at Catherine's court? Some say it is *her* court already!

Propriety demanded Catherine receive the respect due to her as Queen of England. She was still Henry's consort and his partner in affairs of state, though she exercised no power. She had written to her nephew and had been showered with reassurances of his protection, love, and good faith. When she moved about court she clung desperately like a child to its mother, to the Spanish ambassador, and to Thomas More.

Anne believed more and more that he was like a spider. Crawling along feigning innocence, and then just when it has caught its prey by gentle pleadings and merciful whispers, it devours the flesh before it, spraying blood through its fangs in spatters along the wall. This made for a visible warning to all who would follow in the folly of the first. He crept along with Catherine, pledging his allegiance to her and her faith, smoothing his black velvet doublet down with trembling hand and preening his eight legs. Catherine, for all her faults and naiveté, would be resplendent in bright cloth-of-gold, shimmering delicately like a freshly bloomed flower being sucked dry by the nature around her. She pictured Henry as the persistent bee who keeps buzzing and withdrawing pollen from his flower, and then wondering why it does not grow strong and beautiful.

Anne's sympathy wavered in mid-conviction; she could certainly not support Catherine or her religious fervency for the Pope, but she could respect her position and her tenacity in supporting her beloved. But she would not let any woman, or man, stand in the way of achieving her love, and her own desire to declare to the world the Lord's great power.

For in Anne's heart of hearts, she held the honest belief that God had specifically chosen her for this role, chosen for her to be Queen, God's anointed. She would never doubt this simple fact, and it would buoy her through the strongest waves, and the most violent tempests. I can do all things through Christ who gives me strength.

*** 

Anne sat, dubious, as the Latin was read out in monotony to the gathered followers of Christ. She shifted slightly in her pew, her tailbone sore from sitting on the hard glossy wood. Henry's head was bowed obsequiously, Catherine and her retinue of ladies were not present for this Mass, or Anne would not have dared show her face.

Incense choked the room, relics glinted garishly from every nook and cranny, an ugly Christ glared at Anne from the cross where bloodied nails held his hands and feet. Stained glass windows showed scenes of Mary Magdalen, and Paul on the road to Damascus. A series of Daniel and the Lion's Den stained glass took off in a row across the right-hand side of the church, and a lone figure of Solomon sparkled brilliantly with the morning's sun filtering through.

Snoring could be heard emanating from the back of the church and Anne resisted the temptation to fall into a slumber herself. The English people must believe whatever the priests tell them the Bible says because the English people cannot speak Latin. This angers Anne and her neck begins to turn crimson, the color creeping up into her cheeks. "Are you alright Mistress? Do you need some air?" a girl close by whispers, eyes shining emeralds.

"No I am fine thank you." Anne flapped a delicately gloved hand in front of her face to cool her throbbing nerves. If the Bible was only distributed in English then *all* may read it and know God's Word without relying on the bishops and priests to tell them what it said. Every man should be able to read the Bible for themselves and for their families.

Anne's teeth pressed irritably up against her lips, sucking them in and out, breathing steadily while the sermon went on and on....

## England, Chamber of Presence, March, 1529

Cromwell stood resolute before the gathering, papers in hand. "I have here the determination cover letter sent to me by Secretary Stephen Gardiner; he says that the University of Cambridge has decided in our favor on the canvass that he and Foxe sent out to garner. They are the first in agreement, and surely if they agree, all the other major universities shall follow in their humble footsteps." All the court before him was hushed with either trepidation, anticipation, or a marriage of the two.

## England, May-July, 1529

Away at Blackfriars, the opening of the Legatine Court was commencing. In would shuffle the purple robed bishops who believed in sanctimony and swaying votes. And all the nobles of the land would not seek to miss such a great opportunity and would clamor for the best seats in the house. Anne's father, Viscount Rochford would be in attendance with her brother George. Her uncle, the Duke of Norfolk, and her newfound ally the Duke of Suffolk would also waltz in with heads held high, pretending to be removed from the situation. Anne knew Suffolk did not want her to be Queen, his wife, Henry's sister Mary, had grown to strongly dislike her and be moved in hatred towards her. It was not so much *who* Anne was, but rather *what* she was. What Anne represented and the position she was *stealing* is what so moved the Dowager Queen of France to these feelings of perfidy.

Indeed Anne had painted a correct portrait. Cardinals Campeggio and Wolsey sat at the head table, surrounded by clergymen, councilors, and noblemen on every side. It was as though a sea of power, where the tides could swiftly change a life. Decisions were made based off of emotion and whispers, rather than proof and witnesses. Yet, witnesses they would call.

Henry sat in a wooden throne, carved delicately with Tudor roses. Their sharp edges pressing into Henry's shoulder blades and making him wince when he moved. He would scold the craftsman who so carelessly etched these carvings in without thought to the sitter.

Catherine was called to appear and announced before the court. She took her place on an opposite throne, but sat so stiff-backed that Henry imagined her shoulder blades did not even touch the roses.

Anne would have been astounded at the witnesses who were called, those who had attended on Arthur the night after his wedding. An old man, thin wisps of blonde hair shivering over his bald head, stepped up in front of the court to recite his story.

"'Twas on the morning of November 15th, in the fifteen hundredth and one year of our Lord and Savior." The old man's voice was resonant but scratchy. "His Royal Highness Prince Arthur says to me 'Willoughby, bring me a cup of ale, for I have been this night in the midst of Spain.'"

The nobleman erupted into fits of laughter, stifled giggles, and bursts of mirth. Viscount Rochford suppressed a smile on his own face and shushed his son George who threatened an outburst.

"Hush boy! Don't be a fool!"

The Cardinals dismissed their witness and at this moment Catherine stood, her velvet skirts swishing about her stocky legs. She crossed the room swiftly, falling at Henry's feet, grasping his knotted boots and shedding tears onto his hose.

Bishop Fisher, Catherine's staunch supporter and premiere lawyer half-rose from his seat in shock and confusion, but felt a pull on his robes by Thomas More, and leaned back down again, heavily into his seat, his gold cross thumping his chest as he fell.

Thomas More's eyes were hawk-like and drank the scene in, adoring its every twist and turn.

Catherine's quivering form, hunched over her husband's feet was pathetic. Twice Henry bent down and attempted to lift Catherine to her feet, but she remained, heavy as a stone on the ground before him.

"Sir, I beseech you for all the love that hath been between us, let me have justice and right, take of me some pity and compassion, for I am a poor woman, and a stranger, born out of your dominion. I have here no friend and much less indifferent counsel. I flee to you, as to the head of justice within this realm ... I take God and all the world to witness that I have been to you a true, humble and obedient wife, ever comfortable to your will and pleasure ... being always well pleased and contented with all things wherein you had any delight or dalliance ... I loved all those whom you loved, only for your sake, whether I had cause or no, and whether they were my friends or enemies. These twenty years or more I have been your true wife and by me you have had divers children, although it hath pleased God to call them from this world, which hath been no default in me... And when you had me at first, I take God to my judge, I was a true maid, without touch of man. And whether this be true or no, I put it to your conscience ... Therefore, I humbly require you to spare me the extremity of this new court ... And if you will not, to God I commit my cause".

With a final flourish and a kiss of her rosary beads, Catherine stood, head held high, and exited the court. Her name was called over and over again to return, but she did not heed this, as she was already long gone with her faithful retinue.

All the while Anne bit her lip and prayed to God that all would be well. She could have had no idea the impact this speech would have.

***

Cardinal Campeggio has adjourned the court for summer. But Catherine has appealed to Rome. Her cause has been heard, Campeggio is leaving, never to return. Anne knows this, she has feared it for some time, and she has sat and spoken privily with Henry on the matter. His daughter Princess Mary has been secluded in her castle for quite some time now, Henry wishing to keep mother and daughter apart. He fears his daughter, he fears his wife. He knows the love his people bear for Catherine and Mary. Whenever they step outside in front of crowds, they rush to her, lovingly yelling "God save you Queen Catherine! Long live the Princess Mary!" Fat tear drops rushing down their ruddy cheeks, windburnt, sunburnt, leathery and weathered. Crinkled old hags, fat old men, swarthy farmers, vicious blacksmiths, blood-stained butchers, thumb-pricked milliners, witches and astrologers, nuns and priests, they adore them, and they revere them. It frightens Anne too. How is she to win the love of a people when she is usurping the throne of their Gloriana? It is unbearable. Unthinkable. Yet still she grasps the noose round her neck with nimble fingers, teasing it, threatening it, will she do it? Will she take the plunge? Will she hang herself for England?

All around her are constant whispers. Has she slept with the King yet? Is she his whore? How long must this affair last? She can't really mean to become a *Queen* can she? Yet every day she draws closer to that throne, the throne she pictures inscribed for her by God's touch.

## England, Summer, 1529

Eustace Chapuys was a smallish man of general build. He was nothing to take note of, but nothing to dismiss lightly either. Anne saw his hooked face with crinkled eyes and instantly disliked him. Wavy crests of black hair with grey striped in with the fading of age fell lazily across his head. The Imperial Ambassador, here to represent Emperor Charles V of Spain — Catherine's wily young nephew. Indeed, for being the Spanish ambassador he spoke with a French accent. Anne marveled at the traveled air he possessed, and the obvious intellect honed on his personality.

Chapuys' face belied his own instant disliking of Anne. His lips seemed to form words of their own in Anne's mind. She could see him talking quietly in a corner with Cromwell saying eagerly and with wet lips: "She is dark, like a fallen angel."

"A fallen angel? Why when Satan left Heaven the first angel he called to his bosom was Anne Boleyn, my dark raven, my night crow."

And Chapuys would snicker like a lecher.

Anne shuddered as she came to. In reality Chapuys stood before her with a befuddled and slightly amused expression twitching across his face. He seemed as if etched from stone or carved from ice. She felt he was a very hard man. She nearly reached out a hand to feel his chest, to press her fingers deep into his doublet and decide if flesh and blood, bones and veins lay underneath. Almost.

He has asked her a question while she lingered in her reverie and she is forced to apologize. "Do forgive me Ambassador, could you repeat your question?" She batted her lashes at him beguilingly but he was unimpressed.

"I was simply saying, do you mean to reunite the Princess Mary with her father, the King?"

Anne's gasp revealed the intensity Chapuys' blow had taken. Indeed if Catherine or Mary were here to hear this now they would double over in excited laughter. A rebuke nearly issued forth from Anne's tightly compressed lips but she held it in, the taste of it salting her tongue bitterly.

"The Princess Mary has her own will in the matter. She is stubborn and it is of no concern to me. She sides with her mother on all matters matrimonial and contrary to God's law. If she does not mean to acquiesce to her most humble Father, then I cannot put in a good word for her. For who would want such an undisciplined daughter at court? She would merely spread the lies her mother has taught her all too well."

Now it was Chapuys' turn to look pained and injured. A sudden wall was erected then between Anne and Chapuys that was never to be removed. Anne knew this, she could feel the stones being laid one upon the other, but she decided she would rather assist with the construction then break down the barrier.

Thus Chapuys did bow out of the room hunched over and glum. Anne could not spark herself into any happiness over points scored or battles won. For indeed she felt she had lost this round.

\*\*\*

Anne's heart beat wildly in her chest. She stood strong and resolute, imagining silver armor plating her body with protection. The strength she found was through gripping an invisible hilt, gold and heavy, of a sword in her hand. This sword, this striker of fear into the hearts of Popes was *The Obedience of the Christian Man and How Christian Rulers Ought to Govern.*

"Here," Anne shoved the book under Henry's protruding nose and pointed to highlighted passages. "Look at this first."

> *Oh that our kings were so nurtured now-a-days! Which our holy bishops teach of a far other manner, saying, Your grace shall take your pleasure; yea, take what pleasure you list, spare nothing; we shall dispense with you; we have power, we are God's vicars: and let us alone with the realm, we shall take pain for you, and see that nothing be well: your grace shall but defend the faith only.*

Anne flipped the filmy, leafy pages ahead to a new chapter entitled "The Obedience of Subjects Unto Kings, Princes, and Rulers"

> *God therefore hath given laws unto all nations, and in all lands hath put kings, governors, and rulers in his own stead, to rule the world through them; and hath commanded all causes to be brought before them, as thou readest Exodus 22 "In all causes (saith he) of injury or wrong, whether it be ox, ass, sheep, or vesture, or any lost thing which another challengeth, let the cause of both parties be brought unto the gods; whom the gods condemn, the same shall pay double unto his neighbour." Mark, the judges are called gods in the scriptures, because they are in God's room, and execute the commandments of God. And in another place of the said chapter Moses chargeth, saying: "See that thou rail not on the gods, neither speak evil of the ruler of thy people." Whosoever therefore resisteth them, resisteth God, for they are in the room of God; and they that resist shall receive the damnation.*

Henry's eyes glazed over as he read the passage. But Anne was far from finished. Indeed there was a chapter entitled "Against the Pope's False Power", how much more pointed could it be?

> *For if he had done it, he must have sinned against God; for God hath made the king in every realm judge over all, and over him is there no judge. He that judgeth the king judgeth God; and he that layeth hands on the king layeth hand on God; and he that resisteth the king resisteth God, and damneth God's law and ordinance. If the subjects sin, they must be brought to the king's judgment. If the king sin, he must be reserved unto the judgment, wrath, and vengeance of God. And as it is to resist the king, so is it to resist his officer, which is set, or sent, to execute the king's commandment*

Do you see? Do you see? Anne's mind was shouting with words of comfort and promise. Passage after passage, page after page, Anne had collected together the best paragraphs and presented them to her King. A look of consternation swept Henry's features, allowing for no comment and no questions. He kept his face shrouded in this look of contemplation until Anne finally closed the thick volume and slid it towards him. "Keep it, study it, practice it."

"Anne….this book is…"

Anne cringed, biting her lower lip, squeezing her eyes in preparation for the blow, the outrage at possessing this book. The impertinence of showing it to a King!

"Brilliant. It is a masterpiece; Tyndale etched these words straight from God's mouth! I must read this book, I must devour it for the principles it lays out to all of Christendom! Every ruler should possess this book!"

Anne's face was awash with relief. Henry did not seem to notice as he grabbed her hands and spun her about the room. Yeomen of the guard stood by the doors but did not flinch at this display of gaiety. Their King had enough affairs to have given them leave to hear grunts they should never have heard, and see privy parts they should never have seen; therefore viewing the King and his mistress spinning in joy was nothing to be nodded at.

Laughter erupted from Anne as her vision blurred, twirling round and round the room. Flashings of arras and windows swept past her as identifiable objects in this childish game. Her throat, white and creamy was exposed as she threw her head back and closed her eyes. The rush of wind beat at her eyelids, the very thin, soft layer of skin separating her from the outside world. Her eyelashes lay gently across her cheeks, giving the peaceful impression of blissful sleep. Sleep bringing that state in between reality and dreams; that childlike trust at everything that happens; that heaving of the chest while lost to another dimension.

# Chapter 10

## *England, September-October, 1529*

Eustace Chapuys, Imperial Ambassador: "*The King's affection for La Boleyn increases daily. It is so great just now that it can hardly be greater; such is the intimacy and familiarity in which they live at present. May God remedy it all!*"

"Anne." Henry's voice is interwoven with a slight tremor, a slight fear? She can detect it but is uncertain of its origins. "I have received a letter from Bryan in regards to the Pope's opinion, the whores' son! The bastard!"

Wolsey stood with Henry whilst he gazed out the window, afraid to meet Anne's piercing glare. Wolsey opened his hands in a 'What can I do with him when he refuses to listen to reason?' gesture. Anne nodded at him to continue where Henry left off.

"It says, Lady Anne, that he has 'Suspended his cause.' He assures him that the 'Dispensation was a positive and not a divine law; and if the Queen, as she affirms, was not known by Prince Arthur, there is no doubt that the dispensation was perfectly sound in *foro conscientiæ.*' Meaning before the tribunal of conscience; conscientiously, and he begs Henry to consider the danger in which Christendom stands from the Turks, and how much it is enhanced by this dispute. The letter is dated Rome, 7 Oct. 1529."

Anne felt willowy, wispy tendrils of demonic howls sinking into her eardrums. She felt their talons dig sharply into her shoulders and scrape away her flesh. "NO!" the wretched cry broke out. "He *cannot* support Catherine! Someone must pay for this." Her eyes, alert as a cat with a mouse within reach, locked onto Wolsey's. He seemed to cower before her, bowing low and making his leave to Henry. The door slammed with a shudder, the room reverberated with his insolence.

"Anne...." Henry finally turned to her from the frosted window and met her gaze. "I am sorry."

"This is *Wolsey's* fault. He was one of two legates sent to judge this case, and look at the verdict. He wants you to return to your wife!"

Henry cleared his throat but did not respond. Anne decided the time was now; the peach was ripe to be plucked, soft enough for teeth to sink into and rip the juicy flesh away.

* * *

After much deliberation and hard work by the Dukes of Norfolk and Suffolk, Anne herself, her father Viscount Rochford, her brother, and distantly Francis Bryan, the conclusion had been reached that Wolsey could successfully be charged with praemunire.

The exact law of praemunire was vague at best, but the Boleyns had managed to turn this to their advantage, as with all things in life. Anne heard the distant flapping of birds, the settling of soft winged bodies into rafters, feathers floating about like snowflakes as the weather turned dreary and stark.

"The offense of introducing foreign authority into England — praemunire," Thomas Boleyn said with authority. "Wolsey has setup a foreign government in England by choosing to serve the Pope in all matters rather than his good King Henry VIII."

Nods went round the table and Anne stood quietly, like a sentinel, by the door. She turned towards a vase of roses and began arranging them, fluffing their drooping petals while the men finished the calculations.

Soon, soon, she would have her vengeance. Her deep seated bitterness, her rotten hatred of the stinking pomp and incense of Popery would be exorcised from her. She could almost feel the ghost lifted out of her, releasing her from its vicious grip.

## *England, November-December, 1529*

It was St. Andrews Day, and Henry was in no mood to be quarreled with. A mixture of snow and rain splattered against the window. Not only had the King sprained his ankle the previous day, but now Catherine had confronted him with ungrateful words. She said she "had long been suffering the pains of Purgatory on earth, and that she was very badly treated."

Henry would have none of this. One look at her pious, pinched, overweight face gave him the strength he needed. "You ought to know that I am not your legitimate husband! Innumerable doctors and canonists, all men of honor and probity, and even my own almoner Dr. Lee who had once known you in Spain, are all ready to maintain that we are *not* married!" Henry roared at her.

She blanched but did not back down. "No Henry, I am your legitimate wife, and Mary is your legitimate daughter. Put away your concubine and return to my bed."

Henry's face went pale with disgust. "If the Pope does not conform to my opinions Catherine, I will declare our marriage null and void and denounce the Pope as a heretic, marrying whom I please!"

Catherine had gone completely pale with his insensitivity and heretical words and had fallen to her knees before him, praying to God for his immortal soul. She crossed herself and grabbed anxiously at her rosary, tucked safely away in a slit in her bodice.

Thus disgusted Henry had returned to his apartments and summoned Anne to his side. He recounted this version of events and she appropriately commiserated with him. She stroked his soft hair and lightly caressed his cheek, fresh stubble pricking her fingers as she slid her hand up and down.

Her own hair tumbling quite loose, her pearl earrings half-hidden behind dark locks. She brushed her lips against his hair and his ear and whispered words of affection. "Let them grumble my Prince, my King, let them say what they will. For when day is done and our case is won, they will have had their fill. For first light doth break the darkness of night, and all who fear will flee. And thus we shall prevail through all and at long last, together, be free."

Henry smiled with admiration at Anne, adoring her with every fiber making up his person. "You are a treasure, a jewel, of inestimable value, of endless worth. You shine a light where others produce darkness. You are my one true love Anne." He pulled her onto his lap and ran calloused fingers through her soft tendrils. "My Anne. My sweetheart." He buried his face in her hair and breathed her in. "You smell of lilacs and roses." He smiled, she giggled.

"The waiting will soon be at an end, do not give up heart just yet," he said fervently. She nodded in response, her cheeks pink from his stubble rubbing coarsely against them. "I will stay by your side for a lifetime on earth and an eternity in heaven."

\*\*\*

Thomas Boleyn pulled his daughter aside from the dancing and festivities going on all around them. They were giving a banquet in honor of Thomas Boleyn being granted the title Earl of Wiltshire in the English peerage, and Earl of Ormonde in the Irish peerage. The greatest nobles of the land were present, from the King's sister Mary, to the Dowager Duchess of Norfolk, and the Duchess of Norfolk. George Boleyn was dancing gaily with his short blonde wife, and Mary Boleyn flitted from partner to partner. Mark Smeaton was playing his music as always, and Thomas Boleyn sans wife lingered round the outskirts of the party. Thomas More was absent, but Cromwell could be seen lurking between shadows while he wormed his way closer to the King and ambassadors.

Anne smiled at her father benignly. "What is it?" she asked gently.

Diamonds glinted off her throat and fingers, her ears sparkling turquoise and her smile glittering the same. "I have been given the titles Earl of Ormonde and Earl of Wiltshire due to your rise," he said quietly.

The arras behind them fluttered; a breeze or a spy? Boleyn moved Anne away farther towards a giant pillar and resumed, hand on her shoulder. "It is a promotion, a much fought after promotion, for being your father no doubt."

Anne's grin widened enormously and she refrained from giddily clapping her hands. She composed her features and inclined her head. "Well deserved father, well deserved." An eruption of gay laughter sounded behind them where the revelries were taking place. Someone had spilled an entire ewer of water and Henry's fool fell to his knees like a dog, pretending to lap it up. A few guards heaved him up and shoved him back as he began to place tongue to floor, licking up dirt and small pebbles, along with courtier's grime, that *slime* that oozes off of them from too much importance. Much to the delight of the onlookers he was shoved backwards and fell in a tumble over himself.

The Duke of Suffolk looked about him, Anne noted, seeming to seek her out. They had united to take out a common enemy, Wolsey, but since his removal from the palace to his own home, they had not spoken much. The threat of the Cardinal still hung imminent in the air. The King was loathe to commit himself further than he had by having Wolsey removed to placate his councilors. After all, the charge of praemunire was valid, and Lord Darcy was to sit with Parliament in judgment of this crime, but Henry prorogued Parliament until a much later date and sent Wolsey packing. His thick stomach could suck in the air with relief.

Although removed from court, Wolsey still had *power*; he still had the favor of long years in good standing with the King. He could tap into this well of sympathy from Henry at any time. They must keep him back, they must keep themselves afloat.

Anne's main victory in the trumping of Wolsey was his gift of York Place to Henry. She had long coveted the glorious building, abutting the Thames with private staircases leading to the water for barges to dock at. Wolsey had held this house because of his incumbency to the Archbishopric of York. Anne intended to persuade Henry to renovate and restore the building to a great palace. They already changed its name from York Place to Whitehall, and Anne of course would not stop there.

There were also reports from Gardiner and Foxe that they had made successes of nearly every university canvassed in the King's opinion regarding their Great Matter. But it seemed these arguments held no weight with the Pope. This was to be expected but at least it showed the world could be made to agree to Henry's will, or rather to bend to it at the peril of their lives.

Outside, ice fell from the sky like frozen teardrops, shattering, broken-hearted, on the streets. But tucked warmly inside was the English Court of Great Nobility, or so Anne could now regard even her father, Earl of Wiltshire. She hugged him tenderly, his sturdy frame supporting her delicate one. "Oh Father…" she said as she snuffled into his cloak. "I am so happy…and so scared."

"It's ok Anne; it will all come to rights in the end. It is God's will for you to be Queen. Would you not agree?" He laid a reassuring hand on her quaking shoulders and pushed her back to stare into her eyes. "Queens are not made by men, not by flesh and blood, but by God Almighty, our creator."

Anne's eyes were like slivers of black diamonds as they glistened and glossed at her father's words. "Yes Father, you are right. I am glad that the Rochford title passed to George; he was so longing for one that I nearly pitied him."

"Yes one can always *nearly* pity that lad."

With a smile, a bobbed curtsey, and a flick of skirts, Anne rejoined the merry-making by spinning into a dance with her brother. Jane Boleyn smiled approvingly to watch her sister-in-law shimmer in light blue across the floor. Turquoise ribbons peeping out from her stockings, a silver girdle wrapped tight round her small waist. Her every move was accentuated by her grace and poise, that quality which none can name. That essential….Anne-ness.

***

"Ah…the King gave a grand fête in the city, to which several ladies of the Court were invited, the Lady Anne taking precedence over them all, and being made to sit by the King's side, occupying *your* allotted place your Grace, as the crowned Queen." Chapuys rushed from Catherine's side after delivering this blow and left to submit this information to his master, Emperor Charles V.

Anne, meanwhile, went on rides with the King through the forest. She watched gentle snowfalls, hearing the horses' sharp hooves find no resistance to the soft, melting flakes below. Chilling wind bit cheeks and stung them red, eyes watered from the force of it. But deep in the woods where no one made a noise but the gentle cooing of doves tucked in a hollow, peace could be found. The deafening roar of nothingness. Quiet, quiet, quiet, Anne did not dare raise her voice above a murmur for fear of disturbing the quiet. The sun cast rays across the soft white snow, sending twinkling's of light to catch the eye for miles around.

Fur encircled Anne's head, her wrists, her collar, her hands themselves. Henry was also decked out, more fashionably than practically in his own fur. Thickly laced riding boots held Anne's feet and calves snuggly, and her elegant cloth-of-gold trappings kept her horses' muscles warm. She rubbed a palm along the velvet muzzle and the satin nose, caressing, touching, and petting. Her ears ringing with the sound of quiet.

Henry gazing at her in such open admiration as to send drumbeats of blood coursing through her body in excitement. Love! Love and quiet. She felt so at peace, so escaped out here in the forest. Tall trees shot up and loomed high above her, holding great boughs of snow, ready to slough over at the slightest tremor of the earth. Anne prayed it would hold still as her fur-haloed head rode underneath them. She gripped her reigns lightly, trusting her horse. Elegant and regal she pictured herself to be, the very image of queenliness.

A fox bounded out of a hole and raced across their path, the horses ignored this, but Henry and Anne shared a knowing smile.

*** 

Anne and her brother were debating about Thomas More and his burnings of heretics and pamphlets by Martin Luther. "The man should be abhorred," George declared firmly.

"His beliefs do differ widely from what we are trying to establish in the Church. I think he means well though. His translations of the Bible are something to be praised!"

"Erasmus wrote to Father, do you know what he said?" When Anne shook her head George continued: "'I laid a hen's egg; Luther hatched a bird of quite a different species.'"

Anne could not help laughing at this analogy. "Oh what an egg has been laid!"

"The King has spoken out often enough against Luther that the Pope made him 'Defender of the Faith', but now look at how Henry is treating the Pope!"

"Hush George!" Anne said sharply. "You never know who may be listening."

"Then I suppose we should cease this discussion," George said quietly. "You may have the King's heart, but it could easily be swayed."

"I have opened his eyes to the truth! It is not that he so easily changes his mind!" Anne's heart beat wildly, she knew this was untrue; Henry could be swayed back and forth between a subject all too quickly!

## England, Christmas, 1529

Anne sits heavily with hot spiced ale steaming from a thick mug in her hand. She watched as the Yule log burned on the fire. Today was the first day of Christmas and they had just set it into the flames. Although Anne was once more sequestered in her apartments while Henry celebrated Christmas with Catherine, at least she was in the same location. She simply held to Henry's promise of going to the Whitehall jewel house and giving her gifts of her choice. This was a merry Christmas indeed for Anne!

As the log cracked and sizzled under the merciless workings of the fire, Anne thought about food. Downstairs they would be feasting on mince pie, coffin shaped; a predication of their lives to come. The pies were always stuffed with a turkey which was stuffed with a goose which was stuffed with a chicken which was stuffed with a partridge which was stuffed with a pigeon. At the end of the meal no one could say they were in any particular mood for fowl.

The fire hissed as the wood burned, it sometimes amazed Anne that they could burn this log for twelve days and it would still be in perfectly lumped, blackened, condition. Its skin was thick, she decided, as was her own. No matter how many pricks or cuts, no matter how many times the courtiers would slice through a layer, would they ever reveal the scared woman underneath. She must prove to them all she could handle these pressures and stresses, after all, if she was meant to be Queen she would have many matters to settle and attend to.

## England, Greenwich, January-February 1530

Catherine, the Spanish Queen of England was removed to her own residence at Richmond, while Anne was kept at Henry's bosom of Greenwich. She stood, holding her head high, chin jutting out statuesque, and her hands folded behind her. Henry was to her right holding the Privy Seal and her father, Earl of Wiltshire, knelt before the King.

Henry seemed to shimmer with starlight as he appointed Thomas Boleyn keeper of the Privy Seal, his official title Lord Privy Seal. Henry loved to appear magnanimous before his subjects; loved to keep them in awe of him. Thomas Boleyn did not miss his cue, and groveled appropriately before His Majesty. Anne knew her father was in earnest and was proud that the Boleyn's should see this day. And Queen Catherine was not here to spoil it. As he rose from his kneel and the King placed a hand on his shoulder, handing him the seal, the doors were opened and Anne's nightmare was announced into the room.

"Cardinal Thomas Wolsey your Grace." The servant bowed as Wolsey swept into the room, cloak fluttering in his wake, fireworks lighting his eyes. His claws seemed more sharpened than ever, Anne could see them gleaming under the sleeves of his robe. She shuddered but kept her face a study of composition to be guessed at.

Henry immediately turned from her father to greet the Cardinal. "Wolsey! It is good to see you!"

Inside, Anne was seething and wondering how this man could possibly have been restored to favor; and without any foreknowledge to her or her allies! A storm brewed beneath the surface of her calm, like a cool glass lake ready to burst with a geyser, heated and swelling below the coolness of the water.

"Lady Anne," he made obeisance to the King's mistress before turning back to Henry. "I have made progress your Majesty; I do believe we can get you your divorce." It seemed to Anne that he was mocking her, making a joke of her.

"Come Wolsey, look at this painting, it is done by Master Holbein; tell me, what do you think of it?"

Glorious oils of maroon and gold, deep luxurious chocolates and mauve, swirling navy blue, silver as luminous as the moon's cold surface. "It is called *Solomon and the Queen of Sheba*." Henry waved his jeweled hand in a wide sweeping manner, fingers brushing the vellum surface. "Is it not extraordinary?"

Wolsey's face was a mixture of awe and concern. Would this Holbein pollute the godly works of those before? Or would he contribute to their ranks? Would he be a disgrace to their court; a worldly reputedly womanizer, or a man of good standing and faith. Wolsey was yet to discover but he knew the painting was priceless in measure and execution.

"It *is* extraordinary your Grace, it is quite incredible." A little sigh escaped his round lips, thick lips that to Anne seemed to suck the very air out of the room. She breathed more deeply to attempt to take as much as she could before this phenomenon took place.

Wolsey's gut trembled beneath his speech, with the flap of his tongue came a flap of his fat. Anne hid her disgust and instead turned to her father who as yet stood unacknowledged by the Cardinal. He stood, watching the exchange, seal in hand, feeling slighted. Yet was that not Wolsey's purpose?

Anne looked at Henry, caught his eye and bowed low. "Your Majesty, may we take our leave of you to discuss political matters with the Cardinal?"

Henry nodded, a grin lighting his face, as though he and Anne shared some great secret. Anne inclined her head but turned away with wrath writ on her face. She felt the looming force of Wolsey rising up to tear her down. A wave of astronomical proportions, a phantasm of demons and treachery. Anne walked with her father out into the hall and paused to look at him.

"What are we to do with Wolsey?" she asked pointedly, making no preamble.

"We shall have to rid ourselves of him more permanently this time," Wiltshire said with no qualms, no quiver in his voice, not a single tremor to belie a more innocent nature. No shock passed Anne's face either, not a hint of sorrow. She nodded.

"I will summon Norfolk and Suffolk; we will watch him all the more eagerly. He failed the first time; do you not think he will fail again? And we will be there to watch the blood flow, to watch the crows circle, to gather up the leftovers." He had a faraway look in his eyes, as though he could already see it happening.

Anne looked at him with a sliver of trepidation. "And what shall happen to us?"

"You shall become Queen, and we shall all rise in your favor."

England, Hampton Court, June, 1530

The moat's waters shifted murkily as the wind blew gently across its surface. Anne and Henry entered into the court and swept towards the fountains in the adjoining courtyard. Henry Norris, the King's Groom of the Stool struggled to keep up with the group. Chapuys was also clinging to the outskirts begging a conversation with dear Henry. William Brereton and Nicholas Carew hung back a little ways, but it was Cromwell who was pushing through the rush to seek an audience. It was hard to keep up with Henry once he was on a mission, and Anne herself forced her small legs out with great vehemence, attempting to match his stride.

Cromwell's thick head of dark hair swept down in a bow as he finally caught up to the King.

"What is it Cromwell?" Henry asked, slightly annoyed at this intrusion.

"I have someone for you to meet Sire; I think it will be to your great pleasure."

Henry looked about him, as did Anne, but did not see anyone unrecognizable.

"Well who is it?" His face was pinched with frustration. "I haven't got all day."

Cromwell obsequiously clasped his hands. "I thought to bring him to you later; he has information regarding your Great Matter." He here inclined his head towards Anne as well who flaunted herself as Queen though she was as yet only a mistress.

"Very well."

\*\*\*

Henry Norris was attending on the King while Anne waited patiently for Cromwell to arrive with his 'guest'. She was uncertain how to take this turn of events but intended to stay and find out. Henry Norris loomed large and strong, a close match to King Henry at his side. He had blondish hair which was more wavy than Henry's locks, but the color when shone in the light was similar. His broad shoulders and chiseled features were replicated as well. He nodded to Anne every now and again as though reaffirming and acknowledging her right to be there.

Anne watched a lone candle flicker over a bowl of fruit. Apples and delicate oranges wavered in the light. Catherine's parents Ferdinand and Isabella had funded and supplied ships for a man named Christopher Columbus to sail to a New World. He had brought back many fruits and spices, some of which now sat primly in the bowl, looking waxen and taunting those around to eat them. A knock on the door made both the flame and Anne jump in anticipation.

Within moments Cromwell was standing in the King's office of the chamber, with a tall figure attempting to bow behind him. As he straightened his frame up Anne saw he was very tall indeed, soaring high into the ceiling. Hair dark brown, though not as black as Anne's capped his head. He had brown eyes that were soft and endearing. He wore simple robes but appeared pious. Anne liked him instantly. It was his demeanor, his relaxed but nervous offhandedness. His simple placating smile and his gentle eyes. The look of a small puppy or a newborn foal, for there lurked passion within those depths as well. It was a touch of youth and innocence mixed with ambition and knowledge.

"This is Dr. Thomas Cranmer, your Majesty. He is the one who suggested to Gardiner and Foxe that they should canvass opinion of the university theologians throughout Europe. Do you remember when Wolsey sent them on this mission….?" he trailed off lamely, he had suggested the King might have forgotten something important which was quite an insult.

The fire raged in the King's face but Anne intervened. "Yes, the findings were favorable as I recall from the letters I received from Secretary Gardiner and from Francis Bryan in his relatable schemes."

"Indeed Lady Anne." Cromwell looked at her gratefully, Anne inclined her head imperiously.

"So Dr. Cranmer, you are the genius to thank for the progress with the schools? I was very impressed by the argument and ideas supporting this. Cromwell didn't reveal his sources until it had been considered a success might I add." The King smiled benignly. "Nevertheless I will seek to promote you for your hard work."

"Your Majesty!" Cranmer doubled his frame in half as he bent over.

"You graduated from Cambridge I am told?" Henry looked him up and down.

"Yes your Majesty! I studied logic, philosophy, and classical literature. After I received my Bachelor of the Arts degree I obtained a Masters degree in humanists. I had been working at an elected Fellowship of Jesus College."

"Ah, an educated Renaissance man, someone I can admire." The King's eyes glowed with admiration. Henry loved a man with intellect and wit; someone he could spar with.

"Have you more information for us then Dr. Cranmer?"

Cranmer fidgeted about and his eyes alit as though just remembering his reason for this meeting. "Why yes! As a matter of fact I do! I presented this to Cromwell and this time he thought I should show you anything I thought pertinent myself." He rustled inside his cloak and withdrew a stack of rumpled looking papers. They rustled in his hand.

He stretched out his long arm to the King who took them and read the title aloud: *"Collectanea satis copiosa."*

"Yes your Majesty. It is a set of papers scriptural, patristic, and historical arguments which demonstrate claims that there is no warrant for centuries-old assumptions that the Pope is the supreme head in matters spiritual."

"You believe the Pope not to be the head of the Church?" Henry asked dubiously, but intrigued. His own mind had already been swayed like a pendulum towards this direction by his lovely Anne. Angelic Anne.

"Yes your Majesty. I believe *you* to be the head of the Church of England."

A silence filled the room. Cromwell smirked with the knowledge of someone who has seen the future and knows it is good. Anne trembled with something akin to fear and excitement. Henry's impassivity vanished and he embraced Cranmer who stood awkwardly frozen before them.

Henry Norris had all but melted into the background since this exchange began, but now he coughed, as though choking on the vile words spewing from others' mouths.

"I believe *this* will solve your matrimonial problems," Cranmer finished, all eyes riveted upon his person.

"I declare then, that we gather parliament and attempt to pass a law…." Henry began mumbling quietly to himself, Cromwell visibly straining to gather the King's words to himself. Anne sat, still as stone, rubbing her hands together and biting her lower lip. Could this be it? Could this be their breakthrough? The symbolic dove bringing the olive branch? She could only pray, her hand crossed her body by rote and she closed her eyes in quiet prayer. Little did she know Henry Norris was saying the same quiet prayer of thanks.

# Chapter 11

## *England, October, 1530*

"Finally it is done," Anne announced with great pomposity. "I have directed the King to keep Wolsey at his houses doing menial work for the King. No more bombarding us with his great impetuosity. Let him rot."

"I am not certain if it is enough to simply 'let him rot' Anne," George said quietly, his hazelnut eyes glistening with fervency. "I declare that nothing will ever stand firm for you until he has been removed."

"Oh why must everyone push this finality into the picture? Why can we not just have done with him?" Anne's color rose in tandem with her temper. A flash of color a burst of anger.

"Anne your brother is right." Norfolk brushed his chin gently with his aged hand. "If Wolsey were done away with we would have free reign and access to the King."

"Do we not already have that!? I am his love!" Anne raged as she stood up and paced about the room, only to come back to her original position.

"Your uncle does not mean to say that we do not have power and sway, but there is a force pushing us back ever further. It is though we are swimming towards an island, it is within sight; we can taste it, smell it, and breathe it in. But the waters all around us are churning and spitting us back again and again until it forms a whirlpool and sucks us into its depths," Wiltshire said solemnly, staring straight into Anne's deep eyes.

"Wolsey is a whirlpool now? Whatever shall he be next? Is he *every* evil in this country?"

"If I say so," Norfolk said quietly but with great severity. "I mean to make him pay for his pompous demeanor."

Charles Brandon stood stiffly, bearing himself up, itching at his graying hair. "I believe it is best to strike while the iron is hot, and the metal can be made the softest."

"Indeed. So it is agreed? We must devour him. I have spies in his household; there is much to be achieved. I will intercept any letters he sends and eventually he must slip up." Wiltshire closed the conversation even as Anne's rosebud lips perched to protest.

***

"I have received a papal edict ordering me to return to Catherine." Henry looked at Anne sharply. "But she is already removed to her own household at The More. I will never allow her to be brought back."

"So, the Pope is threatening excommunication then?" Anne's eyebrow arched plaintively. Henry Norris and William Brereton were in the background of the King's Privy Chamber, fidgeting with objects Anne could see no reason to fidget with. They merely wanted to listen in. Cromwell stood erect as always, looking absent-mindedly out the window. His eyes were riveted and he seemed to be staring at something of great interest, but Anne knew he was feigning this as he listened to Henry complain.

Thomas More sat at a desk near Henry's left-hand side, taking notes and adding opinions. No one, save Cromwell and possibly Henry Norris, cared for Anne's presence here. And Cromwell only deemed it necessary for his own advancement, she was no fool. But Henry Norris seemed to enjoy Anne just for Anne. She fidgeted with a pin that was causing her head to itch and adjusted her hood. She licked her lips and waited for Henry to answer.

"Yes," he said after a time.

"And what are you going to do about that?" Thomas More looked up, his eyes pleading. Anne knew More despised her, for he loved Catherine and the Church. In his eyes Anne represented nothing more than a temptation, a she-devil.

"I am going to call together all my clergy and lawyers of this country to ascertain whether in virtue of the privileges possessed by this kingdom, if Parliament will enact that notwithstanding the Pope's prohibition, the cause of my divorce be decided by the Archbishop of Canterbury."

"Warham will never grant you your divorce," More said plausibly, throwing a jeweled finger in the air. His black velvet cloak hung on his body like draperies, drowning him in a sea of darkness.

"I do not intend for Warham to judge my case."

"But you said the Archbishop—" More interjected.

"Yes, so I did." Henry looked at Cromwell who glanced at him from his window position, barely moving his shoulders to glance his way.

More's confusion was palpable; it hung in the room like a spider web, glistening like gossamer and easy to tear apart.

"I mean to make a new Archbishop of Canterbury." Henry smiled broadly and pulled Anne to his side. "And thus we shall be married."

## England, November, 1530

"The time has finally come, at long last." Wiltshire nearly jumped with jubilee; Anne had a dream.

It is dark; the trees all around the castle stand stark like soldiers sneaking into battle. They besiege the walls, clamoring, their branches beating the stone and scratching the windows with vehemence. The air spits at the castle, fat raindrops splashing into wet nothingness as they land. It feels as though God is disgusted with the inhabitants.

Inside this castle, Cawood Castle, George Cavendish sits with Cardinal Wolsey at the dinner table. A silver archiepiscopal cross sits propped up in the corner. Wolsey sits under his cloth of estate. Candlelight flickers, sending ghastly glows of silver shafts of light dancing across the room from the cross. Black velvet lining is its cushion, making the silver all the more stark of a contrast. The wind cracks and splits the windows with a long whining.

A sudden commotion, a burst of doors, a rush of feet, a heaving of chests. The Duke of Northumberland trails in with the Groom of the Privy Chamber, Walter Walsh. Wolsey looks at Northumberland with fear, for he had ruined Henry Percy's love with Anne Boleyn when they were but children. Why would he be here now? Storming in on their dinner?

"Cardinal Wolsey, I arrest you of High Treason."

A slammed fist, a loud struggle of Cavendish leaping up from his chair, the wood clattering against the stone flooring. "No! Not my Lord Cardinal!" He blocks Northumberland's path with the bulk of his body. "He has done no harm, what proof have you?"

Northumberland withdraws an arrest warrant, sealed and signed by the King's own hand. Cavendish is trembling, but so is Northumberland. Wolsey looks at him with something akin to pity, no not Cavendish, Percy. He remembers the pathetic way he scampered along, tail between legs, when threatened to lose his inheritance if he continued his dalliance with Anne. Now here he stands; the opponent with the higher ground. Wolsey bowed his head but Cavendish was not ready to relinquish his master.

Anne comes to reality to find her father staring at her strangely. "Are you not happy at our success?"

"Indeed. Wolsey was fraternizing with the enemy. It is unacceptable and treasonable and thus he shall hang for it." Anne's solemn face was as strong of an emotion akin to sadness at Wolsey's demise that she could summon. She was sorry for the way things must end, but end they must.

"Where have they taken him? To the Tower?"

"They have not arrived yet. He is currently residing at the Earl of Shrewsbury's house, Sheffield Park."

"Oh…I see," was all she said.

\*\*\*

"Dead?"

"Dead."

"How?"

"We do not know what killed him."

"Are you certain he is dead?"

"Yes."

Anne sat with her face perched in her hands, balanced precariously as she shook her head in disbelief. "But he never even made it to the Tower!"

"Anne. Cardinal Wolsey is dead. He was taken ill at Sheffield Park, William Kingston the Constable of the Tower arrived to escort him, but they made it only as far as Leicester before Wolsey could not struggle along anymore and died in bed."

"He cheated his fate!" Anne raved. Her father looked at her blankly. "Isn't this what you wanted all along?"

"I…" Anne looked up, trying to envisage God looking back at her smiling and pleased. "I don't know."

## England, Whitehall, 1531

Thomas More rose from his kneel, knees wobbling slightly. Henry had just bestowed him with the chain of office for Lord Chancellor. The position had been vacant since Wolsey's death. Anne had heard More and Henry had argued about the position, More did not want it but Henry sequestered his conscience and won in the end. As he would always do.

She watched him thoughtfully, accepting the weight of the chain hung round his shoulders. The sobering effect his face had made Anne feel the tendrils of fear. This man has the power to undo me, and I know he should like to, Anne thought to herself. He did not admire Anne, but he did not openly defame her either. Anne was uncertain rather trusting him in their Matter was a wise idea, but Henry promised he would never publicly speak against them, More had promised as much himself.

His black velvet cloak flapped gently against his body as he shuffled to an upright position. He looked down and then back up, his hat slipping slightly on his head. Insufferable. Unsupportive. Demonstrative.

Now his eyes stared straight at Anne's, meeting her soul in midflight. She felt caught unawares and gasped a little at the effrontery this provided. At the provocative way he emboldened himself to meet her gaze. A shiver of antipathy raced through her but no words spluttered out as she stood rooted to the spot.

"Lady Anne." For what else could they call her? Some still dubbed her 'Mistress Anne' but all knew it was in their best interests to refer to her as a Lady, rather this was earned or entitled they had yet to discover.

Her name passing through his lips seemed to sour his countenance; he seemed to taste the word Anne and spit it out with an ugly face. Screwed up lips and squinting eyes peered at her while the spittle dribbled down his chin in disgust. Anne.

## *England, Whitehall, February, 1531*

"Oh you should have been there Anne." George looked at his sister with excitement. "Do you want me to paint a picture for you?"

"Only if you make it as vivid as if I were standing there living and breathing the moment in."

"Our great King stormed into the church, throwing the great doors open wide. The reverberation this caused made my bones rumble. A murmuring had started in the crowd but hushed to an utter stillness as King Henry made his way down the long carpeted aisle. Ministers lined every possible nook and cranny, purple and crimson and black velvets and robes shimmered like waves in the ocean Anne, like living stones. For you know how very serious they are. How they adopt those pursed lips and religious stares. '*In nomine Patris, et Filii, et Spiritus Sancti. Amen.*' Their droning filled the hall like bees in a beehive. I swear the windows shook with the force of the humming. The great pillars soaring high into the ceiling mumbled *their* distaste. I had to tell them to 'hush!' before Thomas More caught wind of their dissent."

Anne giggled and begged George to continue.

126

"Well, as Henry made it past all those lovely priors, and bishops, and archbishops, the aged William Warham of Canterbury turned up, he stood before them and proclaimed that Convocation must recognize 'King Henry VIII of England, Ireland, and France as sole protector and supreme head of the English church and clergy.' Oh and the tide came in!" George spread his hands wide, simulating the tumultuous churning depths of the black water. "They would not agree to anything, Henry became rather despotic with threats of imprisonment and excommunication. He said: 'Whom do you make your allegiance to? You swear oaths to Rome, to the Pope, but you are living in *England* where *I* am King!' This seemed to cow the teeming masses and Cromwell, shady as always, appeared behind the King as if by witchcraft with the catchall phrase 'so far as the law of Christ allows.' The clergy agreed to this and Henry was sent packing."

"But doesn't that negate the entire title?" Anne asked dubiously.

"Supreme Head of the English Church so far as the law of Christ allows works *both* ways Anne. The clergy saw it as a compromise, as a way of pulling rank on Henry if they don't agree with him, but in reality it is to Henry's favor because *he* is the one who determines what Christ's law is. Don't you see?"

"I do. I do."

"And we are now to call the Pope the Bishop of Rome, so watch your tongue, as sharp as it is it may wound someone."

"George!" Anne swatted her brother playfully and ducked when he attacked her back. "So Henry is happy?" Anne asked finally, settling into a pile of green silk.

"Yes, he is now anyway." George chewed on a fingernail and Anne slapped his hand. "He needed placating when he believed Cromwell had betrayed him to the church. Once Henry understood it and the thorn was plucked from his paw he went from throwing Cromwell against the wall and screaming insults in his face such as 'whore's son' and 'blacksmith's son', to promising him promotions and offices."

"Well, at least we have won this round. I cannot imagine what Catherine would say now." But indeed, it was most pleasurable for her to imagine this. To fantasize about trumping Catherine right to her face. She could see the horror spread across in wrinkles on her pudgy face. It was a sweet victory indeed, coated with sugar and juicy to taste.

\*\*\*

"It seems we now understand our enemies entirely." Anne looked at her father disinterestedly.

"I have always had enemies Father. There is nothing new in that."

"Nicholas Carew, Charles Brandon, Duchess of Norfolk, Bishop Fisher, Thomas More, Reginald Pole….and…"

"Yes, and? Anyone else cannot be much worse." She huffed sarcastically, blowing a tendril of hair out of her eye.

"The Nun of Kent."

\*\*\*

Anne's maid twisted her hair up gently, pressing pins into the thick mass as she worked. Pearls now dotted her head in perfect rows. Crushed lilac scented these locks and she studied her face in the glass as her maid worked. She was laced into her dress loosely, feeling shabby and untidy. She pictured Elizabeth Barton, the Nun of Kent raving about her across the countryside. Cardinal Wolsey had met with her once, years ago, due to her 'visions' of the future. She knew also that many nobles of the court sought her advice. It was foolish, the girl was demented. She had an illness, severe mental attacks that had first started these 'visions'. She relied on the Virgin Mary and paid pilgrimages to her. But too many people were listening to her, ears wide open, believing every word. Elizabeth Barton hated Anne and believed Henry should return to Catherine.

Anne's mood was sour and twice she snapped at her maid for pinching her head while sticking the pins in. But really she just wanted to diffuse her anger before she met Henry and lashed out at him. Painstaking efforts were taken to make her appear effortlessly beautiful every day. She knew she had a sort of 'clean' quality, a simple sheen of newness and purity, but she did not want to lose Henry by becoming lazy in her toilette.

Anne turned her black thoughts to brighter ones; today renovations would begin at Whitehall, Anne's favorite new palace confiscated from Wolsey's greedy hands. Their plans for this castle were no less than four tennis-plays, two bowling-alleys, a cockpit, a pheasant-yard, and a gallery for viewing jousts. As it stood, one could enter the court through the northern gatehouse which led into a courtyard. On one side of the courtyard stood the great hall and next to this was the King's and Queen's outer chambers and chapel. From there ran privy lodgings, overlooking the most lush, green, and extensive gardens one could hope to find. The castle was large and extensive; Anne treasured it for its beauty and location.

***

Stephen Gardiner has been appointed Bishop of Winchester.

# Chapter 12

## *England, New Years', 1532*

"Thank you your Majesty." Anne smiles, pleased with the set of hangings Henry presented to her as her gift. He in turn was effusive about the boars' spears she presented him.

Anne and Henry sat ensconced in the court, Anne sitting in Catherine's rightful place, finally being recognized. Courtiers were summoned before their 'majesties' to present their New Years' Gifts to the King and 'Queen'. Henry lifted his hand and waved a man forward, he was small with darting eyes and pale blonde hair. He bowed his head reverently.

The man held a jeweled box aloft and placed it before His Majesty. Henry lifted the lid gently; velvet lining ensconced a gold cup. Anne's eyes sparkle as they alight on this gift; Henry smiles widely, noticing the fine craftsmanship. "It is beautiful! Who does it hail from?"

The servant before him bowed low. "From Queen Catherine your Majesty."

Anne leapt from her seat, sending an eruption of noise from the gathered crowd. "How *dare* you show your face here and present a gift from *her*!" She balled her small hands into fists. "She is not his rightful wife, how dare you call her Queen in my presence!"

Henry watched Anne's reaction and stood from his own seat, beckoning Anne to be seated herself lest she strike the servant cowering before them. "We will not accept the gift," he said plaintively. Anne somewhat mollified still glowered at the pale man. "Now leave us."

He got to his feet, scrambling, half bowing half falling over his own feet. He trailed out of the hall awkwardly, courtiers parting to let him past, trying to stifle their own embarrassment or amusement at the scene.

"Sweetheart, we must calm ourselves." Henry patted Anne's hand gently, but his face was hardened. "No more outbursts like that."

"Yes, forgive me your Majesty."

England, June-July, 1532

"It is nothing against your Majesty, but I cannot countenance my conscience by weighing the differences in opinion."

"I cannot understand you Chancellor More." Henry looked at him with a bored expression, Anne sat to his side stitching quietly in a window seat, pillows plump all around her, light trickling in tantalizingly close.

"I mean to resign as Lord Chancellor your Majesty." More's hands were clasped in front of him, his chin nearly touching his chest as he bowed his head in mock-severity.

"Resign?!" Henry demanded, Anne looked up from her work to peek at More's facial expression, stoic, indiscernible.

"I cannot stand against you, I must resign."

"It is a meeting of your conscience against the meeting of my will?" Henry asked with fury. "You mean to say you quit because you cannot approve of my actions."

"You claim yourself Supreme Head of the Church, but you know my feelings on the matter."

"You would yet support Catherine against me?"

"I merely adhere to my Faith your Majesty; as you once did." More winced even as the word left his mouth, he could feel their sting; hear the resounding *smack* as they slapped Henry across the face. It smelled like betrayal.

"Fine. Your chain of office."

More handed it to him reverently, straining to bow and return the medal at the same time. Anne's jaw hung open ever so slightly as she watched this scene. Were they all to flee from her service?

When More left Henry screamed and threw his fists in the air. He demanded of God why his friends must abandon him. Anne thought it best to leave her King to his own lamentations.

\*\*\*

"Thomas Audley is the new Chancellor," Thomas Boleyn, Earl of Wiltshire, says as he chews thoughtfully on his food.

Anne bowed low to his ear and whispered fiercely: "I think we can count him as an ally. He is a great friend of Cromwell and Cranmer."

"Very good," her father said, lips smacking, juice leaking down his chin. She looked away in disgust and returned to the dancing.

## *England, September 1st, 1532*

Thomas Cromwell appears ubiquitous. Anne can never seem to escape his ever watchful presence. He lingers at the fringes of her mind, the outskirts of her conscience. She fears he would manage her downfall if he put his mind to it, but he was committed to their Matter, it seems he believed his promotion could only come from that direction. This was probably true. He could end up like Wolsey if he did not get the King what he most desired.

Anne's hair flowed loose down her shoulders, a staple, a statement of virginity. Anne wore red, bright crimson Wolsey red, in luxurious pools it formed about her legs as her skirt melted against her body, her dress clinging to her provocatively. Jewels adorned every available orifice and visible surface on Anne's body; her ears, her neck, her fingers, her slim wrists where veins throbbed. Delicately laid across her shoulders in all regality was an ermine trimmed velvet cloak. As she walked into the Presence Chamber where Henry and the Nobles were gathered, Mary Howard, the Countess of Derby, and the Countess of Rutland held her train and assisted her, while leading her was the Garter-king-at-arms.

Silence fell as she walked through, feeling lighter than air, looking like a rose petal drifting through the room.

She reached Henry and fell on her knees. He was flanked by Charles Brandon, Duke of Suffolk, and Thomas Howard, Duke of Norfolk. They stood regally in ermine cloaks as well, Suffolk attempting to invoke a serious countenance but failing miserably.

Bishop Gardiner stood holding Anne's new letters patent and proceeded to read them aloud. Anne was being made into the Marquis of Pembroke, which was the male title, and had once belonged to Jasper Tudor, forming royal connexions for Anne. She was also being granted five manors in Wales, another in Somerset, two in Essex, and five in Hertfordshire including Hunsdon and Eastwick.

After the patent was read, Henry placed upon her head the golden coronet of the marquis, and cloaked her in an ermine mantle, of crimson velvet, matching her dress exactly. Her lands were worth over £1000 per annum.

Anne felt proud as she stood and knew that she was the only woman to have ever held this title. No one was strong enough nor willed enough to have received such an honor. Anne's pride was mingled with a sense of thankfulness and praise to God for giving her this opportunity. She placed one crimson slippered foot forward, beginning her exit as a well-titled woman. Bows and curtsies went round the room, Henry held her hand delicately, and exited with her.

Let them grumble. Let them feast on a scandal if they like. For Anne had no more worries, no more doubts about her future. I am the Falcon and I will arise. Anne smiled to herself as she felt her black locks bouncing gaily against her back, brushing her shoulders delicately, falling in glorious ribbons. She flicked her satiny hair back, and held her eyes up to the ceiling, thanking God for this opportunity. She gripped her patents in her hand tightly, the scroll feeling thick and heavy.

It was time to partake in the banquet hosted for her honor. They would feast and be merry; laugh and sing; dance and whisper. But nothing could spoil this day, this hour; nothing could make every second tick slower nor taste more glorious like a fresh spring rain washing away all the dust and grime of the filthy winter. She felt renewed and replenished. Here was her step forward, her fate decided.

Marquis of Pembroke, Anne Boleyn.

\*\*\*

"What do you think of this design?" Holbein's face looked up, quick as a bird, as fierce as a tiger, as cunning as a fox. His hooked nose protruded from his face and seemed to get in his way; for he would oftentimes stare cross-eyed at it when speaking.

"Wonderful, wonderful," Henry said very pleased.

Anne caught glimpses here and there but Henry would push her back from the table again and again while he studied the parchments Hans was presenting.

"I like this idea here." Henry placed a thick finger on the paper and smiled. "This is very good."

"Yes. Yes. I thought you'd like that Majesty." Holbein's solid frame moved back and forth with strain. The light would filter across his eyes once in awhile when he turned towards a window and Anne would watch in fascination as the grey sparkled like living stone or faded diamonds.

"Lady Anne's coronation will be the most spectacular the city of London has ever witnessed before!" Hans Holbein gesticulated widely. His mouth open and his hands spread. He shook his hair fiercely as he spoke. "The Lady Anne is fiery and saucy, but we must make her appear docile and pious to the people. They must adore her for her goodness and kindness."

Anne opened her mouth to argue this point but found it moot. "I *am* docile and pious, good and kind." She huffed and crossed her arms.

Henry guffawed and slapped Holbein on the back. "I like you very well Master Holbein. These coronation constructions are exactly to specification. Please do continue." Here he turned to Anne. "We have already begun work on refurbishing the Tower of London to house you in preparation for the coronation. The Queen's Lodgings are being completely remodeled. All for you sweetheart."

Anne ran to him gaily and wrapped her arms around his waist. "I love you." She buried her face in his neck and sighed. Soon. Very soon.

\*\*\*

"The Nun of Kent has begun prophesying that if Henry marries me, he shall die shortly afterwards." Anne shuddered. "I want her finished!"

## France, October, 1532

Her eyes are black like onyx, her skin pearlescent, her hair like satin or velvet, and her steps purposeful but dainty. She is adorned in the Jewels of the Queens of England. She stands tall and erect, elegant and regal. She smiles and those around her simper. She is the Marquis of Pembroke. She is Mistress to the King. She is Anne Boleyn.

She whipped a small fan across her face; its paper is thin like gossamer or wasp's wings. The handle is jeweled with ivory and turquoise. She sits at her dressing table; she replaces the fan and picks up her pomander filled with sweet smelling herbs and perfumes, crushed flowers and grasses. She breathes in the scent and smiles, she is ready to face this new day.

The bloodstone flashing in her ear is honest-faced like Mary Boleyn. The pearls breathing on her neck are virgin and pure. Anne heaves a sigh and picks herself up. She is very pleased that Henry stripped Catherine of her queenly jewels; for only a true Queen should wear them!

Today they would leave for France, to Calais, to meet Francis I, so Anne could be recognized as Henry's consort. Anne knew Francis could be counted as an ally; after all she was almost as French as he!

\*\*\*

They travelled slowly, as befitted their rank of royalty. They went from Gravesend to Faversham by sea for there was plague in Rochester and Henry was determined to avoid sickness at all cost. All knew of his great paranoia of disease and of his medicinal cabinet that if a woman possessed would be deemed a witch.

On the way to Calais they had stayed with Sir Thomas Cheyney, the Lord of the Warden of the Five Ports, in the Isle of Sheppey. But now, the sky was swirling with topaz, amber, and emerald as Anne lifted her eyes to watch the drifting clouds and the setting sun. The golden orb which hovered, hazy in the near twilight.

Anne was impatient to disembark and be alone with her King. Her precious gems now glowed faintly in the fresh spattering of stars blanketing the growing darkness. She looked up at these twinkling jewels and breathed in the spray of sea salt. Cromwell had just been made Master of the King's Jewels and was in charge of the royal plate and jewels. He seemed to be worming his way into every part of her life; as small and slimy as the worms that hook themselves in teeth causing aches.

The boat finally rocked to a stop and Anne alighted from the *Swallow* with glee; indeed swallowing more salty air than she had intended and feeling the edges of green creeping onto a sallow complexion. The ground felt solid beneath her feet, the weight of her body falling between the sheets of gravity. She grappled with Henry's outstretched arm and fell against his soft doublet, crushing her weight into his. He barely flinched, her small frame being no great struggle, and together they hobbled into the royal lodgings awaiting them.

*** 

"My Lady Marquis!" Anne's maid pranced about the room excitedly, waking Anne from a deep slumber where she was being rocked to sleep on a wave that tossed her higher and higher into the air until she reached the sky and danced amongst the stars. They were cool to the touch but burned the eyes.

"Yes Bess what is it?" Anne groggily sat up, angry at the sudden jar from her sleep.

"King Francis has sent a gift Madame!" She skipped like a trollop about the room with a velvet box and Anne leapt out of bed in her shift, racing to where she was. She snatched the box out of her hand and opened its hinged lid.

A loud gasp escaped as if from one body as the women simultaneously inhaled. Snug inside the box sat an enormous diamond. A fat chunk of a star, a scraping of the moon, a sliver of Heaven. It caught the morning light streaming through windows and seemed to trap it inside itself. It almost appeared to have its own light source as it sat there glowing on its velvet pillow.

"I could swear I hear it humming my Lady!" Bess's red face was alight with pure pleasure. "I daresay you have arrived Miss!"

Anne laughed gaily, caressing the stone gently, careful not to disturb its quiet sleep. "Why, it is snoring Bess, we mustn't wake it!" She clapped her hands and snapped the box shut. "Well, I see I must be ready early! Help me get changed Bess, I want my hair fixed quickly too. We will have breakfast soon no doubt."

"Oh no doubt Mistress." And the inner-workings of the female household were set in motion. Fabrics were thrown in the air and landed on whatever surface they happened to flutter to. Ladies maids dashed to and fro consulting Anne on various ribbons and hair pins. A handheld mirror with a topaz studded handle was pressed into Anne's palm for viewing her plucked eyebrows and powdered face.

Water splashed about and the smell of fresh cut flowers emanated from her room. Slippers and boots were thrown haphazardly about. Earrings and bracelets lay in unorganized piles. Various girdles, jeweled prayer books, pomanders, furs, and sheer stockings with ribbons and diamonds piled every surface. In one heap alone sat her French hoods, and in another were cloaks, hats, buckles, and brooches.

"Enough! I must be dressed!" Anne finally called. The women stopped in midstride, all attempting to put together Anne's outfits for the duration of her stay. "We must be orderly, I cannot think in here!" Then she started laughing happily. "It is just as I would have it!"

***

The French and English courts were joined together in royal matrimony for the first time since the Field of Cloth of Gold back when Anne was just a young lady-in-waiting to Queen Claude. Now with Claude long dead and Wolsey triumphed at last, the scene has shifted to one of more gaiety and mirth rather than political dalliances and furtive meetings.

Henry and Francis sit delightedly in conversation at the head table in the great hall. Cloth of silver and cloth of tissue are draped along the walls. The shimmering effect this had was like raindrops glistening on a spider web. Ornamented across these fabrics were golden wreaths encrusted with pearls and emeralds, rubies and diamonds. A miasma of precious gems to catch the eye. Twenty candelabra of silver and gilt were filled with a hundred wax candles that melted under ones glare. This is what lit the scene and set the mood. Waxy teardrops raced down the tallow to fall in a heap, hardening under the cool of the silver. Tables laden with food nearly collapse under the weight of the many sumptuously prepared meals. One-hundred and seventy different meals decorated this table. Meats steamy and luscious sit ready to be succulently chewed on; having undergone slaughtering and plucking and many bloody procedures that the nobles prefer to stuff their ears to.

Henry and Anne had been lodged here at the Exchequer to await the arrival of King Francis; he had come to a 3,000 gun salute; the snapping and popping of gunfire sounding like fireworks bursting into the night sky. This had kept Anne up the night before, causing her late slumber in the morning.

But now Henry sat without Anne, gesturing as he spoke with Francis of war and the Pope and religion. He had nearly forgotten his purpose was to introduce Anne as his consort when he was caught up speaking of long-bows and sieges. A flurry of activity in his peripheral vision alerted him to the change in scene. Seven ladies floated out from behind the cloth of tissue hangings, the fabric singing as it was brushed, and they ran into position before the head table where Henry and Francis sat.

Francis' dark chocolate locks simmered under the candlelight, like amber and honey congealing together. His eyes were eager to drink in the beautiful women, his large nose making it difficult to catch those eyes for a locked gaze. He stroked his chin and adopted a dignified posture as the ladies became statuesque before him.

Each of the seven ladies wore a silver mask studded with pearls. Droplets of pearls hung from their soft earlobes, and pearls studded their necks in thick chokers. The ladies flapped fans in front of their faces, hiding their mouths, weaving in and out amongst each other as the music started and they began to dance. It was slow and seductive. The candles flickered and protested the movement, shivering in their candelabras; the silver and gilt glinting under the subdued lighting. Henry's mouth curled up in anticipation and the women began to twist and turn, spinning and swinging round.

Their cloth of silver skirts swished against their legs, clinging to their thighs, and revealing gossamer stockings, satin garters holding them up. Elegant jeweled shoes shone out from underneath and pale skin glowed like the moon before him.

The lady in the middle, with the coal-black hair and ember eyes stood out even to Francis. She purposefully flicked her fan back and forth in front of him and reached out her hand for him to take. The other six ladies also chose dancing partners and soon the floor was awash in color as the men stepped in to play a part of this charade.

Henry sat, smiling, pleased. Anne had done it yet again. As the music ended on the final note, Francis clapped and smiled eagerly at the lady before him. Henry bounded up, young and fit as ever, and joined Anne's side. He tugged gently at the ribbons holding her mask in place and enjoyed the gasp of delight when he revealed his mistress to King Francis I.

"Why it is little Anne Boulan! My little Frenchette!" He hugged her tightly and kissed her palm elegantly. "You danced quite elegantly Lady Anne. I was deeply impressed with your rhythm and sense of theatricality. It is much to be applauded." He smirked at Henry and then pulled Anne away for a more private conversation. He waved the servant away who tried to serve them wine.

"I must thank you for the jewel you sent me." Anne smiled and her cheek dimpled.

Francis looked at her with something akin to lust. "It is nothing. Its beauty cannot compare to its beholder." He grinned mischievously and pulled her into the next dance.

Anne laughed as she was spun round and twirled about. Flashes of silver stars spangles twinkled in the room. Some shielded their eyes; others looked on with awe as Anne floated about as though on clouds. "I feel like I am dancing amidst the stars," Francis said gaily.

When the song ended he pulled her into an alcove and looked deep into her eyes. "Anne. Lady Pembroke. Marquis." He made a half-bowing gesture.

"Your Majesty," Anne replied gamely.

"You see, though there are those who may not think it best for you to be named Queen of England, I do." He paused and checked his surroundings. "I believe you love France almost as much as you love England. You would support us in policy and politics. Am I right in saying so Lady?"

"Indeed you are your Highness. I almost consider France my homeland."

He smiled wide. "This is what I wanted to hear you see. I have no qualms as recognizing you as Queen, I cannot speak for my people, my council, or Rome, my religion, but I can speak for myself."

"I am surprised."

"I am not Henry."

"He breaks with Rome."

"This is unwise…." He stroked his nose, obscuring Anne's view of his face.

"He is the head of the church now."

"Yes but how far will he take that?"

"As far as he must."

"All for you Lady Anne?"

Anne paused, at a loss. "For me?"

"All for you." Francis stared her down. "You would rip Christendom in half for your marriage; do you think this is wise?"

"I think it is what God has called me to do."

"We can spar all day Lady Anne, I do not think we will come out unscathed. I must say you have sharpened your sword rather fine, would you care to look at mine?"

Anne laughed. "I am not my sister."

"That is not what I meant!" Francis adopts mockery and gasps with flippancy.

Anne notices Henry lingering and suspects he is growing jealous. "I must return to His Majesty." Anne says abruptly, turning to go.

"I have enjoyed our chat Lady Anne. I hope that we shall remain great friends."

"I am certain that we shall." Anne gave him a generous and genuine smile before going to join hands with Henry.

When she reached his side she whispered into his ear. "Now you may have me as your wife."

***

A hiss of silk falling to the carpet. A rustle of fabric being removed. A tingle as a kiss is planted. A hand brushing skin. Silence that envelope all around.

Anne is finally mistress in more than name and determines herself to now be Queen. She must wed at once.

# Chapter 13

## *England, St. Erkenwald's Day, November 14th, 1532*

The White Cliffs of Dover shine like an angel, beckoning Anne home. The purity of these cliffs makes Anne's heart leap and she remembers seeing them as a little girl. Childish memories flit through her head out of order, in a sort of collage. Running through a field with Mary. Playing Blind Man's Buff with George. Learning to play cards with her father. Stitching with her mother in her bed chambers. Combing out her freshly long locks while her uncle comes to visit. Having her first dress made with fabric of her choosing. She feels tears prick her eyes and she hurriedly brushes them away.

Anne has a secret. A dark secret. A secret that could change the world.

Henry and Anne have married.

A secret she longs to shout at the top of her lungs. A secret she longs to declare and say 'I won!' with fervency and vehemence.

I have won.

## *England, Whitehall, January 25th, 1533*

"Why are you getting married *again*?" Mary Boleyn asks Anne gently as she helps her place the last pin in her head and straightens her silver girdle.

"Well, since the last marriage was in France he decided he wanted to marry me in England as well. Nothing wrong with getting it right.... twice."

"It is a reassurance that he's really married to you is what I think. He doesn't quite believe it and wants to prove it to himself." Mary laughed, flipping honey hair behind her.

"Oh Mary! Quit fussing!" Mary was primping and picking at Anne all over.

"I just want you to be perfect." She squeezed Anne's cheeks, making them instantly redden. Anne slapped her hands and giggled. "Stop!"

Lady Berkeley entered the room then and asked: "Are you ready Marquis de la Pembroke?" She winked and held out her hand. Anne grasped it and smiled at her, walking slowly out of her chambers, Mary's face glowing with pride behind her.

In the Upper Chamber above Holbein's Gate the King and Anne joined hands in front of George Brown, prior of the Augustinian Friars of London. He was an aged man, made of bones, and wrapped in brown cloth. Henry Norris, William Brereton, and Thomas Heneage stood next to Henry while Lady Berkeley adjusted Anne's long cloth-of-silver skirts behind her in an elegant train.

Prior Brown asked the King for the marriage license from the Pope, but Henry waved him aside impatiently, eager to have done.

"I need the license your Majesty."

"The license is in my office chambers Prior. If I should now that it waxes towards day, fetch it, and be seen so early abroad, there would rise a rumor and talk thereof other than were convenient. Go forth in God's name and do that which appertained to you!"

Henry's mop of flame hair burned as did his cheeks. Anne smiled sweetly, bringing his temper down instantly. They said their vows and kissed before all the privy attendants. "It is done in the eyes of God." The prior looked at them solemnly, somewhat afraid. Penchant perhaps?

Anne could not but feel elated. Twice married to the King of England should seal it surely? Indeed, Anne already felt a stirring in her belly. A jelly forming, a fist beginning, a life growing. Was she certain? She had not bled for a long time. Maybe it was time to consult with a midwife.

A baby? Surely. A prince? Surely. Security? Surely.

"Now you are my Queen. And I shall make you known to the world." Henry closed his mouth over Anne's, and crushed her small frame against him. He felt the swell of her breath as she inhaled and tickled her cheek with his rough skin.

"Anne…oh my Anne."

## *England, February-March, 1533*

"I have had *such* a craving for apples! I cannot fathom why!" Anne's eyes flashed, rainbows danced before her eyes, hoped dawned with every morning.

Thomas Wyatt eyed Anne with suspicion. "Apples Queen Anne?"

Anne brushed out her skirt, purple, the color of royalty; she brushed it merely to draw attention to the rich and banned color to all but those of her status….royal. The velvet felt thick against her hand, rough but soft, dense but supple. Anne had these layers to her own personality, why not have a dress that corresponds?

"Yes. The King says it is because I must be pregnant! But I tell him that is not so!"

Wyatt studied Anne's stomach as best he could through her thick fabrics and girdle. He thought he could detect a faint swelling. "Anne…?" he said quietly so none of the courtiers round them could hear.

"Ha ha ha!" Anne threw her head back and laughed, her doe-like eyes wide, her white throat exposed, a mole flecking her skin poked its head out.

The courtiers waiting in the hall all whispered amongst themselves at this astonishing news. Did Wyatt call her *Queen*? Did she say she was *pregnant*? We must find Queen Catherine!

\*\*\*

144

"Convocation has been asked to pronounce the validity of a papal dispensation allowing a man to marry his brother's widow." George eyed his sister with obvious delight. Of course they will decide in Henry's favor.

Anne nodded. "Of course."

\*\*\*

"Queen Anne is a virtuous Queen. She is pious and devout, holy and saintly. The Blessed Virgin Mary looks down on her and smiles. We can thank our Good God and our most Holy King Henry VIII for bringing this Christian woman into our fold and setting her as an example before us all."

King and Queen sat together with the court in church. Anne has now been recognized as Queen of England before all. She smiled, smug. Let them grumble.

\*\*\*

"Thomas Cranmer. You are now consecrated as Archbishop of Canterbury. You may rise."

\*\*\*

"And you shall conduct yourself with virtue and religion. You must be humble and contrite. You must be honest and kind. You must help those who are poor, giving alms and praying to God. You must read daily from the Bible, I have an English translation all may use. Take nourishment, draw strength, from the Word of God. You must not visit whorehouses or have immoral dalliances at court. You will behave and conduct yourself with diligence…and perseverance. I will hold each of you accountable for your actions and will dismiss you if I find you in violation." Anne's sharp head turned and stared down each one of her newly formed royal household.

Among her new ladies were her sister Mary Boleyn, her sister-in-law Jane Rochford, Jane Seymour, and her cousin Margaret Shelton.

Anne dismissed her men, her yeomen of the guard, and immediately turned to her ladies. "I do not want improper conduct from any of you. You must embody the angels, have souls meant for heaven, destined for greater things, do not put earthly ambition before that of holiness." Her eyes grew misty and she turned away. "You have duties to perform," Anne said when no one moved. "We will embroider bed hangings and coverlets, shirts for the poor, tapestries, and rugs. We will stitch until our thumbs grow sore and our minds are numb with the effort."

Jane Rochford studied her new counterparts; Mary she knew well but the other two were fair mysteries to her. Margaret was very pretty; a dimpled face, caramel colored hair, and a button nose. Jane on the other hand was rather plain and pale. She was flat-chested but amply waisted. Dowdy and whey-faced. Jane had a notion to label her rather mealy-mouthed though she had yet to find this true of course. Her blonde locks lacked luster and fell rather flat on her head. She wore an English-gable hood as opposed to Anne's French ones, and figured she would soon be reprimanded for it.

"I will have your new dresses provided for you, and your hoods as well…" Anne looked pointedly to Jane Seymour. "We wear the French cut dresses, and French hoods. We adopt styles foreign from our own and promote unity within our Kingdom."

Jane Seymour blushed under the sudden scrutiny. Lady Rochford thought this suited her better; it made her prettier, well, almost.

"Cousin Madge," Anne said suddenly and Margaret looked up. "Will you please retrieve the sewing materials so we may commence at once on our work?"

"Yes your Majesty." Madge bowed and left the room.

"We will have our fun too," Anne remarked dryly. "We shall have singing and dancing and feasting. We shall gamble amongst ourselves and recite poetry. Never fear the specter boredom looming at your shoulder, or eating at your conscience."

The ladies smiled in obvious relief as Madge returned with a large basket of sewing materials.

## *England, April, 1533*

Catherine must now be referred to as Dowager Princess of Wales, her title by right of being Arthur's widow. Princess Mary must now be referred to as the Lady Mary.

## *England, May 29th-June 1st, 1533*

Anne looked around her in awe and delight. She was being taken from Greenwich in a water procession to the Tower of London for the start of her coronation. Anne sat in a wherry mounted with a mechanical dragon. At sudden intervals the dragon would groan forward, creaking, and belch out great bursts of flames. Men covered in coal and powder wearing extravagant furs depicting wild men and monsters shrieked and threw fireworks, frightening anyone who saw them.

Anne's wherry was leading the procession, behind her were no less than fifty great barges of the London livery company, and many smaller vessels as far as her eye could see. These boats were all decorated with extravagance. Flags and bunting draped the sides and the canopies overhead. Gold foil shimmered in the afternoon sun; little bells tinkled when the wind blew. Musicians were on board multiple barges and their howling and melodies could be heard across the water; echoing eerily. Cannons lined the Thames on both sides nearly the whole procession, and *boom* after *boom* resounded war-like as Anne floated down the water.

Directly behind Anne came the Mayor's barge with all the aldermen and councilors. The bachelor's barge was behind that with the Haberdasher's arms covering it.

A special barge was right next to Anne, looking like starlight and sunbeams in cloth of gold and silver. Trumpets shattered the air with their noise and the flags of the Merchant Adventurers billowed softly as the wind puffed its breath across the barge. The rigging was spun with streamers, silver bells jingling at the ends of the colorful fabrics. Two banners were hung up depicting the arms of Anne and Henry, and on the starboard gunwale were thirty-six arms of Anne and Henry, but these were impaled to form one badge.

But Anne's favorite attraction of all was a floating replica of her badge — a barge carrying a giant white falcon, crowned, perched primly on red and white roses growing from a golden tree stump. The tree stump sat on a green hill surrounded by the song of virgins. It was a haunting scene but it spoke to Anne. It was her taking her rightful place amongst the Tudor line. She represented the bringing together of the Lancastrians and the Yorkists with both colored roses. She would become that falcon; she would embody its symbolism.

Anne jumped, the wind caressing her face as gunfire salutes commenced and the *pop, pop, pop* of the shots ricocheted from the shoreline. Its sound was reminiscent of icy water splintering under a great weight. A smile replaced Anne's decided and adopted look of regality. She could not hide the mirth and gaiety threatening to overwhelm her.

The procession finally reached Tower Wharf, the waves lapping gently at the sides of the barges, and Anne was helped out and greeted by Tower officers and heralds. They were all dressed like soldiers, in their finest uniforms, metal gleaming off of their coats. Gold and silver seemed to sparkle from every corner. The stone walls of the Tower did not seem so confining; she walked out in an open courtyard and breathed in the fresh scent of the coming summer. Walking through the postern gate Anne was greeted by Henry himself. He kissed her full on the lips and hugged her small frame delicately to his large one.

"My sweetheart. This is all for you." He swept his arms wide and they walked together inside.

***

Anne has had days to rest and awakes this morning with a knot in her stomach. The baby kicks and moves irritably inside her. She rests a quaking palm to her tumultuous round lump and rubs gently. Her heart beats wildly like a lioness begging to be let out of her cage, her eyes shine bright like freshly lit candles, and her forehead begins to sweat small tears. "Today is the day I become Queen."

***

Crowds line the streets and are held back by a line of constables. Rails are put up to help keep back the populace. The roads are gritted so horses have footholds. The houses all through London are decorated with cloth of gold and silver, deep crimson velvets and tissue. Cornhill and Gracechurch Street are hung with arras; there are tapestries and carpets on display, scarlet and crimson bedecks everything in sight. Rich colors, royal colors, thick fabrics, shimmery fabrics, it is all provided by the King.

Anne exits the Tower, she is dressed as French as she possibly can be. Her procession is headed by twelve servants of Jean de Dinteville, the French ambassador; she is quick to associate herself with everything French. De Dinteville and his servants are dressed in blue velvet; their sleeves are slashed with yellow and blue. Great white plumes extend from their hats like peacocks. Even their horses have trappers of blue sarcenet and are powdered with white crosses.

The gentlemen of the royal household come next, two by two, paired off like animals to mate. The nine invited judges are next; they are dressed in their scarlet gowns and hoods, looking like monks of the devil more than judiciaries of the law. The newly made Knights of the Bath walk regally behind them; the young men feeling they are royalty themselves. The royal council, ecclesiastical magnates and peers, the chancellor, the two archbishops, the Venetian ambassador, the lord mayor, the deputy earl marshal, and Suffolk, the Constable of England, all follow after. It is a gathering of all the greatest individuals of the realm. Henry means to show Anne off as the penultimate Queen of England.

Now Anne is coming in her litter. The crowds gasp, they hush, and silence descends like a halo from heaven. Anne is wearing a filmy, sheer, silky, creamy white dress. It hangs from her body, yet clings to her body. It gropes her body, yet falls from her body. It is like frothy white waves descended in a waterfall over a cliff. It is beaded and shimmers in the light of the morning sun. A glittering princess for the world to behold; who could hate her now? A gold coronet crowns her luscious dark locks falling loosely to her waist. Her eyes are sharp but they hold crystal tears. Her cheeks are flushed pink with emotion, but it only endears her more to the people. They doff their caps and yell "God save Queen Anne!" Her lips quiver with emotion.

Over her head is a canopy of cloth of gold held aloft by the barons of the Cinque Ports. Following her is her own palfrey trapped in white, white as snow, white as virgins. Her ladies follow, twelve ladies, in crimson velvet on horses with matching trappers. Carriages bedecked in cloth of gold and cloth of red trot solemnly alongside these great women. The sober procession of gentlewomen of lesser rank filing along on horseback in black velvet is last.

On each side of the procession marches the King's guard in files. Their armor shines like molten lava; it simmers and glows as the yellow and orange of the sun mix together to form red. It is like the embers and ashes of an awakened phoenix. Anne's eyes are riveted by the sights around her.

Henry has arranged for displays to be setup all along the processional route for Anne. She is now presented with the first of these as she nears Leaden Hall. The front of this display is open, wide and long, it is a castle structure roofed with a cupola. The inside of the roof is painted a deep blue, clouds drift across the surface, and stars of heavenly bodies accompany them, igniting both night and day into one.

The floor is green and Anne is again presented with a hill with a tree stump sat high atop it. But on this hill sits St. Anne and her descendants: the Virgin Mary with Christ, Mary Salome, and Mary Cleopas. "Most excellent Queen and bounteous Lady!" they shout at her when she draws near. Then a young boy, supposedly Cleopas' son steps forward and begins reciting:

"For like as from this dearest Saint Anne
"Issued this holy generation.
"First Christ, to redeem the soul of man;
"Then James th'apostle, and th'evangelist John;
"With these others, which in such fashion
"By teaching and good life, our faith confirmed,
"That from that time yet to, it hath not failed.
"Right so, dear Lady! Our Queen most excellent!

"Highly endued with all gifts of grace,
"As by your living is well apparent;
"We the Citizens, by you in short space
"Hope such issue and descent to purchase;
"Wherein the same faith shall be defended,
"And this city from all dangers preserved."

A gentle creaking then resounded and out from the tree stump poured red and white roses; colorful blooms of paper and tissue. A cloud on the roof appeared to grow misty, the eye drew towards it as it floated forward, and from behind it descended a white falcon that settled with a rustle into the roses below.

The *coup de grace* came from the cloud last; an angel, glowing, shimmering, as it descended and placed an imperial crown on the falcon's feathery head.

"Honor and grace be to our Queen Anne,
"For where cause an Angel Celestial,
"Descendeth, the falcon
"To crown with a diadem imperial!
"In her honor rejoice we all,
"For it cometh from God and not of man.
"Honor and grace be to our Queen Anne!"

The words floated down to her, seeming to come from the angel's rosebud lips. The wings were made of swan's feathers and seemed to move of their own accord, as a living breathing thing. The people watching this scene all cheered and a man dressed as a herald stepped forward blowing a trumpet as gold as the coronet round Anne's head.

Anne's hair languished softly in streamers down her chest and to her waist; it was a stark contrast to the purity of the snow white gown she wore. "She is like a diamond!" a woman with a ruddy face and a kerchief wrapped round her head whispered to her child. The herald cleared his throat and recited a poem in Latin while a small boy beside him translated it into English for the commoners to understand.

"Of body small,
"Of power regal,
"She is, and sharp of sight;

"Of courage hault,
"No manner fault,
"Is in this falcon white.
"And where by wrong
"She hath flown long.
"Uncertain where to alight;
"Herself repose
"Upon the Rose
"Now may this falcon white.
"Whereon to rest
"And build her nest,
"God grant her most of might!
"That England may
"Rejoice always,
"In this same falcon white."

Now the litter moved on from the scene, Anne feeling magnanimous and generous, loved and adored. I will be their true Queen. The procession halted once more at the gate into the precinct of St. Paul's. A throne was set high up with three holy virgins sitting beneath it. They held gold placards with words painted in blue '*Veni amica coronaberis*' Come, my love, thou shalt be crowned. Two angels in gossamer with wings of thinly spun silk held an imperial crown at the base of the tableau. The whole scene seemed to shimmer before Anne's eyes. The crowd's "oooooh's" melted in tune with Anne's heart beat.

The horses began walking serenely once more, passing a tower in Fleet Street erected with four turrets upon which were painted Anne's badge. On the turn from Fenchurch into Gracechurch stood a likeness of Mount Parnassus. Anne felt herself gasp, could *feel* the crowd smile in anticipation of this display. She strained her long pale neck and tilted her head. She settled her hands into her lap and filmed out her skirts of stardust.

Beneath the giant mountain stood a fountain made of fake white marble; it gleamed like the architecture of Rome; giving the appeal an authentic feel. In this fountain sat an antique basin with a column rising from it with a smaller bowl mounted atop this. Rhenish wine spouted out from four nozzles, filling the bowls and basin with its dark liquid. It ran like blood and made Anne shiver.

On the mountain sat Apollo, god of music and poetry, an eagle perched above him giving that added flair of other-worldliness. The Muses gathered round him in harmony. Calliope, the Muse of epic poetry played the lute, the strings twanging like shooting stars beneath her knowing fingers. The other muses held instruments of their own and sang out together in harmony. Clio, the Muse of history then sang out in a beautiful husky voice rising pure as the angel's breath:

"Anne comes, the most famous woman in all the world. Anne comes, the shining incarnation of chastity. In snow-white litter, just like the goddesses. Anna the Queen is here, the preservation of your future."

Anne clapped, tears rolling freely down porcelain cheeks. The Muses bowed to their Queen while Apollo looked on in mock-severity. He inclined his head in reverence nevertheless and her litter moved on. Anne looked up to the heavens and said a silent prayer to God in thanks. Thanks for this day, this momentous occasion, this making of history before her very eyes.

All around shouts were heard. *Regina Anna! Prospere, precede et regna!*

On the rooftop of St. Martin's Ludgate a boy's choir sang ballads in praise of her. Their procession halted again and again at tableaus and artistic displays, plays, miniature theatres, poetry, and music. It was enough to move the most hardened heart to tears. Tears to honor England, tears to honor the Queen, tears to honor God.

Just when Anne thought the seams of her dress might burst from her joy she was stopped at Westminster Abbey. The coronation may finally begin.

***

Anne entered Westminster Hall, a cloth of blue ray stretched seven hundred yards from the dais of the hall to the high altar of the abbey. Anne sucked in a deep breath; in fear, in excitement. In the audience sat the peers of the realm, their parliamental robes hanging limply on their shoulders. The lord mayor, aldermen, and judges, again in their scarlet robes. The monks of Westminster, the bishops and archbishops, the staff of Chapel Royal, twelve mitred abbots, the full regalia of pontificals making them appear as ornaments and relics of the church rather than priests of the Lord. Anne found she preferred the simplicity of monks to the scholarly ambition and pride of bishops.

Anne herself was draped with coronation robes of purple velvet, furred with ermine. The weight of it bore heavily on her shoulders; the weight of the world on her shoulders. Her gold coronet nestled against her loose hair, wind-swept, flowing to her waist. The lustrous curls slightly unbound into wavy angles and curves. As tradition would have it, Anne was barefoot, and the cool dampness of the marble beneath her feet could be felt through the blue carpet. The barons of the Cinque Ports held the cloth of gold canopy over her head as she walked slowly down the aisle. She was supported by the bishops of London and Winchester on either side of her, taking her elbows and hands into theirs. The Dowager Duchess of Norfolk carried her long train, with ladies of Anne's royal household following behind in scarlet.

Anne was following the scepter of gold and the rod of ivory, the gentle dove nestled on top, and the lord great chamberlain, Earl of Oxford, carrying the crown of St. Edward. The crown used *only* for reigning monarchs. And this was to be Anne's crown.

Hidden from sight, even from Anne's knowledge, her conscience mind, her very thought, was Henry. Behind a lattice-worked screen in a special stand, he peeped through like a young boy at a brothel. He smiled serenely at his queen; walking as though meeting the Throne of God, the smile of the angels on her face. Her soul alighted from her body and came to join Henry in that room; joined with him as never before.

Anne was allowed to rest when she reached the altar. A solemn high mass was sung by the abbot of Westminster and then Anne knelt prostrated before the altar. Archbishop Cranmer anointed her with oil then helped her to her feet. She shuffled up a platform carpeted in red, then walked up a dais of two steps covered in tapestry, and finally sat in St. Edward's chair draped heavily in cloth of gold.

Archbishop Cranmer raised the crown of St. Edward high into the air before bringing it down in one slow motion unto Anne's dainty head, the coronet being placed on a pillow and removed. He then handed her the scepter and rod of ivory, consecrating her finally as Queen of England.

A *Te Deum* was sung, and Cranmer helped Anne switch into a lighter crown, especially made for her, as St. Edward's was heavy and made for the head of a male. Anne took the sacrament and made an offering to the shrine of the saint before rising to be led out of the hall.

Anne would finally have a chance to rest before the great banquet given in honor of her Queenship.

***

The hall was hung with arras; great gleaming dishes were laid out on the two tables sat lengthwise on the blue carpet padding the cold floors. Henry had even gone so far as to have the windows reglazed for the occasion.

Anne's seat was twelve steps up, on a dais, and only Cranmer was invited to sit at her table, though he was such a distance away Anne feared she would have to shout to be heard by him. Her cloth of estate hung lifeless around her and the marble tabletop was cold to the touch. The Dowager Countess of Oxford and the Countess of Worcester stood beside Anne, holding a cloth in front of her face whenever she had the desire to spit, or be otherwise unladylike. Under the table sat two young maidens waiting to do anything Anne might bid them to do. The other tables were sat with Lords and Ladies and Peers of the Realm. The Titles and the Nobles and Anne found her head spinning with the weight of it all. Her stomach protruded as the baby inside grew bigger with every second.

She thoughtlessly nuzzled her belly with her hand, making tiny circles against her flesh. She chewed all of her dishes thoughtfully and smiled pleasantly to any who made eye contact with her throughout the feast.

Suffolk rode through the room on a horse, guarding the proceedings, as did Lord William Howard, all in crimson, his horse in purple velvet embroidered with the Howard white lion, which was slashed to reveal white satin lining. Anne sighed wistfully wishing George were not on an embassy to France and were here witnessing this.

The Knights of the Bath carried in all twenty-eight dishes served to Her Majesty.

When Anne felt she could keep her eyes open for not a moment longer she made her leave of the court bidding them all farewell: "I thank you all for the honor you have done me this day." She inclined her head to everyone, raising a small jeweled hand to the candlelight and leaving by escort of her ladies. Her reduced train collecting dirt from the ground as she exited, one hand cradling her stomach tenderly.

"Tomorrow there shall be balls and feasting, jousting and dancing, and I cannot stand another moment of it." Anne said to Countess Worcester as they walked silently down the hall. She saw the woman's lips twitch; in sympathy or disdain she was not certain. Anne brushed her long locks off her shoulders and let them tumble down her back. "I am so very tired; I must rest, for the health of my son." She indicated her swollen bump with her hand and Worcester smiled and nodded, looking every inch tired herself.

Small careworn wrinkles meandered across her face. "It has been a tiring day for your Majesty. You must keep up your strength. I am sure King Henry was very proud this day." There, Anne decided, it must have been sympathy.

The Dowager Duchess of Norfolk said nothing; her lips sealed as though with wax. Anne sensed her black thoughts eagerly slipping across the threshold into Anne's mind. She shook her head. "I do so hope the people love me."

"They did your Majesty! Didn't you hear them shouting your name and begging you to rule them! They loved you! To see the men doff their caps and hear the children speaking of your beauty, and watching as the women's faces crumpled in thanksgiving; tears leaking out of their flint and steel eyes! It was a moment to mark down in the pages of our history."

Anne looked at Lady Worcester with thanks brimming in her eyes. "My Lady Worcester," she said sweetly. She pulled her to the front of her procession to walk side by side. "Thank you for that. I know that you do not always approve of my methods or my means, but I do hope you approve of my goals. I have lofty ones you see. I have high hopes for the Church of England, and I mean to see them through."

Anne watched as a flicker of torment and doubt passed across her face; she loves Catherine then, to be sure. Anne hung her head and sighed. "Today was a success and we must never forget it!"

"I am sure no one shall Majesty. I am certain no one shall ever forget this day, but that they themselves are forgotten. This is a day that shall live on for an eternity, blazoned into the hearts and minds of the people to tell their children in times to come. The sun did not awaken until Queen Anna floated down on a cloud from heaven, dressed in white like the saints." A sigh and a gasp passed through Worcester in a moment of weakness for pageantry, royalty, tradition, and romance. She would not forget Catherine again.

# Chapter 14

## *England, June 25ᵗʰ, 1533*

"Your Majesties," Cromwell said, entering the room, bowing low. Anne did not much like this secretary-cum-servitor of all the King's needs, and his peevish looks. He sauntered in as though he himself were royalty. Anne felt ready to spar; he was not unintelligent, his accomplishments boasted that far and wide. He was someone to contend with; she admired him in so many ways, and agreed with many of his principles. But if he crossed her there should be danger.

"What is it Cromwell?" Henry waved him into the room; he sat cuddling with Anne on a chaise.

"I am afraid I have some bad news for your Majesties." He paused, as if for once, unsure how to continue.

"What is it Master Cromwell?" Anne asked gently, probing him on.

"It is your sister Mary…she died at her home of Westhorpe Hall in Suffolk today."

"What? No!" Henry leapt up from Anne and shoved his fists to his mouth, stifling a cry of anguish. Anne looked on in genuine pity; she knew Mary was his most favored sister and that this would hurt him very much.

"We knew she was sick Henry, we knew this was a possibility," Anne tried to be consoling.

"I know but she was so delicate, so fragile, she did not deserve this. Where is her lowly husband Suffolk!? Why does he not appear before me on his knees in grief?"

"He is mourning his loss sire, at their home. He weeps over her body and keeps a vigil I am told. He has lit candles and sits by her shrouded dark form."

"That is not good either." A tear trickled down Henry's face and he brushed it away in frustration. "She must have a royal burial. And tell Suffolk to return to court; he is needed here."

Anne felt a sadness blooming inside her. True Mary had never really liked Anne; and when she attended on her when she was Queen of France she had seemed rather snobbish. But she also knew that Mary loved Henry dearly, and he her. And that this would be a great blow to his happiness. It would be a blow for Catherine too, and in that alone Anne took consolation.

## England, August-September, 1533

A troublesome hangnail eludes Anne's small teeth as she tries in vain to rip it off. Sweat pools above her eyelids, dripping down, stinging her eyes; splashing in droplets from her eyelashes, hanging there for a moment, suspended in time, appearing to be infant diamonds, before resuming their liquid form, shedding their ice-like state and burning Anne's coal eyes. She whimpers. The room is dark, the curtains are pulled, they are black velvet, it is like mourning. Death. But this, this is life! She is confined to give birth to her son.

If life could be thus compared to death what state are they in? An awkward limbo where one foot is surrendered to heaven and one is bound to the earth. Shadows leap across the walls, snaking down and slithering up, writhing and niggling at Anne's conscious thoughts. She shakes her head hard, loosening the stiff muscles in her neck and attempting to banish her morose mind.

Heavy curtains hang round the bed; her chambers are cordoned off, partitioned for only females to enter through. The men are banished, banished to a world of men. A world where they rule and they decide fates. Where in the confinement, the birthing room, a woman was the ruler, a woman the Queen, a woman the decision-maker. It was out of *her* womb after all that the baby would exit. *She* would bring it into existence. Though it was not by her efforts alone, it would be recognized as Henry's entirely should it be male. If female then the fault lay with Anne. For only *women* would decide to have other *women*. Their very coding and make-up must be deformed. For Anne could be seen as an oddity if sometimes a commodity. Plump breasts and ample hips, long limbs, and pale hair; this was not Anne. Meek and submissive, humble and subservient to a husband; this was not Anne. A fire, a spirit, a determination rested inside her small frame. Her delicate features were complemented by her waspishness, her sauciness, her attitude. Who was to blame for her repartee? Margaret of Austria? Anne herself? Who is to say?

She struggles under the covers holding her captive to the bed. I do not want to be here. I do not want to be here. A circle, a ribbon, a trail of thought looms up in her mind and twirls itself around in delight; freedom. The sun's face, the stars' naked delight, no, her King to snuggle up to. Not this utter loneliness in the black, in the gloom, alone.

The women came in and out. Her ladies maids, her midwives, instructions from the doctors. Reports from Henry's astrologers; they predicted a boy. Well, they would wouldn't they? Who would risk the King's wrath? But if they were wrong...? Would his wrath be set free upon them? To eat of their flesh like a lion may destroy a lamb? The lion will lay down with the lamb. But not in this life. Anne reminded herself of her mother in this moment; this dark moment, alone with her thoughts and God.

Catherine would not countenance, would not answer to anyone but God and her conscience. It made Anne sick to think that Catherine's conscience was higher than the King's wishes. In thought at least one may consider such notions; but in speech! It was a hateful act on her part — the Spanish Queen no more! Now who is she? Charles cannot rescue her. Will he risk war on England in support of the Pope and his aunt? Would he do it? Time would tell.

The tales time must admit to! The history lost, slipping through fingers. History is what we make it after all. It does not write itself — it is not an empty story, but full of faces, thoughts, and ideas. Simple words make history complete. Now Catherine has written into history that her conscience is a higher being to submit to than her King. The secrets of the world are mine to keep. Anne's discordant mind tossed itself like the ocean back and forth, back and forth. The cabin rocked her into seasickness and lost in this reverie Anne was sick all over the side of her bed.

No matter, the servants rushed in to clean it up, as though it were a royal favor bestowed upon them. Anne smiled drunkenly at them, waving a hand in the air. "I want to *breathe* in here. Can I please *breathe*!?" Anne's smile now wavered, faltered, fled. Her hair was damp, damp from sweat. Beads of sweat forcing her locks into lumps and knots. She tugged at them in earnest, straightening them, picking at the ends, laying them perfectly across her chest. "There, my hair is done." A tired glow emanated from Anne like an aura. She shrugged, her white night gown slipping from her shoulders. She brushed the cotton fabric, rubbing an embroidered rose and tightened the lacing round her neck and breasts.

Her stomach formed a large camel-like lump from up out of the coverlets. It was like a great hill in the midst of a valley. It reminded Anne of the hills protruding up from the great grassy areas in her coronation procession, and on these hills sat the golden tree stump of the Tudors. Anne used her trimmed fingernail to trace outlines of tree stumps on her stomach, lifting her dress up to expose the naked skin. She tickled it and then traced roses along its surface.

A midwife came in with instructions to feed Anne. She poured her a glass of water upon request and Anne drank it greedily. "Mightn't ye be wantin' somethin' stronger Maj'sty?" The aged woman grinned rows of brown teeth at Anne and she turned her head slightly in disgust.

"No I want water."

The woman dampened a rag and dragged it slowly across Anne's forehead; mopping up sweat and cooling her feverish skin.

161

"It'll be startin' soon," she said with mirth and left Anne again, beyond the partition to the world of men. The world Anne wished to escape from.

"A man did this to me." She lamented her state now; bordering between madness and mirth. "To be free....I want to be like the falcon, white and angelic, free...free....free..." An image of herself came to her then, talking to her father in earnest. "I want a man who loves me." A man she thought, a marriage she thought, a title she thought, those things would fulfill her. But is she fulfilled? No.

God must sustain me, she thought. This child must sustain me. Then, maybe I can sustain myself? No. God must.

The pains began.

\*\*\*

"It is a beautiful baby girl your Majesty." The midwife handed the baby to Mary Boleyn who slowly, solemnly walked the Princess of England over to Anne's exhausted frame. Dark half-moons ringed Anne's eyes, her hair in heaps of tangles, her bedclothes wrapped round limbs and damp.

"Here you are sister, a beautiful, beautiful Princess." Tufts of reddish gold hair were in clumps upon the infant's head. One would assume this scene to be rather peaceful, light trickling in through freshly opened curtains, stifling air being choked with fresh overpowering fragrance, a flattened stomach hanging on the Queen's frame, and an infant so awash in love as to forget about wailing. But this was not the scene as it were. The curtains were still shut, the air still feverish, Anne's stomach had not changed in size, and the infant screamed like someone was holding a hot iron to her bare flesh. But Anne reached out her arms and grabbed the baby to her as though she were her rock amidst a stormy sea.

"My Elizabeth," she murmured and cooed into the girl's soft head, her cornflower-blue eyes captivating her from the first moment. "She is mine, I made her," she said to Mary who looked on with gemlike tears in her eyes. They were not tears for beauty or sweetness, but tears of fear. What would happen when Henry came in here? What would happen when he found this was not his longed-for son? What then?

Mary slid a finger through the soft wisps of hair anyway, fingering the fluff with curiosity. "It is so new Anne. Doesn't it feel incredible?" She reminisces of her own births.

"It does. I love her. She will be a great ruler some day; you can see it in her intelligent eyes. She smells like honeysuckles and buttercups. What a sweet child." The baby had stopped howling and made gaggling sounds akin to a dove's gentle coos.

Splotches of red on the newborn skin and a few bloodstains still exist, but Anne ignored these.

The world of men was opening slightly, the crack in between was widening. Henry came in.

"So, it is a daughter," he said dryly. His normally supple locks of hair fell flat on his head, matted there with sweat and anxiety.

"Yes," Anne answered feebly, a sleepy smile enveloping her face. She would choose to ignore his subtle disapproval. "Elizabeth."

This brought a smile to Henry's face. "My mother's name."

"And mine," Anne rejoined.

He took the baby from her and held her gently in his arms. "She is perfect isn't she? Exquisite." He looked at her and held her as though she were a dainty doll; a plaything. A toy to show off to his court. "My little Elizabeth."

Anne felt relief awash her in multi-color; she swam in purples and danced amidst greens. She was swallowed by blues and tickled by yellows. Bliss…she sank into her pillows, throwing the covers about her in disarray, and fell into a troubled slumber.

Henry looked at Anne with something akin to distaste before handing the baby over to her new wet nurse. "Thank you." He bowed his head, swept one more glance in the direction of Anne's exhausted form, and then left. The servants fluttered into bows as he passed them by, not daring to raise their eyes until his presence could be felt no more.

"Well. I am glad that's over," Mary Boleyn said.

***

A *Te Deum* was sung while the baby was brought forth to be christened. The Marquis of Exeter held the taper of virgin wax while the Duke of Suffolk escorted Elizabeth. Lord Hussey walked alongside the unusual pair, struggling to hold the canopy over the new Princess. The Marchioness of Exeter stood as a godmother, begrudging herself as a great supporter of Catherine. Thomas and George Boleyn lined the hall with the other twenty persons present. Thomas Cranmer stood as godfather, and Cromwell and William Brereton lurked near the sidelines. Anne was furious that Catherine had not turned over the christening robes she had tucked away in a trunk somewhere deep in her exile.

Anne lamented that she was unable to attend her daughter's christening, but again and again reminded herself that she must be churched and purified before she would be allowed in the public sanctum again. The process must be accomplished before she can be clean again and fit to appear before her subjects.

She shuddered and imagined Elizabeth's round pudgy face glowing brightly under lit candles. She tried to imagine her frustrated gurgling as they dipped her in water and splashed her small tummy. Her tuft of golden hair clinging damply to her skull. Her soft hands grasping at Suffolk for comfort; but he would give her none.

\*\*\*

"I have arranged it with the King. Your daughter Mary shall marry the King's son Henry." Anne's hair was swept back, revealing a face full of life and color, though drained of a quality no one could quite finger. Anne knew what it was; hope.

Her uncle, the Duke of Norfolk, stood imperiously before her, dark hair gleaming with menace. "You are placing her in a position to be Queen if the chance should befall her."

"It *is* possible," Anne conceded; she had foreseen this conversation and was prepared for it. "If, God forbid, the King has no male issue from our marriage, he may in time see fit to place his bastard son Henry Fitzroy on the throne. And if your daughter, Mary Howard, is wedded to him, then indeed she would be Queen by his side. The

164

problem with this theory is the court itself. They would never allow a bastard on the throne."

"Have you no idea of what went on before the Tudors reigned? Before the King's father defeated Richard III at the Battle of Bosworth?"

"Yes Uncle, I know about the wars. The civil strife and the economic strain and the instability of the kingdom that resulted; we cannot be placed in such tumultuous times again. That is why it is most beneficial to this nation if the King's *wife* and *Queen* gives birth to a son; a prince."

Norfolk inclined his head, aware of the thin ice he was treading on. One small slip and he would crack open a plot of treason. "Your Majesty." His eyes were swallowed by his lids as he looked to the floor in obsequiousness. "I must thank you for this honor you are granting me with His Majesty."

"Yes. You needn't worry about a dowry either. His Majesty will provide for everything."

Now her uncle's face betrayed surprise. "No dowry?" Wonderment was an emotion she had rarely seen on his face. "It is a thing unheard of!"

"Not for His Majesty." Anne was growing bored of the conversation and looked towards her outer chamber where her ladies were busily stitching, red fingers flying across garments and tapestries. Norfolk noticed her attention stray and bowed before her.

"I will take my leave of your Majesty," he said graciously while Anne tilted her sharp chin and rested her eyes on him once more.

"Uncle," she said in response as he exited her room.

***

"They have arrested the Nun of Kent," George said earnestly to Anne, attempting to bring her some much needed happiness.

## *England, April 17<sup>th</sup>, 1534*

Parliament is passing acts; the Act of Supremacy and the Act of Succession. Mightn't she be thrilled about these? Why, yes please, but the underlying fate, the streak of malice lacing her heart with turmoil. The fear under the skin; the belly of the beast. The breathy scales that snore with hatred. The sparkling eggshell that cracks under the thinnest weight? Whatever can be done now?

The Act of Supremacy is an oath to be sworn stating that Henry VIII becomes Supreme Head of the Church of England; the oath of the Act of Succession states only the offspring of Henry VIII and his Goodly Queen Anne are lawful heirs to the throne. This act bastardizes Princess Mary. Last year the King had declared Catherine must now be the Dowager Princess and Mary simply a Lady; but now Mary is a bastard, a bastard indeed! But not a bastard *in deed*.

Anne could not pay attention to her ladies or the gentlemen surrounding them. Francis Weston was busily reciting witticisms for his rapt audience and flirting with her ladies rather brazenly. She would have to put a stop to it when she could think clearly. Thomas More had been imprisoned in the Tower today; he refused to take the Oaths — of Succession and Henry's Supremacy. He was a dear friend of the King's, regardless of his alliance to her. It would sour Henry's temperament; he would lash out at her. Bishop Fisher had been imprisoned as well for refusing the Oaths. They were the only two in all the kingdom staunch enough supporters of Catherine to throw their weight thus far. Now they would both pay for it.

She nervously fingered her embroidered sleeve, plucking at a loose thread and rubbing her fingers raw. If Henry could not be swayed towards leniency, if More and Fisher refused to swear the Oaths, Henry might make an example of them. If they were executed wouldn't the people blame Anne? Wouldn't they hate Anne all the more for making these two great men into martyrs? She began to nibble at a fingernail. The laughter and gaiety of the courtiers beyond her current frame of mind was but a distant murmuring as she dwelt upon the heaviness of her heart. If they did not support her marriage and the succession of her children to the throne, then how could they claim loyalty to the King? And yet they were. They claimed loyalty to Henry and to God, but they could not chide their consciences.

Jane Seymour's piercing laugh cut through the air like glass. She jarred herself into reality and stood to approach Weston's antics.

## England, Summer, 1534

Mary bowed low before her sister, the Queen of England. "I am back your Majesty," Mary said politely.

"Well you were not gone long Mary, but I missed you most terribly." Anne's hair was beaded with pearls and was a beautiful stark contrast to her onyx hair. She fluffed out her blue skirts and smiled, her 'B' necklace clinging to her neck for dear life. Un-powdered moles could be seen spattered over her pale smooth skin. Mary averted her eyes.

"What is it Mary? You look like you have some secret!" Anne smiled conspiratorially and the other ladies of her chamber giggled likewise. Mary noticed a new face in the retinue, a fiery red head with a saucy lilt to her head. Her chin dipped elegantly like a painter's brush, and her eyes were languorous and swallowed up their beholder. Her lips were plump yet dainty and curved to accentuate her face. Her fire hair was swept up in pins and crowned with Anne's adored French hood. She was breathtaking.

Anne caught her gaze and nodded. "This is Lady Elizabeth Burton. She is quite a beautiful young maid is she not?" Anne's look was soured, Mary detected hostility; she chose to merely nod. "Now what is it sister? Do tell me, you look so troubled." Anne's face cleared of her anger and an expression of sisterly confession replaced it.

"Oh Anne, do not be angry with me."

Anne was silent.

"I have gotten married sister."

Anne remained silent.

"His name is William Stafford, he—"

"He is a nobody."

"Well, yes…" Mary's golden locks seemed to simper in fear, hiding behind her shoulders for confidence.

By now the other ladies were looking on in bafflement and wonderment. Anne did everything possible to check her vehemence.

"You are hereby banished from court Mary Stafford."

"No Anne please I beg you—"

"You have married without the Queen's permission; you are related to royalty- you had no right to do as you have done! And you married a commoner at that! You and your husband are banished from court Mary. Get out of my sight!"

"But I love him Anne! And he loves me! You know I am called the infamous whore! Please do not do this!" She was tripping over her long skirts, trying to bow and grasp Anne's small hand. "Please sister!"

"Out!" Anne yelled. The other ladies were open-mouthed and gaping. Anne whipped round and furiously ordered them to return to their duties. They fell all over themselves to get out of her way.

Tears were pouring down Mary's splotched face; she hobbled out, still half-bent over in a bow. She took one last long look at her sister's face before taking her official leave.

***

"Move a little please." Holbein did not bother with scruples, titles could be discarded on cue, and he did not simper in Anne's presence. "No, into the light. Yes, yes, there!" He removed his paintbrush from between his thick lips and attended on his canvas once more. Anne faced towards the window and watched the streams of light trickle in, she lifted a hand to shield her eyes. She wore a gold beaded French hood and her 'B' necklace hung in strands round her neck. She wore black velvet which deeply accentuated the darkness of her hair and eyes. She pursed her lips in a budding pout and looked just beyond Holbein as he stood assiduously laboring over her likeness.

"Hold the rose just so." Holbein shoved his fist into his chest, pounding it like a whip to horseflesh. "Right at your chest.yes.up, a little higher, okay." Anne held the rose in her right hand and brought it to meet her left in a gesture of grace and elegance.

"You look not pretty your Highness…." He must be placating her to adopt a title. "You look…somehow eerily beautiful. Yours is not an obvious beauty; your beauty it comes from," he pointed towards his heart, his moustache trembling as he spoke, "Your heart. It comes from inside you. You generate a beauty far greater than these other flouncing ladies adopt. You are naturally graceful and elegant and show that to the world through these flesh and bones. Others must work at their looks painstakingly powdering and rouging their complexions to be admired by the gentlemen. You have a quality that most women lack. Generosity, genuineness, veracity, and....spirit." He swept an exaggerated and dramatized arch of his brush across canvass. "I am capturing your essence now. Your grace shall speak through this image; it will come to life and walk amidst the onlookers. Hah!"

Anne smiled, a tear rolling down her porcelain cheek. No one ever seemed to notice her or study her in such an infinite way any longer. She was the pushed aside wife; she could not be weak and submissive as a wife aught, she was who she was. Henry was supposed to love her for that. Did he not? Did he not?

\*\*\*

"I know you have mistresses! I know you sleep with the whores of this court. You do so right under my nose! You treat me like an imbecile!" Anne fumed and raged, fire lighting her eyes.

"You need to rest Anne. Think of the baby."

"Leave me alone you rabid fool! I will not abide this infidelity! You married me because you *love* me!" Tears dangled precariously, threatening to overflow at the slightest tremor of the head.

"Sweetheart! I *do* love you. But the affairs of men should not concern you." His tone was gentle, probing, but stern.

"They *do* concern me; you are my husband! Does that mean nothing?"

"Of course it means something Anne! What do you take me for? I am the King of England and I shall do as I please! You must shut your eyes and endure as more worthy persons have done!"

The tears fell, one by one, splashing to the stone floor beneath their feet. Anne felt her world change instantly. Henry had loved her and only her. His passion had rose and rose always threatening to overwhelm her. Heated moments of desire and lust had been enough to undo him. He had broken with Rome for her. He had changed his whole idea of love for her. He fell for the first time, for a woman that was his equal. And now they are married, she is pregnant, and he is bored with her. The faint beating of her heart grew weaker and weaker. She felt suddenly numb. How could this have happened? Where had she gone wrong?

"But I love you…" she said meekly. He did not answer her.

***

Every day Cromwell conspires with His Majesty to close more monasteries. They raid the friars and the monks, they pillage their goods, they reap their profits and gold. Cromwell claims it is for the good of the church, that they only take from the corrupt and depraved, but who is he to be the judge? Is he not corrupt and depraved himself? And where does that money go? To fill the King's coffers? Into the Exchequer? Why not funnel the money into educational institutions — give it to the poor! Redistribute to the needy why reline the pockets of those who run afield with the devil? The consorters of demons? The prostitutes of the destitute?

Anne shoos her lapdogs and they fall scurrying in small particles of fluff across the floor. She sighs, frustrated, clenching and unclenching her fists.

Anne could feel her blood bubbling inside of her, boiling over like a witch's cauldron. She could feel the steam rise and smell the salty ingredients, she nearly vomited. She thought of the life growing inside her. As though the very thought can give rise to evils Anne clutched her stomach in sudden pain.

Jane Seymour rushed to her side, her stitching falling like an avalanche to the floor. "My Lady! Are you alright?" Her pale face was etched with worry; a genuine concern spread across her features.

"I…I…" Anne was in a pool of fabric as she sat on the floor, not understanding how she got there. She pulled her hands down as she felt a rush of sticky wet liquid drip underneath her. By this time Madge was kneeling beside Jane, crowding her, the air getting denser.

"Too much…" she whimpered, laying her head back on the cool stone floor.

"NO!" Madge yelled, splashing Anne's flushed face with tears. But Anne was too tired, too weak to see why. Why the yelling? Why did the pain stop? Why am I all wet? Oh well….

\*\*\*

"She has lost the baby your Majesty."

\*\*\*

"The Nun of Kent has been hung for treason at Tyburn gallows. I hope your Majesty shall be pleased." Cromwell cowered before Anne.

"Very pleased."

## England, July 1st, 1535

Thomas More and Bishop Fisher are executed. It is done. Until the end they denied hostility against Henry. Until the end they claimed they had never spoken out against His Majesty. They lay crumpled up in their stone cells, barred windows, bleak light. More stooped over parchment, etching his final thoughts onto paper as though writing in his own blood. He seemed to think it might save him. His constant outpouring of Godly wisdom and holy ideas; what had it given him but his own death? Why could he not have simply sworn the Oaths?

Bishop Fisher was no less the pious papist; the Pope made him a cardinal while he was imprisoned, as though daring Henry to martyr a church's prince, a church's high noble. Henry should never be dared, should never be tempted, he will take the bait every time. He did not prove false, but stable and steady; he had Fisher's head struck off with a blade.

Fisher knelt down gripping a silver cross, praying fervently, believing Henry to be a just ruler. What is justice? More fell into a sopping pool of blood, his severed head carried away by his most favorite daughter, weeping salty tears onto the drying flesh. His body lay limp, twitching, in the crimson liquid, seeping into his humble clothes, turning his white shirt red. The vision is eerie, the consequences resounding hollowly in Anne's ears. The drums of change are beating loudly; the call for reform is echoing through the land. Who will be next on the chopping block they ask. Who will be next?

A swollen pompous noble is soon taken down by a tyrant-royal. Who Henry? Never. None would dare call him a tyrant. Tyranny is what despots use; Henry may be narcissistic but he knows when to quit. Doesn't he? Anne swallows a hard lump knotted in her throat. She feels the blood of Fisher and More lies on her hands. She looks at them in sudden fear, believing she will see them coated with the sticky substance. But they are clean, they are white, they are pure as a fresh snowfall.

Her conscience did not subside. Her heart beat wildly with images of More's head and Fisher's head floating round her in a circle; praying, praying, praying. A silver cross rose up between them, casting a ghostly reflection round them; Fisher's cross. His lifeblood, his heart, his passion for Christ. She has made them into martyrs!

"It is *my* fault!" she screams aloud. Jane Rochford looks at her in sympathy; she seems to read her very thoughts. No one else dares glance at her face, none seeking to be reproached.

Anne's fists are clenched tightly now, she attempts to draw blood from them, just so she can see the image swirling in her mind made into a reality. Her purple gown shifts under her straining and she catches herself losing her control. "What am I doing?" she whispered, a hiss of muted breath, air shifting across the white lips.

More and Fisher will not be her undoing. She must stand firm in the face of adversity. So what are two deaths? They cannot taint her reign, her belief in the ultimate good they were establishing. They were blocking their path to greater success!

# Chapter 15

## *England, October, 1535*

Mark's eerie haunting melody floated through the hall. Anne felt she could palpably reach out and touch the notes as they hit her ears. Revenge, fear, fury, peace, happiness; these emotions flood Anne's senses as the song lingered on. The court was dancing gaily, procuring nothing but ambition from the music; senseless of senses.

Anne is pregnant again. She has not told Henry yet. She is afraid to. She feels the weight of her satin dress pulled her down. Her embroidered sleeves, beaded and glistening, cling irritatingly to the soft fabric. Her head is crowned with a coronet of turquoise and pearls. She looks at Henry with a wild fear in her eye; the fear a horse senses and thus imbues to a rider. That animal panic, that sense of flight, that spooked uncertainty that sends a horse thundering off in the opposite direction. Anne shivers, shaking her dark mane, her lips are pressed into a decided line; a mosaic of beauty and concern. "Sweetheart, your feet are all over the place," Henry chides Anne as he pulls her close and spins her round. She is dizzy from the dancing, the heat; she is sweating.

Should pregnant women dance? Anne stops, pulse reverberated in her ears in time to the music. She looks bewildered, like a stag caught between the hunter and a cliff. "Anne? What are you doing?" Henry's blonde eyebrows shoot up in confusion; is anger lurking there? Rebuffed, Anne turns away.

"Wait! What are you doing?" Henry grabs a sleeve, a bead pops off and rolls across the floor. Anne washes a slipper crush it as the courtiers round them keep up their lively dancing.

"I do not feel well," Anne said, not meeting his eyes, looking to see if she can locate the bead. She does not know why but it keeps her attention off of him. Anywhere but him.

Henry looks at her, waiting. He waits. He tilts his head. The dancers roar around them, they are an island in the midst of a hurricane. "I am surprised they do not stop to see if we are alright," Anne says.

"Yes but then they fear they would interrupt a lovers' tryst."

"We are out in the open."

"Tryst of words Anne, wanton."

Anne sighs in fatigue. "I am pregnant."

Delight washes his features like a fresh rain on a field expired with draught. "Pregnant! My son! Finally your duty will be fulfilled!" A wave of his hair falls into his eyes. Anne reaches up and brushes it away, out of habit more than affection.

Her lips squeeze out a smile, just barely, she is angry. Her face is white, her eyes are large, and her nostrils flare. Does he notice? Of course not. He is looking eagerly at her stomach as though he would rather be married to it. "Henry," she hisses. "Stop."

"I am to have a son!" Henry shouts to the room in general. The music stops, the dancers stop, the conversations stop, the tinkling of glasses and plates stop, Anne feels her heart stop.

"My Queen is to have a son! Let us celebrate this joyous occasion!"

"I must rest Henry," Anne says urgently, she wobbles on her tiny legs. "I must lie down."

"Yes, yes." He nearly pushes her aside and then remembers she carries the heir. He turns back to her, gazing fondly at her stomach though there is nothing but fabric to see. She is flat as of yet.

"Here, let me escort you." He grabs her elbow, somewhat roughly, before again remembering and righting himself, his grip loosens. "Sweetheart, do you know how long you have been pregnant for?"

"No." Anne does not feel like discussing this, she feels like vomiting. Her world is spinning. Henry has two heads but still she detects only one heart. Her vision keeps swimming though she knows she is on dry land. She lolls her head to the side like a martyr and nearly stumbles to the ground. A retinue of Anne's ladies gathers behind them to follow Anne back to her privy chambers. Anne notes Cromwell lurking in the background, watching with…happiness?

Happiness at her pregnancy or at her illness Anne was not certain. His shadowy figure was not due to her dizzy spell but rather to his true form. She shuddered. Henry held her firmly until they arrived at her rooms. They put her in bed and attended on her until she fell into a fitful sleep.

*** 

"Oh Majesty!" Jane Rochford nearly fell over trying to tell Anne the news. "The King was just here."

Anne lifted her head from her pillow, wakefulness flooding into harsh reality. "Oh," she said weakly.

"He said that he 'loved the Queen so much that he would beg alms from door to door rather than give her up.'" Her face was awash with happiness at being the one to deliver this good news. The King and Queen's relationship was so tumultuous and stormy that any good comments must be passed on posthaste.

"He is impotent Jane," Anne said suddenly, her face turning hysterical, her eyes wide. Flayed eyelashes nearly touched her hairline as she exaggerated her expression all the more. "Impotent! He is not always able to…"

Jane touched Anne's hand is sisterly sympathy. "I am sorry your Majesty. I know it is so very hard for you, and so much pressure is placed on you to bear a son. It must be heart wrenching and very frightening when it does not work. It is not your fault. None of it is your fault."

"Thank you Jane. And please, do not tell anyone." A weak smile faltered on her face and she fell into a waking dream.

***

"Jane, come here." Anne beckoned to her from where she sat, recovering, in her great canopied bed. The embroidery shimmer as Jane sent a slight breeze fluttering through the room. Anne was plumped up and a freshness lingered about her. A sense of renewal. Jane walked slowly, afraid of what Anne might request or say next. Secrets were deadly and she already carried an arsenal.

"My Lady." She curtsied but Anne pulled her closer until Jane sat on the edge of the bed by her head. "Listen. We must do something about Lady Burton. She is Henry's mistress and I will not have it."

"What would you have me do Majesty?" Jane's blonde eyelashes beat furiously against her cheeks. "I am not certain this is for me to get involved in…I…"

"Jane! Heavens no! I am not asking you to take her place. I merely wondered if you would…start a fight and help me get her sent from court."

"Start a fight!? Your Majesty?" Pink crept up Jane's neck as a flush of excitement washed through her. Courtly intrigues.

"Yes. Claim that she stole something from you or that she is after your husband, I do not know, but cause a scene. I will go to Henry and have her banished."

Jane smiled wide. She did not like Elizabeth anyway; she was haughty and rude. She was new to court yet thought she was its new mistress. She may have ensnared a King, but his passionate flares soon ended. And Jane would see to it that it ended sooner rather than later.

## England, January, 1536

"Your Majesty!" Mary Stafford rushed to her sister's side. "Thank you for having me back at court your Majesty."

Anne smiled at her piteously. "Oh Mary, I am sorry I ever banished you. You found love and happiness and I suppose I was jealous."

"But you have love and happiness too, do you not?" Mary's angelic face was bewildered. She had seen the passion and heat between the King and Queen, what was wrong?

"Jane Rochford is banished from court. Did you hear?"

"I had from George, yes."

"It is my fault Mary. I went to the King, I had Jane fight with Elizabeth Burton, but it seems the King sided with Elizabeth and sent Jane from court, suspecting my involvement. The winds have blown over and Elizabeth is out of favor, and no longer the King's mistress, but that does not sweeten the distaste souring my mouth. And poor Jane…"

"George is not angry with you. And neither shall I ever be."

"You wrote to Cromwell. He has interceded on your behalf."

"I love my husband Anne; I do not know what else to say."

"You really love him that much?"

"I had rather beg my bread with him than to be the greatest Queen christened."

"Oh sister…" Tears welled up in Anne's eyes. "That is truly beautiful. I am very happy for you."

"Anne…" Mary's eyes searched her face steadily. "You are very frightened." She could see it now, it dawned on her. "You are very alone. You are pregnant and you are scared."

"You must help me Mary. If I lose this baby….I do not know what Henry might do." A shudder passed through her at the sheer terror his anger wrought in the Kingdom; she did not think kindly of it being used on her. "I had been his true love for so long, but now the feisty desire has left. He is hollow, an empty shell. He looks at me and sees through me. He does not long for me or dream of me any longer. I am a past for him that keeps lingering in the present. What am I to do?"

"I will help you Anne, I will take care of you. Why did you not tell me of this sooner?"

"How could I? He loved me and I loved him. This was not a marriage of diplomacy or politics; we were a meeting of minds and passions. Now it has fizzled out but I am left carrying his heir and should I drop it…"

"Anne, stop it! Stop! Think what you are saying. His Majesty loves you! He does! Look what he has sacrificed for you!"

"He says he has raised me up and can put me down again just as quickly! He says if he had it to do over again he would have passed me by; not turned an eye my direction. He has lost his fervor for me, but I *do* love him sister. I love him still."

"A drowning man loves air Anne."

Anne shivered; the halls were hollow and drafty.

\*\*\*

"Catherine is dead!" Henry raced into Anne's apartments and shouted with joy. He brazenly wore yellow and danced about gaily. "I have had the Princess's household ordered to make her ready for a gay day of cockfights, jousting, and dancing! Come sweetheart! Let us celebrate! There is no shadow to overhang our marriage now!"

A great foreboding dawned on Anne. He swept her up out of her seat, her sewing clattering to the floor. Jane Seymour leapt to gather the materials and Anne watched as his gaze lingered on her bent form. He sharply looked back to Anne once more. "Come, make ready, we will commence the festivities at once!"

Anne and her ladies were ready within an hour; Anne adopted a more pious dark colored dress, but jauntily donned a feathered bonnet. Henry was busily parading the Princess Elizabeth around in a cloth of gold dress, holding her high, her golden red hair shining like the sun. Golden teardrops splashed down from heaven and stained her lovely daughter.

It was a day of celebration because a Queen had died; a Queen whom Henry had loved and coveted and married when his father died, leaving him the throne and the decisions of the kingdom. He took his brother's wife for diplomatic and romantic reasons. But now that she's dead he rejoices; he wears yellow, a mockery to his dead wife. Where does that leave Anne? Who will she be in the years to come? How much longer can she hold Henry's heart, flaming in her hand?

\*\*\*

Anne watches Henry's eyes; they follow Jane Seymour everywhere. Every hand tucked daintily across her mouth. Every blink of her filmy eyes. Every toss of her pale blonde hair. Every dip of her shoulders and heaving of her bosom. Every breath escaping her lungs; Henry is riveted.

***

Anne studied Jane Seymour while she worked; she sat with her Psalter and appeared lost in deep thought and contemplation on her heavenly life.

Mark Smeaton was in the corner playing his lute as always; it seemed an extension of his arm if not a separate part of his body. Henry Norris lingered about near Madge, whom he claims to be courting yet makes no matrimonial offers. This irks Anne; she catches him staring at her...often. More often than makes her comfortable.

William Brereton, the court's rogue, is hanging about as well, dancing gaily when the mood takes him. Francis Weston stands with Thomas Wyatt attempting to woo the ladies. George speaks quietly to his wife when chance admits it; otherwise he must admit to manly rivalries and contend chivalric games. He looks bored with them but earnest with Lady Rochford. Anne smiles.

She is thinking how to rid herself of Jane Seymour when her uncle bursts in unannounced and in a great hurry.

"Your Majesty." He sweeps a shallow bow, holding his hat in his hands, feathers tickling fingers but he seems not to notice. His face is red, his breathing is rushed, his doublet is crooked, and his hose are torn. Whatever could be the matter? His dusty muddy boots he shuffles back and forth before bowing again.

"What is it Uncle?!" Anne asks in utter exasperation, throwing a hair behind her ear.

"It is the King." He pauses and looks at the expressions of horror written on the faces of the ladies around him. Jane Seymour seems most particularly alarmed.

"What! What! What has happened to the King?" Anne is frantic, fear lacing every breath, strangling it, choking her life from her.

"He has fallen from his horse and has been knocked unconscious your Majesty."

"How long!? How long has he been like this?" Tears raced down unchecked from her gem-like eyes to her dainty chin.

"An hour your Majesty."

"Shows he any signs of recovery?"

"Not at this time your Majesty. We suggest you prepare yourself for the worst."

Anne fell to her knees in agony. A great pain began in her stomach, a kicking sensation, a writhing. She felt faint and grabbed at her dress, attempting to rip the fabric.

Madge raced to her side before anyone else could get there. Anne thought feebly while she helped her to her feet that Madge had also been the King's mistress, and then she wondered if maybe the easier thought would be — who had *not* been the King's mistress.

\*\*\*

"Anything?" Anne asked feebly from her bed, she was covered to her neck in blankets. A fire was blazing in the hearth. Someone had closed the curtains and lit candles. She felt trapped again, smothered in darkness.

"It has been another hour your Majesty, he has not awoken yet."

"God help us."

\*\*\*

Anne awoke to a sensation of rushing water coursing through her. She dreamed she drank a whole ewer of liquid only for it to slide right through her body and slither out of her immediately. But when she woke it was to find it was not water rushing out of her body, but blood, a bloody mass a heap a lump lay in the thick of the crimson mess. It was a boy.

\*\*\*

"Stillborn."

\*\*\*

"His Majesty has awoken! Long live King Henry VIII! "
"It is God's will."
"It is good to see you Harry."
"Good King Harry!"
"Your Majesty, Queen Anne has lost your son."

***

George held Anne tightly in his arms, hugging his sister in her fragile state. "I am so sorry dear sister. I am so sorry. Hush, hush."

She wept silently, wetting his doublet, though he cared not.

"George, what am I to do now?"

"Jane has told me of the King's....issue."

"But she was not to tell anyone! It was a private matter—"

"Anne, hush! I would not tell a soul; we are husband and wife you see, it is natural."

Anne conceded with a nod of the head. "Yes, alright. But since you know you can understand the natural problems that it induces. How am I to manage another pregnancy? Will he even come to me now George!?" The sobs wracked her tiny frame, George imagined she was a doll, made of glass, and easily broken. He must fix her.

"You will be alright. It will come to rights. We can fix this Anne; it can be done."

"But George, you *know* he has mistresses. He goes and sees them and any effort towards making *our* son is lost inside those *whores*!"

"You mustn't speak so loudly or they will *hear* you!"

"What matters it who hears me? They all know Henry is not loyal. He was never loyal to anyone but me and now he discards me! Me! The woman he loves!"

"He is of a fickle nature; you know this." George moaned, his creamy brown locks falling delicately across his head. He shoves a fist onto his forehead, wrinkling the skin. His eyes are full of worry and his nose is pinched in consternation. "You will be pregnant in no time, I am certain. You must retain a calm serenity, be gay with your ladies, do not give way to fear or the devil will latch hold of you. He will shake you until your neck snaps and then we shall truly be in a bind."

"Your morbid humor does not amuse me brother. It does not amuse me in the least."

"Forgive me your Majesty." He bowed in mock-salute and his face lost its mirth. "I will always protect you Anne."

"I'm not sure how much longer you can."

Madge and Henry Norris walked into the room and looked at George holding Anne in a brotherly embrace and smiled together. How sweet are the Boleyn siblings they thought! How sweet indeed.

England, Spring, 1536

Madge sat sewing in the corner, Anne looked to Mark where he stood gazing longingly out of the window, lute discarded for once by a chair. "Why do you look so sad?" Anne asked him gently, as a lover might.

He sighed, his shoulders visibly heaving. "It is no matter."

Anne was furious. "You may not look to have me speak to you as I should do to a noble man, because you are an inferior person!"

"No, no madam. A look sufficed me; and thus fare you well."

He departed abruptly, grabbing his instrument from the floor and leaving. Madge looked at her in confusion and alarm. He should not have treated the Queen thusly. Madge vaguely wondered what it could mean before dismissing the thought from her mind.

\*\*\*

"My Queen!" Cromwell dropped into a floor-sweeping bow as Anne stepped inside his office. She went directly to the window behind his desk and stared out at the sweeping gardens. Fountains trickling in the distance, trees bowing their fresh green heads to the wind, birds mating for the season.

"Master Cromwell. After giving much thought to your closing of monasteries, I must ask you what you are doing with the revenues." Her face was pale but strength was visible beneath the surface sheen of fear.

"Why, your Majesty, it is only going to the King! It has, after all, been stolen from him in the first place—"

"Master Cromwell! It has been stolen from no one. It was a deceit by the church, no doubt, but it should now be given back to those whence it came from. Distribute it to the poor and needy, donate to the scholarly foundations we so long to build up. Do not fill a cup that is already full. For where would the spill go but to make a mess?"

Cromwell's beady eyes shifted back and forth, like a rabbit, or maybe a snake Anne thought with malice. Cromwell could no longer be counted on as an ally. He had set himself up to butt heads with Anne, he had purposefully stepped on her dress and stood there, not letting go. He did not have any idea how strong his opponent was; but he should. He should have known.

"Before you think of making an elegant retort, remember who you are speaking to."

"You Majesty." It seemed all he could say. His hair looked to be graying, aging he was. His face no longer as smooth, cracking under the pressure. Anne smirked.

"I will have you to do as I have asked—"

"It is His Majesty's request that the funds be placed where they are now."

"You dare to interrupt me?" Anne's tongue lashed out, hot as coals.

"I ask your Majesty's forgiveness." Cromwell bowed his head and stared at the floor in fear.

"You *will* do as I have commanded, I am the Queen of England, and you cannot ignore me! I will have you pay for your insolence knave!"

Cromwell attempted to rope in his fears but felt his heart rate increase anyway.

"Do not force my hand," she spat at him and stormed out of the room, a rush of purple satin in her wake.

"Do not force *mine*," he said to her retreating figure.

\*\*\*

Anne danced about while Mark played in her chambers. Henry Norris came in on the ladies giggling in a circle, skirts swishing like slashes of rainbow.

"Sir Henry." Anne admitted him into her presence and took him aside. "Why do you not ask Madge to marry you?" she asked with contempt creeping into her tone.

He smiled and looked down. "I am still courting her your Majesty." He dipped his head.

"You look for dead men's shoes," Anne said. The music stopped, Mark staring at her hard, lightning flashing in his eyes. Sour notes hang on the air from the abrupt end of melody; the ladies look on in something akin to horror. Anne pictures Jane mouthing the word 'No'.

But Anne could not stop herself; the words tumbled out as though in a nightmare. She was not in control of herself. She was scared, confused, upset, tension broke. "For if naught but good came to the King you would look to have me."

Henry Norris fidgeted, fear encompassing his body. "If such a thought were in my mind, I would my head were off." He turned and fled.

Anne crumpled, her face melting like wax from a candle. "I have done it now haven't I?" Anne turned to her silent ladies. "Oh no..." The whisper of wind could be heard in the chamber; no one moved. Finally Mark had the sense to resume the song exactly where he had stopped and the ladies attempted to dance again, but the happiness and joy had dissipated leaving a foul odor in its wake. Anne had gone too far; she had bordered regicide. But what harm could it possibly do tucked safely away in the Queen's chambers?

# Chapter 16

## *England, April, 1536*

"It is done. The commission of oyer and terminer has been setup your Majesty." Cromwell bowed and Henry nodded.

***

"Anne. Mark Smeaton is arrested." George nearly shook her as he spoke. Her dumbfounded expression only infuriated him. "He has been arrested!"

"Well what has he done? Did he steal something? Kill someone?"

"No one knows. He was taken to Cromwell's house for twenty-four hours. Can you explain that? Why would the King's secretary take a prisoner to his home?"

"I do not know."

"We must think what this could mean!"

"I do not know!"

A great shadow settled its bulk across Anne's heart. She slept fitfully that night.

***

"Henry wait!" Anne shouted at him as he walked through the gardens. She ran, Elizabeth dangling precariously in her arms; a bundle of cloth of gold. "Henry…" He stopped and turned towards her, his eyes alighting on his wife and daughter with anger and distaste.

"What is it?"

"Something is wrong. I feel it brewing. I can sense a storm about to break. I can smell it on the wind. Tell me what is happening." Her hair was loose and blew wildly in the wind; she looked like a witch.

"Nothing is happening Anne."

"Why was Smeaton arrested?" She bounced Elizabeth up farther in her arms, the child's golden hair like firelight.

"That is a matter of concern for the state."

"But I *am* the state Henry!"

"No, *I* am. You are just my wife. A wife with no sons. A useless wife. What good are you to me?" He turned his volatile eyes away from her, steel forming over them, melting, gluing itself shut.

"No. Henry. Stop! I love you! Please Elizabeth loves you!"

"How do I even know that child is mine!?"

Anne stopped, Henry walked on, a coldness descended. A metal grip grabbed her heart and squeezed, she lost her breath, and she lost her footing. She nearly dropped her almost three-year old daughter. What could he possibly mean?

"Henry?" she called to him but he was gone.

✱✱✱

"Matthew Parker!" Anne yelled her chaplain's name with a great bellow. She still held Elizabeth in her arms and covered the gap between them quickly.

"My Lady." He bowed to her but she shook her head.

"If anything should happen to me, you will look after Elizabeth won't you?"

"My Lady I—"

"Do not dance round the bush; will you look after her?"

"Yes, yes I will."

### England, May, 1536

It is May Day, the day of the pagans. The day where we rejoice in fertility and happiness. Anne sat shrouded in a cloud of gloom. She wore yellow, attempting in her dress to convey jubilee through her body. Henry sat beside her in the viewing gallery watching the

186

jousts below. Henry's leg was badly injured from his unconscious bout when Anne lost their son. He could not fight today, so instead he had lent Henry Norris his horse; the cloth of gold trappings and tassels bouncing gaily off the stallion's flank.

"Such a lovely day," Anne commented dryly, to no one in particular, and in fact she had not much noticed the weather. It was sunny and bright, the sky as blue as sapphires, the clouds fluffy and white; looking soft as a lamb's wool. Anne tried to feign nonchalance but failed. Henry was distant, not answering. He had a faraway look, as though he was seeing great distances, to the Vatican, to Paris, his mind was gone. Maybe he is having his way with a mistress right now, locked tight in that mind of his. Anne simmered.

A disturbance below; a fluttering of fans. A man was rushing to Henry with a sealed parchment in his hand. "Make way!" he shouted feebly, passing through nobles. Norfolk and Suffolk looked placidly at the scene, Anne turned away nonplussed. Hurry this up, she thought meekly.

"Your Majesty." The man handed the note to Henry and swiftly departed, bowing stiffly.

Henry was silent while he read the letter. Anne tried to look over his shoulder, the print was small and succinct but she could not make it out. He stood up, the paper crumpling in his fist. Anne said something to him but he didn't seem to hear, he walked out of the stands and left with his guard. Anne sat dumbfounded; should she follow? Should she stay? She stayed.

She cheered and let Henry Norris wear her favors that day. He won the tilt and Anne smiled endlessly. Smiling, smiling, smiling. Baring her teeth to the world; it is rather my soul they are being shown.

"What is happening?" her father sidled up to her throne and whispered fiercely in her ear.

"I do not know father." Anne's tone was vicious; she was careworn and tired. "I do not know! Why must everyone always conspire against me?"

Wiltshire looked at her in confusion and a little malice. "Watch your tongue daughter."

"That is Queen, Earl."

"My Queen." He bowed his head.

\*\*\*

"Henry Norris has been arrested and taken to the Tower."

"What!?" Anne exploded, this was it, this was the storm, this was the thunder clapping and the lightning striking.

"They took him right after the jousts; the King!" Madge was hysterical, fluttering like a newborn bird unable to spread its wings in flight.

"Madge! Enough! What are we to do?"

"What *can* we do your Majesty?" Jane Rochford wailed miserably. "We do not even know what is happening."

"Make haste, we must sew. We must do our duty. Do not linger! Gather your things and work! We must be diligent in our mission to clothe the poor."

\*\*\*

"More men have been arrested!"

"We do not know who."

"We do not understand what is happening."

"Anne."

"Yes father?"

"Prepare yourself for the worst."

"Yes father."

\*\*\*

Anne sat with her ladies, sewing tirelessly. Everyone's nerves were taut as strings on a bow. The merest twang could send them flying. Her gaze was steely and it lingered on her ladies individually. Madge fidgeted overmuch, Jane Rochford looked guilty. What was the matter with them?

"My Lady." Jane jumped up in a panic. "I have to tell you. Cromwell came to us …. He …. Well you see…. He questioned us about—"

"You cannot Jane!" Madge bounded up. "We swore an oath not to tell!"

"Not to tell what?"

The doors to her chambers flew open. A smell of danger hung on the air. The guards marched in; there were six of them.

"Your Majesty, you are hereby arrested for treason against his most high Majesty the King, Henry VIII."

"What?" Anne asked bewildered.

"For adultery and compassing the King's death."

"No." Anne quivered but remained strong; she would not let them see her falter. She looked at her ladies and understood. Cromwell had questioned them and they had told him what he wanted to hear. It must be it. He had plotted this. She had threatened him and he had taken his revenge; as she had done to Wolsey. She should not have said those things to Norris; she should have dissociated herself from Smeaton. But she had not committed adultery! Of what were they speaking?

They helped her from her seat but she commanded them not to touch her. They walked with her, the six of them, surrounding her, and she a small flower in the midst of a towering dark forest. She would not wilt in the darkness, but would bloom brighter than ever. Not a single petal would she let cascade.

*** 

Jane Rochford wept miserably. "They have arrested George. My husband; they have taken him!"

*** 

Anne is taken by barge; she feels the water lapping at the sides like a dog licking up the last droplets of water. She is reminiscent of her coronation; she had taken this same route after all. They dock at Tower Wharf; there are neither nobles nor Henry her King to greet her. There is William Kingston, Constable of the Tower. She walks through the gate and he leads her to the Tower. "Have mercy on me oh Lord." She prays gently. The Duke of Suffolk and the Duke of

Norfolk, her escorts on the barge, take their leave. Her own uncle and one of her worst enemies part ways with her. They leave, without a word. They are silent as the trees that she imagines them to be. They may have life, but they do not show it. They may be blown by the winds of change, but they do not bend.

"Mr. Kingston, shall I go into a dungeon?" Anne asked hesitantly.

"No Madam, you shall go into the lodging you laid in at your coronation."

"It is too good for me! Jesus have mercy on me!" She fell on her knees and wept and laughed hysterically. Emotion finally overcoming her. She righted herself with the help of Kingston and came to her senses. "Mr. Kingston, I would like to have the sacrament in my closet if it please his Majesty, that I might pray for mercy. For I am as clear from the company of man as I am clear of you, and I am the King's wedded wife." She paused; looking at the sky for what she felt may be her last time. "Mr. Kingston, do you know why I am here?"

"Nay."

"I pray you to tell me where my Lord my father is?"

"I last saw him at court before dinner."

"And where is my sweet brother Lord Rochford?"

"I last saw him at York Place."

"I hear there are men accused with me. I wish I could open my body and show the world I am clear." Anne began to unlace her gown before Kingston placed a stopping hand on her arm.

"There is no need my Lady."

"Oh I lament for my mother; the sorrow her children must bring her. I pray for my dear brother, and Mark, and Henry Norris. I am sorry they should be here on my account. For they have done no sin in the eyes of our Lord."

Her gaze was so sad and depleted of all hope that Kingston smiled at her and nodded his head to proceed up the cold stone steps before them.

"Mr. Kingston, shall I die without justice?"

"Even the poorest subject of the King hath justice."

Anne nodded, unconvinced. Once Henry had determined his mind on something, he set out to accomplish it. He had meant to have her, he did. Now he meant to be rid of her, and so he would.

\*\*\*

"Lady Kingston, Lady Shelton, Lady Boleyn." Anne nodded her head at the women chosen to wait upon her in her cold tower prison. Lady Shelton was Madge's mother, her father's sister. Lady Boleyn was the wife of her father's younger brother James. And Lady Kingston was the Constable's wife. They were an interesting selection, and Anne knew Lady Shelton and Lady Boleyn were not supporters of her; regardless of familial connection.

The women stared at her through cold glass eyes. They looked with distaste and disdain, imagining her doing all sort of malicious and seditious acts with the gentlemen also arrested. Anne shook their hawk-like stares from her mind, kneeling down on her knees, the stone floor biting her flesh. She folded her hands and said a humble prayer to the Lord. She asked for forgiveness for all her sins and for mercy during all the proceedings. Her ladies looked on with suspicion and each went about what business they could manage with so little to truly attend upon.

Anne stood on her tiptoes to peek out of a small barred window. Her view was limited but she could breathe in fresh air. The scent of the Thames wafted in to greet her; it was refreshing. She smiled at God for this small blessing and returned to her prayers once more.

\*\*\*

"I feel my Lady, the need to tell you that William Brereton, Francis Weston, Mark Smeaton, and Henry Norris appeared in court today. Mark Smeaton pled guilty, the rest pled not guilty, but all were condemned. They are sentenced to be drawn, hung, then cut down and quartered." Lady Boleyn licked her lips with relish. It was obvious that if the men condemned for adultery with Anne were to be killed, then it should follow that Anne would also be condemned and killed. If one then the other.

"I pity Smeaton; that he should burn in the fires of hell for his lies. It is sad really. I suppose being a commoner they tortured him. I hope he is not too severely punished for this." She looked up as though reasoning with God. Lady Boleyn chuckled quietly and left the room.

\*\*\*

Thomas Wyatt is arrested, but he is not tried. He sits in a cell, souring, choking on rumors and disgust. Thick with hatred for the court and his King, he sits feebly scratching out poetry, lamenting his dear Anna. Now she will never be his, and he may never be his own. Thunder splits his mind, he shall not break.

\*\*\*

"The Lady Anne, Marquis of Pembroke." Anne walked forward into the court room. Her heart beat wildly in her throat, a strange sensation, her muscles quivered, her knees shook, and she held her head high. A great scaffold was erected in the middle of the hall, benches and seats lined the walls all round where the lords sat with their chests puffed out and their faces drawn. On a high throne before the platform sat the Duke of Norfolk, her uncle, underneath the canopy of estate bearing the royal arms. He held in his hand the white staff of his office, and his son, the Earl of Surrey, sat at his feet holding the golden staff of the Earl Marshal of England. Thomas Audley, the Lord Chancellor, and Charles Brandon, stood on either side of her uncle. Already she felt outnumbered and thwarted.

Among the men Anne could sufficiently pick out with a quick glance at the jury were the Marquis of Exeter, the Earl of Oxford, Henry Percy, Ralph Neville, the Earl of Worcester, Lord Morley who was Jane Seymour's father, and Lord Dacre. None of these men whom she quickly identified were friends of hers. She knew they despised her. She knew that Suffolk despised her; he stood there sucking at his teeth and looking at Audley with a glimmer in his eye. Audley was a great Cromwell lover and friend and would never speak out against him. Norfolk, her onetime ally, would bend where the King commanded. He would have no scruples against condemning his own niece. He shifted in his seat as though Anne's glare unnerved him. She turned her face to stare into the eyes of her old suitor, the Earl of Northumberland. He immediately looked away, a bitter taste lining his lips like venom. He looked as though he may be ready to be sick. Anne smirked inside herself; one look from her could undo these men.

Anne wore a black velvet gown, her petticoat was of scarlet damask, and she tucked up her hair in a small cap decorated with a black and white feather. Anne started when she noticed her father sitting amongst the gentlemen, but did not let any fear show on her face or in her countenance. She stood, undismayed, not exhibiting any token of impatience or grief or cowardice. She curtseyed before the men and they seemed rather moved by her expression and display of coming to honor and triumph rather than sitting before a court to be judged.

Anne knew she must contain this composition and flicked her hands absentmindedly across her velvet skirt. The black swishing ominously as she moved. She felt the nobles before her had more to fear than she herself did. She knew she had right on her side, and that no matter the outcome she could not be held accountable.

She proceeded to the seat on the platform and sat down with much grace and dignity. Her indictment was read out and she kept her face in a neat line as the words tumbled out making her heart race:

"Record of the Indictment found at Westminster on Wednesday next after three weeks of Easter: that whereas Queen Anne has been the wife of Henry VIII for three years and more, she, despising the solemn, not to mention most excellent and noble marriage between our lord the King and the same lady the Queen, but even at the same time having in her heart malice against our lord the King, seduced by evil and not having God before her eyes, and following daily her frail and carnal appetites, did falsely and traitorously procure by base conversations and kisses, touchings, gifts and other infamous incitations, divers of the King's daily and familiar servants to be her adulterers and concubines, so that several of the King's servants yielded to her vile provocations...."

Anne could hardly believe that anyone would lend credence to such accusations. Yet it did not end. After they listed the "divers times" that Anne had slept with each of the gentlemen in question they ended with the regicide charge.

"Furthermore, they being thus inflamed by carnal love of the Queen, and having become very jealous of each other, did, in order to secure her affections, satisfy her inordinate desires; and that the Queen was equally jealous of the Lord Rochford, and other the before-mentioned traitors that she would not allow them to hold any familiarity with any other woman without exhibiting her exceeding displeasure and indignation. Moreover, the said Lord Rochford, Norris, Brereton, Weston and Smeaton, being thus inflamed with carnal love of the Queen, and having become very jealous of each other, gave her secret gifts and pledges, while carrying on this illicit intercourse; and the Queen, on her part, would not allow them to show familiarity with any other woman without her exceeding displeasure and indignation; and that on 27. Nov. 27 Hen. VIII [1535] and other days before and after, at Westminster, she gave them great gifts to inveigle them to her will. Furthermore that the Queen and other of the said traitors, jointly and severally, 31 Oct. 27 Henry VIII [1535], at Westminster, and at various times before and after, compassed and imagined the King's death; and that the Queen had frequently promised to marry one of the traitors whenever the King should depart this life, affirming she would never love the King in her heart."

A voice inside Anne's heart threatened to be her undoing. But instead she lifted her neck high, and stared at Norfolk with much intention and said: "Not guilty," with all the muster available to her.

Sir Christopher Hales, the Attorney General, stepped down from his seat and began to pace back and forth before Anne. "You would deny before this court that you have carnally known the following men; Weston, Brereton, Norris, and Smeaton, who have all been condemned of the crime already?"

Anne smiled faintly. "As you say Sir, they have been condemned of the crime, but I have not, would I then admit to a crime I am neither guilty of nor proclaimed guilty of?"

He looked at her in anger. "You would deny compassing the King's death? A treasonable charge of regicide?"

"What proof has anyone of this claim? In all my life the only time I ever even imagined the King's death was when he lay in the throes of it, unconscious of the world, and I pregnant with his son. The mere thought of losing his life cost the life of that son. Do you therefore think I would compass his death? What profit would I gain? Tell me."

Hales looked perplexed. He scratched his chin thoughtfully. "But it is true that you have slept with these men. We have the dates listed out, would you like to look at the indictment?"

"I heard the dates you claimed. What is most impossible is that half of the dates can be disproved! I was not at Greenwich when you claimed, but at Whitehall. I was pregnant for part of the charges, and the rest was being churched! I have had miscarriages that led to my imprisonment in my room, shut away in dark airless beds. Have you arrested any of my ladies? For at least one if not more of my ladies would have had to have been complicit in these 'affairs' for them to have happened at all! You have not, have you? As there is no one." She paused to wet her lips. "After all, when am I ever truly *alone*? There are always servants attending on me. How would no one know of these 'divers affairs' Sir?"

Hales paused theatrically and then spread his arms far. "You see! She says herself when is she ever truly *alone*! She never sleeps alone your graces, and that is why she is an infamous whore!"

Images of Mary's sweet face flicked through her mind. She imagined herself as a small girl wheedling Mary about, begging her for things. Mary was a strong girl, as Anne viewed herself; her strengths simply lay in different areas. She didn't deserve the title infamous whore. She shivered at the mere comparison.

"I am free of touch of man. How shall I prove it to you?"

"You cannot Lady Anne!"

"Would you have me but open my body to you!"

"Ah you see! She is wanton! She would freely give herself to me! The attorney of the state!"

195

Anne shook her head sadly at the game these men were playing. "I do not say I do not deserve death for the sins I have committed in life. I have not always properly conducted myself; I have often been jealous of my King. But I do not deserve the trial I am put in now; I have done no wrong with any man and you have no proof thereof."

"You deny that you carnally knew your own brother? That you enticed him with your tongue in his mouth? And that said same tongue in yours?"

Anne knew she blanched but she didn't show a lack of strength, she overcame her sudden fear. "It is true I am close to my brother and love him very much as any sibling should; but may God strike me dead now if I ever carnally knew him."

The court paused as if waiting for lightning to strike through the room and singe Anne to her very hair. After a moment passed they seemed to breathe a collective sigh of relief.

"Is it not true that you gave money to Francis Weston?"

"Truly I did good sir! I have often leant money to those in need, and he was a young courtier in need. I see it as the Christian, goodly, charitable thing to do. In fact I would like all the revenues derived from closed monasteries to also go to the needy and helpless. All excess funds she be redistributed to those in need. My books may be checked, it is not the first person I have helped."

He paused. He looked to Audley. He seemed to come to the conclusion that they would not win in a battle of words. So be it, it was over.

"We will announce our verdicts then."

One by one the gentlemen inclined their heads and said the hollow, heart wrenching word Anne most dreaded to hear: "Guilty."

"Guilty."

"Guilty."

"Guilty."

Anne could hear it echoing in her mind as each man repeated it in turn. A pulse, a beat, a breath, it was over and done. The guard in the room turned his shiny axe towards her, a symbol of the condemned.

She shuddered, tears glittered like diamonds in her eyes, but she did not let them fall.

Norfolk inhaled deeply and then spoke with a grating rumbling voice like that of thunder issuing across a sunny sky: "You are hereby condemned to die; to have your head struck from your body or to be burned at His Majesty's pleasure."

Anne stood, her skirts swishing round her stockinged legs and slippered feet. She bowed her head.

"You are hereby stripped of your crown and titles." Her jewels were passed from a waiting servant to Norfolk. They did not mention her title of Queen and Anne could not fathom it. She opened her mouth and spoke her heart:

"My lords, I will not say your sentence is unjust, nor presume that my reasons can prevail against your convictions. I am willing to believe that you have sufficient reasons for what you have done; but then they must be other than those which have been produced in court, for I am clear of all the offences which you then laid to my charge. I have ever been a faithful wife to the King, though I do not say I have always shown him that humility which his goodness to me, and the honors to which he raised me, merited. I confess I have had jealous fancies and suspicions of him, which I had not discretion enough, and wisdom, to conceal at all times. But God knows, and is my witness, that I have not sinned against him in any other way. Think not I say this in the hope to prolong my life, for He who saves from death hath taught me how to die, and He will strengthen my faith. Think not, however, that I am so bewildered in my mind as not to lay the honor of my chastity to heart now in mine extremity, when I have maintained it all my life long, much as ever Queen did. I know these, my last words, will avail me nothing but for the justification of my chastity and honor. As for my brother and those others who are unjustly condemned, I would willingly suffer many deaths to deliver them, but since I see it so pleases the King, I shall willingly accompany them in death, with this assurance, that I shall lead an endless life with them in peace and joy, where I will pray to God for the King and for you, my lords."

Guards swept forward to escort her from the room. When her back was turned one of the diamonds fell from her eye and shattered on the ground. A million pieces of beauty from one small droplet; this was Anne in the court of England.

\*\*\*

"Your brother has also been found guilty Madam," Lady Boleyn said haughtily after Lady Kingston informed her of the news.

"What less could one expect? God save his soul."

"That may be beyond His means Mistress."

\*\*\*

The day Brereton, Smeaton, Norris, and Weston are beheaded, a commuting of sentences as befits the King's 'kind' nature; Anne will not get out of bed. "Bring me Archbishop Cranmer, I wish to make my confession."

\*\*\*

William Kingston escorted Cranmer into Anne's rooms. She quickly stood and curtsied, then asked her ladies to leave. Kingston turned to exit with them, in the wake of their swirling skirts, but Anne stopped him. "I would like you to stay Master Kingston," she said quietly.

"As you wish my Lady," he said, his kind face crinkled in consternation.

"I know you are a good man sir, and I wish you to hear that I am a good woman. I wish you to pray for me in my final hours and remember me always in your thoughts."

Cranmer stepped forward and looked at Anne with tears in his big eyes. "Anne, my Queen." He bowed to her but Anne lifted him up.

"Please don't Archbishop; you will only make this harder for me."

"What do you wish to confess to me Anne? What burden do you plan to place on my conscience?"

"You well know I am innocent."

"You swear it in confession! Anne, do not be blasphemous; this is your eternal soul at stake!" His purple robes swayed eerily in the shallow lighting of her rooms. The cold walls emanated a damp smell that Anne nearly choked on.

"It is true; I am innocent of all charges laid against me."

Cranmer's face fell in anguish, tears leaked out of his eyes. He crushed a hand to his head. Kingston stood in the background; hurt swelling in his own face. He was silent.

"I would like you to pray for mc Archbishop Cranmer; I am in much need of the comfort of prayer. Is it self-effacing?"

"No, no it is not," he managed to squeak out. "I always believed you were a goodly woman, the best I have ever seen. You have done many good things for the Church and our Faith; I could not believe the crimes of you. I could not believe them."

"And there, your faith in me is proved just. As my faith in God shall prove once I leave this earth."

"You know the King wants his marriage annulled. His is going to declare your daughter a bastard just as he did with the Princess Mary."

"No!" a horrified gasp whispered past Anne's teeth, inflaming itself in the room. "It cannot be! What grounds Cranmer!? What grounds!?"

"Consanguinity. The fatal degree of affinity."

"Because he slept with my sister Mary."

"Yes."

"But that was all allotted for in the original dispensation he drew up!"

"I know. But he must be out of it, you know that Anne."

"He…he cannot."

"But he is. He is and you know who has helped him to accomplish all his goals."

"Cromwell."

"Yes."

"He gave his rooms to the Seymour family, so that Henry could be closer to his sweet dainty love affair, that whey-faced Jane."

"Oh do not speak so harshly Anne."

"I am sorry. But do you know what I am most sorry for in all I have done?"

"What is that?"

"My cruelty to Mary."

"Your sister?"

"The Lady Mary, the King's daughter. I....I had her established in Elizabeth's household, to wait upon her. I thought that was just punishment as she would not recognize me as her Queen, I thought she could recognize my daughter as Princess." Tears rushed down her cheeks as she spoke. "I told her I would intercede with her father to have them reunited if only she would recognize me! But she said 'I recognize no Queen but my mother. But if the King's mistress should wish to intercede on my behalf, I would be much indebted.' The King's mistress she called me!" Anne wailed and wept on his robes. "I am so sorry for the cruelty with which I treated her! I would write to Lady Bryan and ask her to beat Mary and whip her to straighten her out. I had her shut up in her room for days at a time. I wanted her dead with her mother! Dead Cranmer!"

"We all say and think things we cannot mean when we are scared and hurt and troubled. We all wish we could take things back but we cannot. We can seek forgiveness."

"I pray she forgives me. I destroyed her mother and then I destroyed her."

"I do not think she is quite destroyed my Lady."

Kingston looked on with wonderment at this conversation. He would report Anne's innocence to Cromwell as he reported everything of interest his wife told him about her time spent with Anne.

Anne knelt and sobbed her heart in her tears. "I suppose I deserve death for all the evil I have wrought."

"You could never deserve death Anne. Do not make yourself a martyr."

"I would not presume the title. I am not dying for my faith."

"The King is commuting your sentence to beheading by sword. It is much quicker and nobler."

"Yes the French use this tactic."

200

"They are sending for a swordsman from Calais; he is supposed to be very good…" he trailed off understanding the lameness of the sentence. He steepled his fingers and looked at Anne with sorrow and pity; waves of grief threatening to overtake him.

"I will pray with you now."

\*\*\*

"It is done. George has been beheaded."

Anne fainted. When she awoke she wept so hard she retched twice. She fell into a fitful sleep at long last, dreaming of death.

# Chapter 17

## *England, Tower of London, May 18th, 1536*

Anne took the sacrament twice. She stood up and paced the room, waiting for death to come and take her. Waiting for the cold talons to sink into her flesh and lead her on her way to the other world. She felt mists floating before her eyes and a deep depression settling on her shoulders. She determined she was ready.

But when the hour of her death at 9am came and went Anne sent Lady Kingston to fetch her husband. He came in looking guilty.

"Master Kingston, I hear say I shall not die afore noon, and I am very sorry therefore, for I thought to be dead by this time and past my pain."

"I am sorry my Lady. He shall not arrive until tomorrow. The headsman that is. But I hear the blow is very subtle and you shall not have pain."

"I heard say the executioner was very good, and I have a little neck." Anne roared with laughter, her black humor overtaking her in her tormented state of mind. She stopped abruptly and looked at Kingston quite seriously, her ladies gathered round her now in fright and affection.

"I pray that for the honor of God you would beg the King that, since I am in a good state and disposed for death that I might be dispatched immediately. It is not that I desire death, but that I thought myself prepared to die and I fear the delay may weaken my resolve."

Kingston looked dreadful, a pain writhing like a living thing across his face. "I am sorry; it is not until tomorrow now."

After he left Anne turned to her ladies: "I shall be Queen Anne Lackhead."

## England, Tower of London, May 19th, 1536

Anne awoke at dawn, grey light trickling in her small window. She said her last Mass and received the sacrament one last time. A sick pit sunk in her stomach, the knowledge that everything she did she did for the final time in life. She thought back to the last time she had kissed Henry, felt his loving hands on her body, and held her precious daughter. She thought back to the last time he said 'I love you' to her, but found it hard to place. How had their passion died so quickly? How had their fervor ebbed away?

She tried to eat breakfast, but kept choking on her meager portions, and finally pushed the plate aside. She sat there, at her table, waiting. Her ladies were around her, tears leaking from their stubborn eyes. Anne was strong, she was firm, and she was innocent. She kept waiting and waiting to hear the dreaded footfalls outside her door, and finally as though in a dream, they resounded hollowly through the room.

"No!" Lady Shelton cried in sudden terror.

"Do not fear, I go to meet my Lord today. For I am judged by no man, but by God alone." Anne smiled patiently while Kingston opened the door to escort her out.

Dressed in a grey robe of damask trimmed with elegant ermine, a crimson kirtle peeping from underneath, and a pert English gable hood on her head, Anne exited the Queen's Lodgings. She solemnly walked past the Great Hall, through the gate, and down the side of the White Tower to the scaffold. It was draped in black and looked menacing even from a distance. Anne thought, I will die on that scaffold in mere minutes. My spirit shall leave my body, crumpled and bleeding on that black cloth.

Kingston grabbed Anne's hand gently and helped her up the wobbly scaffold steps. She braced herself as she looked into the densely packed crowd. She caught the eye of Suffolk, and Cromwell, Audley, and the King's bastard son Henry Fitzroy. They shivered when her eyes met theirs. They seemed to feel cursed, and Anne felt pity reach out to them from the depths of her soul:

"Good Christian people, I have not come here to preach a sermon; I have come here to die. For according to the law and by the law I am judged to die, and therefore I will speak nothing against it. I am come hither to accuse no man, nor to speak of that whereof I am accused and condemned to die, but I pray God save the King and send him long to reign over you, for a gentler nor a more merciful prince was there never, and to me he was ever a good, a gentle, and sovereign lord. And if any person will meddle of my cause, I require them to judge the best. And thus I take my leave of the world and of you all and I heartily desire you all to pray for me."

Her hands trembled but no one noticed. Her ladies moved forward and removed her mantle from her shoulders. Anne grasped her hood tentatively, and swept up her raven locks into a plain white cap. She did not want anything to detract from the swordsman's blow. She looked to where he stood, dressed all in black, a half-mask guarding his face where only his eyes could peep out and look on her with abject pity. Anne handed the man his pay, coins tinkling wrapped in a small cloth sack. He humbly asked Anne: "Do you forgive me?"

"There is nothing to forgive."

Anne stepped forward on the scaffold, straw shifting beneath her feet. She knelt on her knees and looked to the executioner in fear. He had expected this, that is why he stood empty-handed, no sword in sight. Anne's confusion melted into peace when her ladies stepped up to her, placing gentle hands on her shoulders and tied a blindfold round her eyes.

"Oh Lord have mercy on me, to God I commend my soul. To Jesus Christ I commend my soul; Lord Jesus receive my soul," Anne's mouth moved quickly, the words spilling out in a rush. The wind blew gently kissing her face with the breath of God, Anne did not sway.

To distract Anne the executioner called out for someone to bring him his sword. Behind her, he pulled it out from under a cloth himself. Thus while Anne was still waiting to hear footsteps bringing her death to her, the executioner silently approached her from behind. The sword gleamed in the light of the fresh morning sun, shafts of silver and prisms of rainbow cascading in brilliance over her head. A solid arc weaved over Anne's head. A steady swing of the sword over his head and it fell in a crushing blow to Anne's unwitting elegant neck.

The last thought Anne had was of her precious daughter bundled up in cloth of gold, clinging to her neck and whispering 'I love you Mama,' with that childlike innocence of pure contentment.

At last her head fell to the ground, her ladies weeping and gathering it up quickly, her lips still moving silently, forming the words: "Lord Jesus receive my soul." And the falcon flew to greater heights than any shall ever know.

# Epilogue

Archbishop Thomas Cranmer studied the small white flower in his hand. His thoughts of Anne, the Queen he so admired. He said aloud: "She who has been the Queen of England on earth will today become a Queen in Heaven." The wind blew in the trees, bare and stark against the sharp cornflower blue sky. This seemed to Cranmer to be the kiss of God and the affirmation he had sought that Anne was sitting in His lap even now. "Just so my Queen, just so."

# Author's Note:

I have attempted to stay as historically accurate as possible in all areas of this novel. However, owing to the fact that it *is* fiction, I have sought to edit the story where needed. I would like to think if Anne were alive today, she would be proud of this retelling of her life's story.

If you are interested in researching more about Anne Boleyn's life you may find the following resources as beneficial as I did.

Websites:

http://www.theanneboleynfiles.com

http://www.the-tudors.org.uk

Books:

*Jane Boleyn, the Infamous Lady Rochford* by Julia Fox

*Six Wives, the Queens of Henry VIII* by David Starkey

*The Life and Death of Anne Boleyn* by Eric Ives

*The Lady in the Tower* by Alison Weir

*The Royal Palaces of Tudor England* by Simon Thurley

*The Tudor Age* by Jasper Ridley

*The Obedience of a Christian Man and How Christen Rulers Ought to Govern* by William Tyndale

# Would you like to see your manuscript become a book?

**If you are interested in becoming a PublishAmerica author, please submit your manuscript for possible publication to us at:**

**acquisitions@publishamerica.com**

**You may also mail in your manuscript to:**

**PublishAmerica
PO Box 151
Frederick, MD 21705**

# www.publishamerica.com

Lightning Source UK Ltd.
Milton Keynes UK
UKOW03f1808130314

228116UK00001B/52/P